"In the Haxan series, Kenneth Mark Hoover is recreating the Old West. Or rather he would be, if the Old West was equal parts *Gunsmoke* and John Brunner's *Traveler in Black*. . . . Fans of the western and dark fantasy genres alike should give this series a serious look."

—Richard Parks, author of *Yamada Monogatari:*
Demon Hunter* and *To Break the Demon Gate

". . . Kenneth Mark Hoover's *Haxan* is a classic pulp western with something coiled and wintry nesting at its heart. . . . The result is pure entertainment, mesmerizing moment by moment, surprisingly moving in retrospect."

—Gemma Files, author of The Hexslinger Trilogy

"The *Haxan* universe is rich with character, history, and mythology. Every story is a joy to read."

—Jennifer Brozek

"You know those terrible Z-grade horror movies? Imagine if Sam Peckinpah directed one, and brought his aesthetic of poetic violence to the proceedings. That's *Haxan*."

—Nick Mamatas, author of *Love is the Law* and
Bullettime

"Kenneth Mark Hoover's worlds are real, and the people in them are just as real. It's only when you hear them speak that you realize that their world is not necessarily the same one you call home . . . but you'll be so enthralled, you'll wish you could join them."

—Duke Pennell, editor of *Frontier Tales*

"Mark Hoover's writing style and his dark fantasy Western novel combine to create a magic that draws readers inside and keeps them there, allowing no escape until the thrilling conclusion."

—Matthew Pizzolato, editor of *The Western Online*

KENNETH MARK HOOVER

HAXAN

ChiZine Publications

FIRST EDITION

Haxan © 2014 by Kenneth Mark Hoover
Cover artwork © 2014 by Erik Mohr
Cover and interior design by © 2014 by Samantha Beiko

Distributed in Canada by
HarperCollins Canada Ltd.
1995 Markham Road
Scarborough, ON M1B 5M8
Toll Free: 1-800-387-0117
e-mail: hcorder@harpercollins.com

Distributed in the U.S. by
Diamond Comic Distributors, Inc.
10150 York Road, Suite 300
Hunt Valley, MD 21030
Phone: (443) 318-8500
e-mail: books@diamondbookdistributors.com

Library and Archives Canada Cataloguing in Publication Data

Hoover, Kenneth Mark, 1959-, author
    Haxan / Kenneth Mark Hoover.

Issued in print and electronic formats.
ISBN 978-1-77148-175-5 (pbk.).--ISBN 978-1-77148-176-2 (pdf)

    I. Title.

PS3608.O625H39 2014   813'.6   C2014-900780-9

C2014-900781-7

CHIZINE PUBLICATIONS
Toronto, Canada
www.chizinepub.com
info@chizinepub.com

Edited by Andrew Wilmot
Proofread by Michael Matheson

Canada Council   Conseil des arts
for the Arts   du Canada

We acknowledge the support of the Canada Council for the Arts which last year invested $20.1 million in writing and publishing throughout Canada.

ONTARIO ARTS COUNCIL
CONSEIL DES ARTS DE L'ONTARIO
50 YEARS OF ONTARIO GOVERNMENT SUPPORT OF THE ARTS
50 ANS DE SOUTIEN DU GOUVERNEMENT DE L'ONTARIO AUX ARTS

Published with the generous assistance of the Ontario Arts Council.

Printed in Canada

HAXAN

for Gemma Files, who always believed

Thermopylae. Masada. Agincourt.
And now, Haxan, New Mexico.
We go where we're sent.
We have names and we stand
against that which must be faced.
Through a sea of time and dust,
in places that might never be,
or can't *become* until something is set right,
there are people destined to travel. Forever.
I am one.

—*Marshal John T. Marwood*

PART 1

HAXAN

CHAPTER 1

Haxan, New Mexico Territory
Spring, 1874

I found the old man nailed to a hackberry tree five miles out of Haxan.

They had hammered railroad spikes through his wrists and ankles. There was dried blood on the wood and iron. Blood stippled his arms and chest. He was stripped naked so the westering sun could peel the flesh from his bones.

He was alive when I found him.

I got down off my horse, a blue roan I picked up in Mesilla, and went up to the man. His twitching features were covered with swarming bluebottles.

I swiped them away and pressed the mouth of a canteen to his parched lips. He was in such a bad way, I knew if he drank too much, too fast, he would founder and the shock would kill him.

He took a capful of water and coughed. Another half-swallow.

"I can work those nails out," I said. "You might have a chance if a doctor sees you."

He raised his grizzled head. His face was the colour of burned leather kicked out of a prairie fire. His eyelids were cut away, his eyes seared blind by the sun.

"Won't do any good, mister." He talked slow and with effort, measuring his remaining strength. He had a Scandinavian accent that could float a ship, pale eyebrows, and faded blue irises. "I been here two days."

I tried to work one of the nails free. It was hammered deep and wouldn't budge.

"No use," he rasped. "Anyway, the croaker in Haxan is jugged on laudanum half the time. And the tooth-puller, he ain't much better in the way of a man."

I let him have more water. "Who did this?"

"People of Haxan."

I tried to give him more water but he shook it off. He was dying and he knew it. He didn't want to prolong the process.

"Why?"

"They're scared. Like children are scared of the dark."

He was delirious and not making sense. "Scared of what?"

"Me. What I know about this place." His words and his mind grew distant together. "The ghost voices frozen in the rocks and the grass, the water and the sky. The memory of the world carried high on the wind."

His head dropped onto his naked chest. He was losing strength fast. I tried to give him water again but he wouldn't take it.

"What's your name, mister?" he asked in a hoarse whisper.

"John Marwood." I had other names, but he wouldn't be able to pronounce them. Sometimes I couldn't remember them all.

"I waited for you, son," he said. "I called . . . but you didn't get here fast enough. This moment . . . in time."

I felt showered with ice.

"So you help her instead, Marwood. My daughter, I mean."

"Let me help you first, old man. My horse can carry us both."

"Thank you for the water. At least you tried." His head rolled back. His breath sawed in his throat. "Did I tell you it snowed the day she was born?"

He gave a long, trembling sigh. With a sudden jerk his body slumped forward.

He was dead.

I cut him down and buried him in the shade of the hackberry tree. The sky was purpling in the east when I placed the last stone on top of his grave.

An hour of daylight remained. Across the empty landscape a single mourning dove flew to water. I walked over the hard ground looking for tracks. Two single-rider horses, well shod, and a wagon, had come from the north and gone back that way.

Headed for town.

The stirrup leather creaked when I mounted up. It was the only sound in the desert and it carried like a scream.

I shook the reins in my hand and pulled toward Haxan.

CHAPTER 2

I rode across a stone bridge that spanned a dry wash, remembering the old man. He was at rest now, but it took someone with a lot of hard bark on him to do something like that to another human being.

I knew what that was like. Carrying so much hate around inside until it blew you apart with dry, quiet winds.

I knew exactly what that was like.

The town of Haxan was a tumbled mix of old low-lying Spanish-style adobe buildings and brand new structures of ripsawed lumber going up around them like sawteeth. Some of the buildings were so new you could smell the resin seeping from the boards.

Haxan had all the earmarks of a boomtown. There were more saloons than schools, more dance halls than general stores. For those who couldn't find lodging in town, a dirty tent city and clapboard shacks sprawled on the flat beside a foul-smelling creek.

It was the same story all over the *frontera*. Down in Texas, because of the war, cattle ran four dollars a head. They could be sold north for twenty along the Goodnight-Loving Trail. That brought money, but it also brought gamblers, drifters, thieves, and a bevy of soiled doves.

Enough to keep any lawman busy for a lifetime. However long that lasted.

There was a railway depot in Haxan for shipping beef, with a jumbled maze of cattle pens, corrals, and warehouses on the north side of town. A long street served as the main thoroughfare. It was bordered by weathered saloons, gaudy hotels, and painted store fronts. The outer facing of a mercantile emporium was covered in stamped metal panels, ordered from a mail catalogue. Beside it, two men rolled water barrels down a dirt ramp for storage in an underground cellar below a fancy French restaurant.

There were many waist-high stone walls throughout town, quarried from the San Andres Mountains that towered to the southwest. A roadrunner raced back and forth along one wall, seeking small lizards in the sun.

The livery stable stood on the other side of a wide-open plaza where a central public water well was surrounded by crude mesquite benches. Mexican women drew water for a cook pot. Their children bounced and chased a red ball.

In one corner of the plaza were several cottonwood trees, leaves rustling in the dry, desert wind. There were drifts of white gypsum sand, like snow, piled against the base of buildings and wooden sidewalks.

As I rode through town I noticed there weren't many people around. It was much too hot despite the late hour of the day and they were in siesta. The only road traffic I saw were two ox-drawn *carretas* wobbling and screeching down Front Street.

The wire I received in Helena said the main freight office was in La Posta, a formidable adobe structure built by titled Spanish for the king's rest. Those days of high royalty were long over, however. Now it was used as a mail drop for overland stages.

The mayor's office was next door to La Posta. I drew rein and stepped out of leather. After tying my horse to the rail I pushed my way through the heavy wooden door.

It was cooler inside. The old adobe house had been converted to a way station and general office with walls a yard thick. The office had dark-stained furniture, chairs stuffed with horsehair, and a cochineal rug dyed from kermes bugs. Hand-hewn vigas supported a low ceiling that brushed the crown of my hat.

A blue-eyed man with balding red hair, and a nose with a bulbous tip, looked up from his paperwork. His shirtsleeves were rolled to the elbows. His hands were split by hard work and fishhooks, and his face wasn't much kinder.

"Help you, stranger?" he asked.

"Looking for Mayor Polgar. I'm John Marwood. The War Department in Washington, D.C. sent me."

He rounded his desk. We shook. "Glad to meet you, Mr. Marwood. Or should I say, U.S. Marshal?"

"John will do me fine."

A smile split his seamed face. "Then you can call me Frank." He hooked a thumb over his shoulder. "I own the freight service next door." He chuckled. "Along with what little mayoring the good people of Haxan allow."

He showed me to a horsehide chair. "We figured you to arrive on the eleven o'clock stage days ago, John."

He offered me a Havana. I declined. I had a habit of taking an old briar pipe after supper and I hadn't eaten yet. Polgar struck a lucifer against a sandpaper block and lighted his Cuban cigar.

"Got here fast as I could," I explained. "Took a train partway and staged down from Montana Territory. Most of it I had to saddle."

I had covered a lot of country after I received the telegram from Judge Creighton concerning my new appointment. Once I hit St. Louis I had some overdue paperwork in the U.S. Marshal's office shoved under my nose. Finally, after I reached Mesilla, I picked up my horse and rode toward Haxan.

That was when I found the dying man in the desert.

However, I was certain Polgar didn't want to hear about my cross-country travails. He had a directness about him, cold and sharp like the hooks that had scarred his hands.

"I wanted to get a feel for the countryside," I said, expecting that would satisfy him.

He nodded. "Good idea, seeing how you'll be stationed here for some time."

"I hope so." Now that the preliminaries were out of the way I thought it was time to discuss the job. Despite his open bonhomie I felt it'd be better to keep this part of the conversation on official terms. "Mayor, the telegram I got in Montana Territory sounded pretty desperate."

Polgar waved his cigar in an off-hand gesture. "I must admit we didn't know where to turn. We even set up a Haxan Peace Commission to show Washington we were serious about maintaining law and order."

I didn't like the sound of that. I preferred to work alone without someone gawking over my shoulder. A lawman that has to straddle a fence doesn't live long.

"It's bad enough answering to Judge Creighton when he's sober," I replied. "I don't know if I want a busy-body commission full of old women telling me how to do my job."

Polgar's chair squeaked when he leaned forward. "You misunderstand, Marshal. All the propertied men in town are part of this commission. Men like Pate Nichols who owns the Lazy X. Hell, I'm on the commission, too. They're all good men."

I shook my head slow. I thought I had settled this with Judge Creighton when I accepted the badge. He knew when I took a job I preferred it my way or not at all. Now I had to make Polgar understand that as well.

"That's even worse, Mayor. Propertied men sometimes feel they have a special provenance when it comes to the law."

Polgar slapped his knee. "That's not what we want, Marshal. We wired Washington and mailed a blizzard of letters requesting federal intervention in Sangre County. We wanted someone with a reputation." He was a good politician. He liked to hear himself talk.

I decided to give up some ground. "All right, so long as we understand one another." I was under no illusions this problem would not crop up again. I didn't mind oversight, of course. That was expected. But men who pull political strings to get a certain lawman in their town often think they own him body and soul.

My soul had already been bought, and paid for, a long time ago.

Polgar looked relieved. Our first political skirmish had resulted in no serious bloodletting. He kicked back, legs crossed at the ankles. Like the rest of him, his boots were scuffed and marred. The man was a walking knot of flesh.

"So tell me, Marshal, how do you like our little corner of the world?" he asked. "I mean, from what you've seen."

"Not much. I found a dead man south of town, nailed to a tree."

Polgar's sandy eyebrows came together. The silence between us lengthened like tempered chain. "Who was he?"

"He didn't give a name. He was too busy dying."

Polgar watched me with studied care. He laid his cigar aside. "The Navajo are peaceful and on reservation," he said low. "Apaches, maybe. They get stirred up by the Army once in a blue moon."

"I don't think so." I fished one of the iron spikes out of my grey duster and tossed it on Polgar's desk. "Not unless the Apache have taken to pounding railroad spikes into people. It's been my experience they are more civilized than that."

Polgar picked up the railroad spike and rolled it thoughtfully between his thick fingers. He looked up, his blue eyes wary.

"What are you trying to say, Marshal?"

"Just this, Mayor. I've been in Haxan ten minutes and I already have one murder to solve."

Polgar showed me the Marshal's office located down the street. It was thirty yards west of the stone bridge I had crossed coming into town. It had a good view of the plaza and Front Street. The office was built of quarried stone faced with adobe mud mixed with too much straw. There were iron bars in the windows and thick wooden shutters with gun ports. Inside, the rectangular space was furnished with a desk topped with outdated wanted circulars and telegram blanks, a pine bench under a flyblown window, an iron potbellied stove, a rusted coffee pot, and a yellow map of Sangre County tacked to the wall.

The rifle racks were empty, but the jail cells in back were well oiled and the keys fit the locks. There was a rope cot with a cornshuck mattress for the jailer and a storeroom with enough room for one man to stand. A back door led to a broken hitch rail and a privy in a weed-choked lot.

"It's not much," Polgar apologized. "But long as you keep your appointment with the War Department your room and board will be paid at the Haxan Hotel, guaranteed by our commission."

"Sounds fair enough," I admitted. The office was a dark, lonely place. I had seen worse.

"You hungry, Marshal? Hew Clay owns the best hotel in town. He serves a good beefsteak."

"Not now." I put my Sharps rifle in the gun rack. It looked lonely there.

Polgar struck a match and fired a second cigar. He had a habit of smoking one halfway before tossing it aside and patting his pockets down with his rough hands for a fresh one. I figured a man hard up for tobacco would have a fine time just following him around town.

"John," we were back on first name terms, "the only person who fits your description is old Shiner Larsen. He rode express guard for my outfit from time to time." He was pointed with his next statement. "He built this town, don't let anyone say different. Well, founded it, anyway. Same as."

"What else you know about him?"

Polgar shrugged. "Not much. Kept a shack on the edge of town. Loner."

"Larsen mentioned a daughter. What do you know about her?"

Instead of answering my question Polgar rapped a hard knuckle against the map. "Sangre County. Wild and dangerous, all four thousand square miles." He paused. "You know what Sangre means in Spanish, don't you?"

"I do." Sometimes the very name of a place was strong enough to draw us in.

"John, this county is aptly named. This is a very bloody place. The man you're replacing, Sheriff Cawley, set up a deadline on Potato Road. But after he quit all the saloons moved back into town."

I sat behind the desk in a swivel chair that needed oiling and started hunting through the drawers. "Now they're making so much money they don't want to move back across the line," I suggested.

"Exactly." Polgar hooked his thumbs through his belt. His silver watch chain glinted from a broken shaft of light streaming through the window. "Out here a man must not only fight other men, but Nature herself. Sometimes, during the rainy season, Broken Bow River overflows its banks."

I found a corked bottle in the bottom drawer. There was an inch and a half of good red eye in the bottom and a couple of dusty glasses. I didn't like having liquor in the office, but there was no sense in having it go to waste, either. I set the bottle on my desk and poured at Polgar's insistence.

"Broken Bow?"

"That's what we call this bend of the Rio Grande. Thanks." He accepted the shot of whiskey and we drank. Another splash for each of us finished the bottle.

Polgar motioned to the county map with his empty glass. "We're digging *acequias* to handle overflow. But when the river floods it brings malaria, yellow fever, and property damage. Although with this current drought we'd be glad for a flood about now."

If there is one thing that makes a lawman perk up his ears it is a mention of water rights. I remembered the men storing water barrels under the restaurant. "How bad a drought?"

"Cattlemen are complaining the coyotes are killing stock." Polgar leaned his broad frame against my desk. "John, we need someone like you out here. A lawman with a tough reputation. I realize your jurisdiction is federal, but the Haxan Peace Commission wants to cede you local and county authority as well."

I stoppered the empty bottle. "Sounds more like a double-edged sword than a help."

"It will be," he agreed. "Especially since you are the only U.S. Marshal in the territory."

"I thought Breggmann rode out of Santa Fe." He was a competent man. He shot two nightriders outside the Governor's Palace a year ago after they got the drop on him.

"Guess you didn't hear," Polgar said. "Marshal Breggmann took after *comancheros* and trailed them to Palo Duro Canyon."

Despite what people read in yellow-back novels, lawmen were often the last to learn anything of value. "What happened?"

"Comanches tied him to a wagon tongue and put him over a slow mesquite fire until his skull burst."

I removed my hat and ran my fingers through my hair. "Mayor, you believe in handing a man a job of work." I tossed the empty bottle into the wastebasket. It rattled around with a hollow sound.

It might have been the sound of my future.

"Sorry, John. I thought you had better know what you're setting up against."

"All right." I cut him a hard look. "But you avoided my question about Larsen's daughter."

He made a pacifying gesture. "There's an unhappy history in these parts. It gives people the wim-wams."

"If it's as bad as you say, why not leave?"

"Too much money to be made. Twenty years ago Haxan was nothing more than a sun-baked shack in the middle of nowhere."

"Shiner Larsen's place."

"Right. He came from Sweden and wandered all over the west. When he settled here he named the place Haxan." Polgar fingered his watch chain. "John, Haxan is a Swedish word for witch."

The long purple shadows inched down the street outside my window. Someone lighted a cook fire in one of the buildings across the street. I could see black shadows moving behind the muslin curtains.

"You think Larsen was a witch?"

"Some did, like our town dentist, and others. Larsen believed there are places where spirits get trapped and tied in knots. He said Haxan is one of those places."

"Why did he settle here?"

"I asked him that on a stage run to Albuquerque once. He said life was like flipping book pages. It was a blur until you stuck your finger out and read what was there."

Polgar continued to play with his watch chain. I could tell he didn't like talking about this. He wanted a rational world where things could be calculated and understood.

"Larsen said it was probable Sangre County didn't exist in men's thoughts, but that it was here because it had to be. When Haxan needed it the right spirits would protect what was worth protecting."

Polgar studied the burning end of his Havana. He had smoked it halfway. He gave it a careful puff. "Like I said, most people ignored him."

"Except this time someone didn't." I wondered how far a superstitious person would go to ease his scare. I had lawed long enough to know murder would not be out of the question.

Polgar finally tossed the cigar and faced my desk, hands flat on the surface. "John, I'm telling you this because I want you to be aware of the corns you might step on. But I want this killer caught, same as you."

I had to admit this wouldn't look good on me if it went unpunished. Plus, every year is an election year for a politician.

But it wasn't like I didn't have enough to occupy me already. Tame a raw cattle town, and now hunt down crazy men who thought they were killing witches. Not to mention find the *comancheros* who murdered Breggmann.

I gave a long sigh of frustration. "All right, I'll do what I can. Now what can you tell me about Larsen's family?"

"He married a Navajo woman. Her name was Black Sky. They had a daughter." Polgar took a new cigar from his shirt pocket and started patting for matches. "Last I heard she was on the Bosque Redondo. She teaches kids their books and letters, or something."

That was enough to start, until I recalled something the old man said about the day his daughter was born. "She have a name, this girl?"

"Shiner called her Snowberry. Magra Snowberry."

CHAPTER 3

I mounted my blue roan and rode north out of Haxan. About a mile and half later I cut a shallow creek meandering between boulders.

I rode easy 'tween them. Ancient symbols, pictographs I guess you would call them, were chiselled into the black faces. I'd heard if you studied these old Indian markings long enough you could make their magic work for you.

Did I tell you it snowed the day she was born?

I came on an isolated house in the centre of a circle of stones. Shiner Larsen's home was little more than a broken down hovel with a sod roof. It was a typical wattle and daub that had incorporated an adobe brick foundation for added structural strength. It stood on a rise overlooking a gulch the locals called Gila Creek. We weren't all that far from Haxan and Broken Bow, but out here, a mile and a half from civilization, the empty desert predominated.

I rode around the place. There were a few rows of planted maize for a shoat penned behind the house, a drying rack, and hornos, or beehive ovens, for cooking bread. Not much else in the way of prosperity.

I let my horse stand and walked up on the house. The sun had set and the sky was pocked with stars. There were so many of them it made me feel small.

Out on the desert flat coyotes and wolves were yipping and howling. A lot of them. The mournful chorus cut through me the way it does any man.

When I stepped on the porch the front door, hung on leather hinges, swung open a crack. Twin eighteen-inch barrels of a Stevens 10 gauge coach gun centred on my stomach.

"What do you want?" a voice demanded.

"My name is John Marwood. I'm the U.S. Marshal out of Haxan." I lowered my voice in condolence. "I'm here about your father."

"My father is dead."

"I know. I'm the one who found him."

"Step back so I can look at you." She stood in the half-dark of the jacal, but there was enough starlight bouncing off the desert floor to make her out.

She had long raven hair tied back with red packing string. She wore a heavy Union coat patched at the elbows and one shoulder, and a doeskin skirt that fell below her knees. A narrow blue belt encircled her waist. She also wore moccasins and deerskin leggings. She was pretty, in that hard way the New Mexico desert makes people.

"You must be Magra Snowberry," I said.

"How do you know my name?"

"Your father told me."

Did I tell you it snowed the day she was born?

The twin bores of the shotgun never wavered. "Marwood. I heard talk about you. People said you worked a lot of bad towns in Montana Territory. Helena and the like. They say you killed men. A lot of men."

The way she said it somehow made me feel smaller than the stars ever could.

"Only when they needed killing."

She kept the gun trained on me. "I recognized you right away. Papa said you would wear a grey duster and carry a Colt Dragoon with a bone handle, holstered crossways."

This took me aback. "Your father—"

"Papa had visions," she interrupted. "Not knowing him, I don't expect you would understand his strange ways."

The eastern horizon sparked yellow fire. The moon was rising fast, owning the desert. There was enough light to see she had been crying. Her eyes looked like they had lampblack smeared under them.

"Mayhap I do understand, Magra. More than you think."

"I doubt that very much." She raised the coach gun and parked the heavy stock on her hip. "What are you doing out here, Marshal?"

"I want to find the men who killed your father."

"What is his life to you?"

"Law says they have to be caught and punished."

She looked me up and down. "And you're the new law in Haxan."

"I am now."

She thought a minute before she swung the door open with her free hand. Maybe she felt she had no other choice but to trust me. "All right, come in."

Despite what the place looked like on the outside, inside was neat and tidy and square. There wasn't much room, however. The close mesquite walls were more like a cage than a home. The mud ceiling was interlaced with *latillas*. Magra set the shotgun down and lighted a coal oil lamp swinging from an iron rafter hook.

The feeble glow cast awkward shadows on our faces and the packed-dirt floor.

"I have coffee."

"No thank you, Miss Snowberry. I'd rather talk about your father."

Her shrug was lost inside the large Union coat with its shoddy carpetbag patches.

"Papa was a good man," she began, "but he had a lot of old-world superstitions and queer ways. People didn't understand what he could see, and sometimes when they weren't laughing, they got scared."

She watched me with large, dark eyes. "You said you understood. I'm not sure I can believe that."

There was a chair and a rough-hewn table in the centre of the room. Without being asked I pulled the chair out and sat down. "Magra, it's hard to explain, but I'll try."

She sat on the other side of the table, her long brown hands folded.

"I'm listening," she said.

"Your father was right about some things. This world—everything you see around you and everything you can't see—is like a vast sea made up of crests and troughs. Sometimes a wave raises a person high enough and he can see a long way. I think your father was one of those people."

She watched me with steady eyes. "Go on."

"Other times, you're stuck at the bottom of a wave where the bad things collect." I used my hands to try and show her what that might look like. "I think that might be Haxan. And through this sea of time and dust, in places that might never be, or can't become until something is set right, there are people destined to travel. Forever."

"Papa talked about wandering Norse spirits. The Navajo, my mother's people, believe in skinwalkers."

I shook my head slow. "No, I'm talking about real people. Flesh and blood like you and me. They're taken from places they call home and sent into this stormy sea to help calm the waters. It never ends because it's the storm itself, the unending conflict, that makes the world we know a reality." I paused. "Along with all the other worlds that might be."

I had to give her credit. She didn't gainsay anything I said. I suppose she was used to hearing wild talk from her father. Whether she believed me or not was another question.

"Marshal, how was my father killed?"

"Someone nailed him to a tree with railroad spikes."

She closed her eyes. When she opened them again she looked years older. "Why would anyone do that to Papa?"

"If they thought he was a witch it stands to reason. A witch can be killed with cold iron."

"Papa wasn't a witch. He was only different."

"In this world that will always be enough to get you killed." The words sounded harsh even to my ears. "Magra, I know this hurts, but the men who killed your father thought otherwise. Did he have any enemies?"

"Not outright. Like I said, people were wary of him, but that's all."

"Scared people do bad things, Magra."

She pursed her lips in doubt. "I can't think of anyone who would want to kill him. Not like that."

"That's because you were used to his ways." I stood up. "You can't stay here. Whoever killed Shiner Larsen will come after you next."

"But why?"

"If they believed Larsen was a witch they might think you have powers, being his blood daughter. I know it sounds fanciful, this being the nineteenth century and all. But someone like this, well, that might be how they think."

So you can help her instead, Marwood. My daughter, I mean.

"I was going back to the reservation tomorrow. There's nothing for me here now that Papa is gone."

That was probably why they weren't here already, I thought. They're off riding for her in the country. I grimaced at my limited options.

"Maybe you can stay at the Haxan Hotel until I run these men down," I offered. "But, I have to warn you, that might take time."

She released a dry, ironic laugh. "Marshal, Alma Jean Clay won't let a half-breed sleep under her roof. Anyway, I have no money."

"Then you can stay in my office. You'll be safe there."

"That wouldn't look right, either. People will talk."

"I'm not here to make people like me, Magra. I've got a job to do as marshal. Tomorrow morning I'm going back to that hackberry tree and see if I can't cut their trail."

"You're going to track them down? All alone?"

"It's what I get paid for."

"When you find these men . . . what are you going to do?"

"Haxan is part of Judge Creighton's circuit. I know him pretty well. If they're found guilty they'll be taken to Santa Fe, or the county seat in Coldwater, and hanged."

Her gaze remained fixed on mine. "Yes. That's what the law says. But what are *you* going to do when you find them?"

She had a way of looking inside a man and seeing what was hidden.

"That's my business," I told her. "Now, take what you need for a couple of days and nothing else."

"I don't have a horse."

"My stallion can carry us both." I picked up the break-action shotgun and opened the breech. It was filled with buckshot: killing loads.

"You know how to use this?" I asked.

"Papa taught me. He never used it for hunting, only protection. He rode guard for Wells Fargo."

"So I heard. Too bad he didn't have it with him when he died." I snapped the breech closed and handed it back. "Keep it. You're likely to need it before this is all over."

While riding in I asked Magra about her name.

"I have a foot in both worlds, Marshal," she said. "One white, the other Navajo. Papa said I should be proud of both, even if neither one wanted me."

"He was right about that. The being proud part, I mean."

"When Papa saved a little money, and I got old enough, he sent me east to a boarding school."

"Where to?"

"Pennsylvania. They didn't want me, either, but I learned how to read and write. Now I teach children on the reservation."

Her words got me to thinking about my past. What little there was to remember.

"How did you hear about your father's death?" I asked. "I found him a couple of hours before I met you. No one in town could have told you in that time."

"He came to me in a dream many days ago. He was never one for writing letters. So he night-walked me sometimes to let me know how he was doing. He told me he was going to die soon. I raced back home to see if I could help, but I was too late. The house was empty."

She fell silent. We rode on. Somewhere an owl called across the flats.

"Why don't you ask me what you want to ask, Marshal?"

The girl sure had a way of seeing right into you. "All right, I'll play along. What did your father say about me?"

"That one day you would come to Haxan, or a man like you, because it was the centre of things. He said a man had to be here, in one way or another."

"You believe that story?"

"I don't know." She thought briefly. "You're here, aren't you?"

"I guess I am."

"Maybe that means something," she added.

We didn't talk after that. After a while she rested her chin on my shoulder as we rode through town.

It was true, though. We go where we're needed.

We have names and we stand against that which must be faced.

A dead man had called me to Haxan. I would serve his wish until I was successful or I died. There was no distinction between the two.

For me, and others like me, death and success were often the same thing.

CHAPTER 4

I reined outside the Haxan Hotel and helped Magra down from the tall horse. I unbuckled my saddle wallet, removed my war bag, pulled my .50-90 Sharps Special from the scabbard, and accompanied her inside the wide hotel lobby.

It was pleasant inside. The floor was white pine overlaid with red Oriental carpets. Red portieres fringed with gold tassels looked as if they'd been imported from Paris. Chesterfield lamps gave plenty of light to read by, and there were lots of overstuffed chairs to sit in.

A clerk in a claw-hammer coat and wearing egg-shaped spectacles worked behind a walnut reception desk itemizing receipts. His black hair was slick with macassar oil.

"You the desk man here?" I asked.

He laid his receipts aside. "Name is Hew Clay, mister. I own this hotel. You want a room?"

"I think I already have one, Mr. Clay. My name's John Marwood. I'm the new U.S. Marshal here in Haxan."

"Why, Marshal Marwood, what a great pleasure." Hew thrust out his hand. It was a good hand, warm and strong. He wasn't one to let deskwork get in the way of manual labour.

"Sign here, please." He swivelled the leather-bound registration book around. I signed it with an ivory-handled pen in my usual spidery scrawl. "We've been expecting you for days, Marshal."

"So I gathered."

He lifted a pass key from a board on the wall. "Your room is number three, Marshal. Top of the stairs and to the left. The window overlooks the plaza. I'm afraid the sun will blind you in the morning."

"I heard I can get supper here."

"Room and board paid for by the Haxan Peace Commission, as long as you keep your appointment as marshal. What will you have?"

"Skillet of ham and eggs. Fried potatoes and onions. Hot coffee, black."

His smile was quick. "Coffee is always hot in my hotel, Marshal."

"I'll hold you to that. I also need a room for this young lady."

He squinted over the rims of his glasses. "Why, I remember you. Miss Magra, isn't it?"

"That's right, Mr. Clay," she said in a tiny voice.

"Goodness, how you've grown since I saw you last. How is your father?"

"Her father was killed by unknown parties earlier today," I said.

Hew Clay's eyes widened in shock. "You don't say? Well, I'm downright sorry to hear that. I liked that old Swede. You have my deepest condolences, Magra."

"Thank you."

Hew laid a finger across his lips. "Um, Marshal, may I have a word with you in private?" He gave a slight bow in the direction of the girl. "Excuse us, Miss Magra, if you please."

I followed him around the end of the reception desk. We stood between a potted plant that had been over-watered and a gleaming brass spittoon. Hew leaned toward me like a hungry bird pecking seed.

"Now see here, Marshal," he began in a confidential air, "I don't mind having this girl in my place. I treat all paying customers alike. Well, within reason. But it's going to be the devil to pay if my wife, Alma Jean, finds out a breed is sleeping in one of the upstairs beds."

I started to say something, but Hew put up his hand.

"Not that I care," he said quick. "Girl can't help being what she's born. I'm sorry her father was killed. I want to help if I can."

"What are you proposing, Mr. Clay?"

"I can put a pallet in the stock room. She can stay long as she pays full price. That'll keep Alma Jean quiet." He scratched the back of his head, mussing the pomade. "For a little while, anyway. Best I can do, Marshal. You won't get a better offer. Not in Haxan."

I thought Hew Clay was a nice man who meant well. "I want to see this stockroom first," I said.

"Why sure, Marshal. It's clean. I guarantee that. The house cat sleeps there." He blinked and gulped when he realized what he had said. He rushed on in an attempt to cover up his mistake: "Don't you want to eat first?"

"The girl, too."

He was taken aback. "Why, of course, Marshal. Don't you think we're civilized?"

I didn't think he wanted an honest answer so I didn't say anything.

We went back to Magra. "Clay says he can set you up with a bed in the stockroom. I guess I'd rather you be around people than alone in the jailhouse. Is that all right with you? Leastways, until we find some better arrangement."

The look on her face told me it was more generous than she was expecting. "Of course. Thank you, Mr. Clay, for your hospitality."

"That's what I'm in business for." His smile was radiant.

"All right," I said, "bill my office for Magra's room and board. I'll see you get paid."

"Can't ask better than that, Marshal. Dining room is through those double doors, folks. Food will be out directly. Enjoy your stay."

He bustled away to get everything prepared.

"I'm going to drop this iron in my room," I told Magra. "I'll be down directly."

"I'll wait for you here," she said.

I climbed the steps and found my room. I unlocked the door and stepped inside.

There was a washstand with basin and mirror, and a Morris

chair. The bed had a feather mattress and a thick Navajo blanket folded at the foot. Under the bed was a johnny-pot in case I got caught short during the night. A fire rope was coiled in a wicker basket beside the window.

It wasn't the best room in the hotel, with its bare walls and plank floor, but it would accommodate me fine.

I threw my canvas war bag on the bed and unpacked. Change of shirt, stockings, straight razor and soap. Ivory handled shaving brush. U.S. Marshal's badge. Leather pouch of Virginia tobacco. There was also a double-barrelled .41-calibre derringer, skinning knife with stag handle, whetstone, extra gunpowder cartridges, lead balls, and caps.

It wasn't much to show for my years in law enforcement. Hell, it wasn't much to show for a life.

Then again, I had more than Shiner Larsen did. Maybe I shouldn't complain too much.

I pinned the badge to my vest and slipped the loaded derringer inside my right boot. It fit snug in a special leather pouch I had sewn myself. The skinning knife went into my pants pocket.

Standing before the mirror with a crack in one corner I washed my face and hands with cold water from the basin. I slicked my hair back with wet fingers.

After checking the loads in my gun I went downstairs to find Magra.

We ate at a secluded table in the corner, away from the open window. Hew was right about one thing: the coffee was hot when the waiter poured it from a two-gallon enamel pot.

I cleaned my plate. Magra finished her pronghorn stew and jalapeno biscuits. When we finished with coffee and pie for dessert I asked, "Do you mind if I smoke?"

"Of course not. Papa often smoked at night and told me stories about the kings and queens of Sweden. I like the smell."

I filled my pipe with Virginia Kinnikinnick and lighted it. I waved the match out and tossed it into a nearby spittoon. "I've got to go to work soon," I told Magra. "I'll be back later to see you're all right."

"I want to thank you for everything you've done, Marshal," she said. "This has been . . . a long and trying day."

"I know it has. I hope we can find the men who killed your father." The smoke from my pipe drifted above the table. "I want you to know I won't stop until I catch them."

"I know," she said softly. "I know that much at least."

We talked further about inconsequential things. When I finished my pipe I said, "Come on. Let's see this stockroom you'll be sleeping in."

I put a silver cartwheel on the tabletop to cover dinner and we drifted toward the lobby. Hew Clay brought us around back, through the kitchen, and revealed the bed he had made for Magra.

I still didn't like the idea of her sleeping in a stockroom with the house cat, but once again Hew was true to his word: it was clean.

"This will do for now," I said. "Thanks for your assistance, Mr. Clay."

"Call me Hew, Marshal. Miss Magra, you need anything, don't hesitate to ask. Hear?"

"Thank you for everything you've done, Mr. Clay."

"My pleasure, I'm sure. Marshal?"

We left her to get acquainted with her new surroundings.

"I want that girl protected," I told Hew once we were alone. "The men who killed her father might try for her next."

"I'll do what I can, Marshal." He pulled me aside again. He liked to stand between the plant and cuspidor. Maybe it was his special place.

"Marshal, listen," he began, "I really do want to help that girl. You see, my wife, Alma Jean, well, we lost our little boy a time ago. I know what that's like, losing a loved one. I promise I'll do whatever I can to help."

"I appreciate that sentiment, Hew. You got any protection in this hotel?"

"I've got a head knocking stick under the front desk. A three-foot long hickory stave, capped with iron."

"What about a gun?"

"I kept the Navy Colt I used during the war. Never could hit anything with it, though."

"Best clean and load it and start practicing. Where does the doctor stay in town?"

"Doc Toland's office is down on Front Street. It's the first two-storey building you'll come to, above the tailor shop."

I followed his instructions and climbed the steep stairs on the side of the two-storey building to a wooden door on a small, railed landing. A brass nameplate said:

REX TOLAND, M.D.
SURGEON & GENERAL PRACTITIONER

I knocked and went on through into an empty waiting room. "Doc Toland?"

He emerged from the back surgery, wiping his hands on a boiled towel. He was a narrow-faced man with grey muttonchops and rheumy brown eyes behind a pair of steel-rimmed spectacles. Late forties, medium size, receding chin. The cuffs of his black frock coat were dusty and there were chemical stains of various colours on his vest.

"Can I help you?" he asked. He stood bent forward at the waist, his shoulders slightly bowed.

"I'm the new U.S. Marshal," I said by way of introduction. "I've come to ask a favour."

"Happy to meet you, Marshal."

"Mind if we sit?"

He hesitated a second. "Come on back to my surgery."

We found a couple of chairs in the room behind his front office. Doc Toland had shelves stacked with bottles of all shapes and sizes holding all measure of minerals, salts, powders, and solutions. A weighing balance, mortar and pestle, and fluted glassware used for reactions and distillation were on a worktable.

In a glass-lined case below the window were steel knives, probes of various lengths, and a pair of brass forceps.

The room smelled strongly of lye soap, alcohol, and raw turpentine.

"Brought that equipment with me when I left Atlanta," he explained with a wink, "under, um, fantastic circumstances which we will not delve into for the sake of propriety."

"A lady by any circumstance, Doc?"

He leaned forward, animated. "My boy, she was a red-haired siren of a most tantalizing and dubious nature. She was also the wife of the hospital administrator." He fell back in his chair like a broken doll. "I can still hear the shotgun blast in my sleep." He put a hand out on a nearby shelf. "Anyway, this gear comes in handy. I'm the only fully equipped medical doctor outside Santa Fe."

"Doc, that's what I want to talk about. I've got a real job ahead of me and it's apt to get violent. Both for me and the men I have to go against."

He was dubious. "Not sure what you're getting at, Marshal."

"I'll say it straight out, Doc. I need a man I can depend on. Not one who's drug-addled all the time."

"I see. Well, that's plain enough." He opened a cedar box and removed a black cigarillo. His spidery fingers crisped the black leaf as he struck fire to the end. He whipped the match out, tossed it into an aluminum pan.

"So you've heard about that?" he asked.

"If you're talking about the laudanum, yes, I have. Doctor, I need a man who can patch me up using all his faculties. Same goes for the men I might have to bring in."

Men in this country weren't sheep. They weren't liable to come peaceable because I said please and thank you. I had to know there was someone I could trust on the medical end. If not, I would have to push Toland out of town and get someone I could depend on.

I explained all this to him in clear terms. "Believe me, when it's my life on the line, I'll sure do it. I'll post you out of town."

He squinched through a blue cloud of cigar smoke. "Like coming into a man's office and telling him what to do, don't you, son?"

"No, sir, I don't. We're both professionals. We have to work together. The law needs the support of medicine as much as medicine needs the law. That means you'll have to depend on me, too, Doc. I'm willing to accept that arrangement. The question is, are you?"

He smoked in contemplative silence, weighing it all out.

"I heard stories about you, Marwood," he said at length. "You've got a mean reputation. People say you cut a bloody swath up Montana Territory way. You get the job done, but at a high cost."

"The War Department sent me here at the behest of the Haxan Peace Commission because they thought I was the best man for the job. I'm not out to prove them right or wrong. I just intend to stay alive."

"What you want is to know if I can stay off the laudanum."

"Let's say I'm asking for mutual respect, one professional to another. That's all."

Doc Toland turned my proposition over in his mind. He rose and used a small silver key to unlock a walnut sideboard. He removed a tall square bottle with liquid sloshing around inside.

He pressed the bottle into my hand with some reluctance. "You hang onto that, Marshal. There may come a time when I need it. When that time comes, I request there be no questions asked on your behalf."

"Okay."

He took a deep breath. "However, in the meantime, I'll try and do as you ask."

I got up, slipping the bottle inside my grey duster. "Thanks, Doc. I won't forget this."

"Marshal Marwood, it's been a long time since someone treated me like the professional I once was," he said. "I want you to know that meant a lot, what you said. I thank you for it."

"We've got to pull together on this job, Doc, and that's a fact. Oh, one last thing. Can you perform autopsies?"

"I have all the equipment I need. I left Georgia with every-thing but my pride intact."

"It might be necessary, time to time. Submit your fee through my office. Okay?"

He looked as if an iron yoke had been lifted from his bowed shoulders. He was standing a little straighter and there was more more hope than despair in his face.

"I will look forward to working with you, Marshal."

I touched the brim of my hat. "Take care, Doc. Hope I don't have to see you too often."

A pawky grin tugged the corners of his mouth. "From what I hear that might be a false hope. But I share your sentiment."

I followed the stairs down and walked across the plaza into a general store. It was the one with stamped metal panels on the outside.

"I'm going to need a few things, and provender, for the office," I told the proprietor after I introduced myself.

Mr. Whatley whipped a pencil from behind his ear and pressed it to paper. "Go ahead with your order, Marshal."

"Five pounds of beans. Salt. Sugar. A tin of Arbuckle coffee. Enough to last the week. You got any pemmican?"

"We've got *charqui*."

"That will do, along with hard biscuit or tack. Oh, and one of those new blue enamel coffee pots over yonder. New lamp and coal oil bucket. Potato for the spout. Block of sulphur matches."

I walked across the store toward the gun cabinet. Rifles and shotguns lined the wall, kept under lock and chain. Pistols and ammunition were laid out neat beneath a shining glass case.

"Five of these new Winchester rifles, a hundred rounds of ammunition, and gun oil." I remembered the gun Magra carried. "Before I forget, a box of double-ought shells for a Stevens double-barrel coach gun. I'll also need powder, cap and ball for this."

I swept my grey duster aside, revealing the yellow-bone handle of a Colt Dragoon.

"Nice percussion gun, Marshal. A real stopper, too." His brow crinkled. "That handle made of antelope horn?"

"No."

"Well, it's not ivory or jigged." He watched me close.

"No, it's not."

"Carve it yourself?"

"Yes. I always change the loads every morning in case they get damp overnight." That wouldn't be much of a problem here in the desert, but old habits were hard to break.

"I hear you," he said. "Pays to be careful."

"Therefore I will need enough ammunition for the week," I said. "I also have need of writing paper, pen and ink, lead pencils, and envelopes for office work. Got all that?"

He finished writing it all down in a careful hand. "When do you want this delivered, Marshal?"

"Anytime tomorrow will suit."

"Happy to oblige. I'll box it up myself." I started for my wallet.

He put out a hand to stop me. "No, Marshal. I fought for the Union Army in Gettysburg. I guess I have to believe you're good for it. Anyway, I prefer to settle up a bill like this at the end of the month. Makes booking easier, my end."

"Not a problem with me, Mr. Whatley. Good night."

"Night, Marshal."

I stepped outside. Polgar had said a Texas herd of four thousand longhorns had dusted in yesterday morning, beaten and tired from the trail. Another herd of three thousand was arriving tomorrow, or the day after, though they were scheduled to press north for Denver. Nevertheless, cattle agents were already trying to undercut one another and vying for limited space on the night train. Cowboys had been paid off and were looking to shoot the moon and maybe anyone who stepped in their way. Three of them raced down Front Street on their cow ponies, firing pistols in the air. One or two pistol shots answered in reply around the plaza. Five men staggered down Cutt Street, singing and passing a bottle of rye between them.

It was going to be a long, and busy, first night.

I drew a deep breath and hefted the Sharps rifle in my hand. I walked with purpose across the plaza, pushed through the flap doors of the first saloon I came to—a raucous place called the Texas Star. It smelled of sour whisky, rank sweat, and stale tobacco.

Without any warning at all I discharged the buffalo gun into the ceiling.

"Welcome to Haxan, boys," I said.

CHAPTER 5

I stepped out of the way of yellow plaster sifting down from the ceiling.

"Now that I've got your attention, here are a few new rules," I told the stunned audience. "As set down by the Haxan Peace Commission and enforced by myself, United States Marshal John T. Marwood. These rules are posted outside my office for anyone to see. For those who can't read, I'll make it plain."

I swept back my grey duster so they could see the yellow-bone handle of my gun and the federal badge. No one moved or said a word.

"I've already talked to Mayor Polgar and cleared it with him and the Haxan Peace Commission. First, the deadline on Potato Road remains down long as everyone behaves himself." There was a lessening of tension. People smiled at one another. So far they liked what they heard.

"We want you to have a good time in Haxan," I said. "Spend your wages and buck the tiger. The beer is cold, the whiskey raw, and Haxan girls are pretty."

Laughter.

"Now that's the kind of law I like," someone said aloud. He was a cowboy sitting at a table with another man.

I was aware of people gathering outside, listening through the flap doors.

"You may wonder about your side guns. Keep them. You don't have to check them with my office like you do in other towns." That trick never worked anyway. A man could always hide a gun. You give a man a reason to break a law, he's going to do it.

"However, they must stay holstered," I added. "Same goes for knives and coshes. It's illegal to discharge any gun in city limits unless you're defending yourself, or it's the Fourth of July. Doing so is a ten-dollar fine and a night in jail for every shot fired. No excuses."

I made it a point to look at three hard men clumped around one end of the bar. I could smell the dust, leather, and rank sweat emanating from them.

"If you don't give a man a call, and if eye-witnesses don't testify it was a fair fight, I'll see you kick at the end of a rope. That's all."

"Plain enough," one of the men said with a careless shrug and drank his whiskey.

I walked between beer-stained, cluttered tables toward the bar. It was nothing more than a wooden plank on empty nail barrels. Someone had slapped a coat of cheap varnish on it as an afterthought. Antelope and bison horns decorated the walls. The grimy mirror behind the bar was festooned in red, white, and blue bunting that had never been washed. The floor was thick with old, sour sawdust. A tattered Texas flag hung limp from one of the middle rafters.

Two men stood uneasily behind the bar. "Which one of you is the owner?" I asked.

"I am," the older and slimmer of the two answered. He wore steel-rimmed spectacles and a paisley vest. "Jonah Hake at your service, Marshal. I can't say I appreciate you coming in and shooting up my establishment."

I gazed at the ceiling. There were over a dozen bullet holes in the dark rafters and cheap plaster.

"You find which one I'm liable for and I'll pay to have it plugged," I said.

General, whooping laughter. More of the marked tension in the room eased. So far no one had heard anything unexpected. If anything, with the deadline down, and allowing them to keep their guns, it was better than anyone had hoped.

"You run gambling tables, Mr. Hake?"

"A little faro." He made a side gesture. "The usual draw poker and stud, if the boys can scare up a game."

I faced the crowd, elbows resting on the rim of the bar. The cowboy who had quipped about the laws he liked sat two tables away, big feet propped on a chair. The rowels of his Mexican spurs cut the wood. A scornful smile touched his face as he returned my stare. He had a tall glass of beer in one hand. He was going on thirty, with long, greasy hair and a walrus moustache that was mud-brown at the ends. He wasn't wearing a rig, but that didn't mean he wasn't carrying a gun or some other weapon. The second man sat across from him. He wore striped pants, green suspenders, square-topped boots with mule ear tugs, and a wide-brimmed hat with a frayed horsehair band.

Partners, I thought. Both looked like they had just beat trail dust off themselves.

I addressed the crowd again, and the crowd outside the bat-wing doors. "As for gambling, it's your money. But if I hear of a dealer running a crooked game I promise you he's seen the last of Haxan."

"Marshal," one of the girls across the room piped, "I heard tell a town marshal in Dodge, he caught a card sharp. He broke the man's dealing hand with the edge of a shovel and posted him out of town."

"Is that all? They're going soft in Dodge these days."

A few men thumped the bar and called in high voices for drinks. Even the scornful cowboy joined in the laughter.

"Furthermore, any crooked game run by a saloon, or a saloon turning a blind eye so a card sharp has an easy time of it, I'll shut it down for a week. If the saloon repeats the offense, I'll horsewhip the proprietor out of town and *burn* his place down."

"Marshal, you don't have the authority to do that," someone challenged.

"Mister, you telegraph Helena and ask what happened in the Bucking Sally last winter when they called my bluff."

That grabbed their attention. Everyone west of the Mississippi had heard about that fire.

I cocked an eyebrow at the bartender. "Do I make myself clear, Mr. Hake?"

"I run a square house, Marshal. Never had a complaint and that's a fact."

"I don't doubt it, Mr. Hake. I wasn't singling you out. You'd best prod the other owners and let them know how I stand. The days of running wild in this town are over."

"I got no problem with that, Marshal. I can make more money your way."

I addressed the crowd one final time. There was now a sea of faces in the street outside. Pale blobs in the dim light. Good. That's what I wanted. Word would spread fast.

"As you can see I'm an easy man to get along with." Most people returned my grin. "But the first time it looks like this saloon can't abide by these rules, then the deadline goes back up and I start checking guns. Then I'll push the rest of you out of town. I've said my piece."

I touched the brim of my hat. "Enjoy your evening, gentlemen." Two girls were in a corner of the room. One was perched in a wolfer's lap, her naked arm hooked around his shoulders. "Ladies."

As I shouldered my way through the throng I heard someone clip in a loud, shrill voice, "Just another quack-doodle."

I stopped. There is always one. There always has to be at least one no matter how hard you try and make them understand you want to be fair.

I retraced my steps and stood in front of the cowboy who had his boots resting on the chair.

"What was that you said?"

"You heard me, lawman. You're a quack-doodle. Quacking like a momma duck to get her baby ducks in a row."

"Shut up, Fancer." The other man at the table had a bland, but weather-seasoned, face. "Marshal's doing his job."

"Well, I ain't no duck," Fancer told him without taking his eyes off mine, "and I don't skeer from big talk. I don't like any man thinking I'll fall in line 'cause he barks orders."

He had said his piece. "What's your name, cowboy?"

He turned his head and spat on the sawdust floor. "Fancer Bell."

"Sounds like a summer name."

He laughed under his breath and knuckled his moustache. "Mebbe. There ain't no readers out on me. You can look."

"Stand up, Mr. Bell."

"I'm comfortable where I sit, quack-doodle."

I kicked the chair out from under his feet. "I said stand up, you shitheel."

That got him riled. He rose swiftly, narrow eyes blazing, calloused fists balled. He was ready to go at me hard.

I pointed. "That your beer?"

He paused, blinking with uncertainty. He took in the half-filled glass. "Yeah. I reckon it is."

"Drink it."

He glared from the corner of his eye. "Say again, quack-doodle?"

"Drink your beer."

He mugged in disbelief. "Like I said, them are laws I like."

No one smiled. There was danger in the room. They could smell it even if he couldn't. Fancer didn't like their reaction. People of his sort, hitting out at the world, never do. They never understand if they swing too wide, too far, all they do is leave themselves off balance and defenceless.

To save face he lifted his beer mug and drained it.

He slammed the empty glass down and swept the back of his hand across his lips. A questioning look filled his face. I had flummoxed him.

"Why'd you ask me to drink off that beer, Marshal?"

"Because there's no sense wasting paid-for liquor before I take you apart."

Before he could react I slammed the stock of the Sharps rifle into the middle of his stomach. He doubled over. His hand flicked from under a thick fleece-lined jacket—he was holding a long, cruel knife. I spun on my boot heel and brought the heavy octagonal barrel of the Sharps down across the back of his head.

He crashed to the floor, overturning two tables in the process and sending cards and chips flying. He was senseless.

"You killed him!" one of the girls shrieked.

"He's not dead," I said. "I just crunched him some."

I picked up the knife. It was a long tooth-picker with "G.R." stamped into the blade. I leaned it against an overturned table and broke the tempered blade with my boot heel.

I asked the man who was sitting immobile in the other chair, "This man your partner?"

"Not if it means going to jail, he ain't."

"Take your friend to Doc Toland's and get him patched up. Pour hot coffee into him and sober him. You men ride in with a herd?"

"Four thousand head up from Brownsville. We got paid off yesterday."

"What's your name, mister?"

"Jake Strop, sir."

I returned a respectful nod. "Take care of your friend. Next time he acts up I'll arrest him."

I walked out of the Texas Star. People shouted with joy behind me and clamoured for beer and whiskey hand over fist.

"Right there," I heard someone's nasal cry. "That's where he shot the ceiling."

The night was off to a good start. Word of mouth would see that most people remembered it. I had to make it clear with a kind of brutal finality that the new laws in Haxan were chiselled in stone and irrevocable.

Haxan had to be shaken up. People had to awaken from their stupor and know, once and for all, things had changed.

And changed for the better.

So I wasn't peeved an opportunity had presented itself in the form of one hapless Fancer Bell. If busting up one drunk cowboy like Bell got the word across then it was a good trade, in my estimation.

I went from saloon to saloon, cantina to cantina. The town had had no real law for months. I couldn't help but wonder if that might have been the reason Shiner Larsen's murderers felt so free to act in the brutal manner they did.

When I had a little free time from my rounds, I decided I'd try my hand at some detective work. Playing a hunch, I went inside the livery stable. The night man and proprietor, Patch Wallet, had a broad stomach, thick forearms, and a wide face with many broken teeth in his lower jaw. His shirt was unbuttoned halfway, revealing a mat of grizzled hair on his chest.

"Horse kicked me in the jaw when I was sixteen," he said. His words jumbled together like rocks in a wooden pail. "Kind of messed up my teeth and my talk, and I never had them fixed. Got a pot of coffee boiling, if you're interested."

"I could use some." The long night stretched ahead of me.

We entered a narrow L-shaped room behind the stables with a frame bed, cotton ticking mattress, and a cast-iron stove. You could smell the warm horses, sweet hay, and sharp manure through broken wall slats. The soft movements of the animals in their stalls served as an undercurrent of familiar song on the night air.

Patch Wallet poured me a steaming cup. "I don't have sugar. Molasses do?"

"Black suits me fine."

He nodded. "Coffee ain't good anyway 'less it's black."

We drank in quiet for a space. "Heard you've had a busy night," Patch said.

"It's not over, Mr. Wallet. That's why I'm here. Maybe you heard about Shiner Larsen. I found wagon tracks where he was murdered but I didn't have enough light left to run them down. Have you sold or rented a wagon to anyone of late?"

He rubbed his whiskered face. The broken teeth raised bumps through his skin along his jaw. "Now you mention it, Marshal, I rented a spring-seat buckboard with team only three days ago."

He showed me the transaction in a records book he kept under the bed.

"Fellow by the name of Connie Rand paid in advance for the

wagon. Said he wanted it for a week because he had light freight to move. Two men rode with him. I didn't recognize their faces, though."

"You knew this first man?"

"Yes, sir. Conrad Rand. Tall man, early forties, I guess, with short white-blond hair. Brown eyes. Left eyelid droops. Folks around call him Connie. He doesn't like that name much 'cause he thinks it's girly. He done anything wrong, Marshal?"

"What work does he do, this Rand?"

"Hires out the week on the big ranches, drinks and whores his wages on the weekend like everybody else. Heard he also runs with a gang of *comancheros* out of Texas panhandle."

I thought about Marshal Breggmann. "Hm. Big ranches like the Lazy X?"

Patch Wallet rolled his thick shoulders in a careful shrug. "Can't say for right certain 'bout that. It's not like he's blood kin to me or anything."

"Where does Rand stay when he's in town?"

"Who knows? This is Haxan. He drifts."

"The two men with Rand. Can you describe them?"

"Not so good, Marshal. They kept down the street and had the sun behind them before they all left out."

I drained my coffee. "Thank you for your time, Mr. Wallet. You gave me more to work on than I had five minutes ago."

"Don't go, Marshal. I can't describe the men, but I can describe their horses."

I faced back around. "How's that?"

"I've got an eye for horses, Marshal, even when the sun's against me. One of the men rode a bay with three black points. The other sat a sorrel mare."

I stayed for a second cup of coffee but Patch didn't remember anything else of importance. Before leaving I checked on my horse and made arrangements to stable and feed him.

"I want him exercised every day."

"I'll take care of him, Marshal." Patch cast an experienced eye along the lines of the blue roan. He brushed his rough, broken-knuckled hand along the horse's withers. "Fine animal. If you're looking to sell I'll pay you top dollar."

"Not looking to sell."

Patch shook his head at the lost opportunity. "Can't say I blame you. That's a top piece of horseflesh, that is."

I left the livery stable and rounded the plaza on foot. The saloons were raucous and busy. Lights splashed out on the boardwalks and street corners. Spanish guitar trickled out of a cantina and climbed into the night with a woman's laughter in tow. I checked all the horses at the tie rails out front, but I didn't spot a three-point bay or a sorrel mare.

As I searched I couldn't stop thinking about Shiner Larsen and what he said before he died. It wasn't unusual someone like him had called someone like me into the maelstrom.

All of the places we protect are like that. They spin like a huge storm in time and space, warping reality and sucking people in. Sometimes people disappear forever. Sometimes I make them disappear.

Now I was here in Haxan, alone and called to service, but this time by a dead man. The only connection I had left with Larsen was his daughter, and there were men who wanted to kill her, too.

I would not let that happen. By my life, I would not.

I strolled through tent city. The air was filled with flying wood smoke. There was horse dung and offal between the tents. Men passed bowls of raw whiskey across a crackling fire. I found two miners who tied an old Navajo to a cottonwood tree. They traded shots at a bottle on his head while betting who could come closest without killing him. I cuffed one and the second swung a haymaker at me. I beat the barrel of my Colt Dragoon across his face and opened his nose down to the bone. He fell, whiffling like a baby while blood ran between his fingers. His friend tried to run. I hooked my boot around his ankle and brought him down in a mess of pear cactus.

After this they decided they didn't want to fight. I put them under arrest and told the Navajo, "Go home, old grandfather. They won't hurt you again."

The white-haired man clutched a threadbare blanket around his naked shoulders. His legs poked through his britches like knobby sticks. "Are you Long Blood?" he asked.

"I don't know what you're talking about. Go home."

I shoved my two prisoners toward town. After I locked them up I stopped by a two-storey frame house on the dog end of Calle de Santiago, a tree-lined dirt street running perpendicular to the plaza. Outside, a white shingle swung from a brass rod:

THE TOPSY TUMBLE
GENTLEMEN CALLERS WELCOME
ADELE BOUVIER, PROP.

A skinny, elfin girl, with chestnut hair in drooping sausage curls and a green choker with a silver buckle, met me at the door. She was in full war paint. Her pupils were unnaturally large—many girls swallowed belladonna to get the special effect of "bedroom eyes."

Inside the richly appointed entrance hall stood a red leather sofa and green satin chairs. The walls were panelled in alternating oak and mahogany. In each corner of the hallway stood a white marble pedestal topped with a potted green plant.

The place exuded a quiet air of sex, discretion, and high money.

"Help you, mister?" She was chewing licorice. Her pale yellow chemise was off one brown shoulder. She adjusted the chemise but it slipped off again.

"What's your name?"

"My name is Bertha."

"Who runs this house, Bertha?"

"You looking for trouble?" She smiled, her lips red with grease. Some was on her teeth. "Because we got lots of that."

CHAPTER 6

My name is John Marwood." I showed her the badge.

"I seen them things before," Bertha said.

"I'm a federal officer on official business."

She sobered up fast. "Oh, a federal man. You'll want Miss Bouvier. I'll find her for you. Chair's over there if your legs get tired standing or somethin'."

She flounced and disappeared like pale smoke through a green velvet curtain fringed with gold balls.

I didn't wait long. Adele Bouvier unlocked a door at the distant end of the hallway and bustled through with a practiced, and perfected, smile pinned to her face. Her ink-black hair had a streak of silver and was done up with an expensive jade comb. Her black and beige business suit was immaculate. Her nails were long, cut square, and heavily lacquered. She smelled faintly of attar of roses and stale cigar smoke.

"You must be Marshal Marwood," she said in a lilting accent with a lot of Mississippi mud in the vowels. "I've heard 'bout you. One of my girls was in the Texas Star earlier tonight. I'm Adele Bouvier. Friends call me Miss Addie."

I shook her hand. She leaned close so I could feel her warmth. She let her languid hand linger in mine so I could marvel at how soft and helpless it felt. Like she would be in a four-poster bed inside of a minute if that's what I wanted.

"I'm here on business," I reminded her.

"Oh, too bad."

"I don't want any misunderstanding, Adele. You may remain open long as your girls stay clean and there's no hint of robbery or blackmail with the customers. No girls on the street, either, unless they work the tents. Keep it inside. Get the word out to the other madams. I don't know them, you do. We'll see about setting up a safe district so you ladies can stay together and feel protected, if that's what you want."

She wasn't affronted in the least by my open talk about sex. She knew the give and take with the law, and the wink and the nod with city elders, that went with her business.

"My girls are clean, Marshal. They're checked every month by a doctor. I have a very profitable enterprise here. I have no interest in doing anything to undermine that."

Her hand remained on my arm, as if she had forgotten all about it.

"But you must understand those cowboys can get rowdy, Marshal. I have to bust heads if they hurt my girls. You understand."

"You employ a bouncer?"

"Red Sam—a black foreman off my father's plantation in Natchez. He keeps everything nice and orderly." She flipped a dismissive hand. "He has his own little farm on Crooked Stick Creek and a very nice family. He does this for extra pay."

"Long as we see eye to eye, Adele, I have no problem with that."

"You want your sin money paid every week? Or would you rather take it out in trade?"

"Neither. I'm trusting you to do the right thing. Keep paying your license fee and the commission won't bother you too much. If you have any trouble, aside from the usual bedroom brawl, you let the law handle it."

She viewed me with growing wonder. "I've never met a lawman who didn't want sin money or skin trade in return. Okay, Marshal, we'll try it your way. On one condition."

"What's that?"

"You call me Addie, like I said."

I grinned. "All right." I had a brain wave. "Come to think of it, perhaps you can help me after all, Addie. I'm looking for a man."

She laughed. "Aren't we all?"

"His name is Connie Rand." I gave her the description.

"He wanted for outlawry?"

"I want to question him."

"I'm asking because we get our fair share of spoilers. No, Marshal, I haven't heard of Rand. I think I can trust you. Leastways, as much as I trust any man. If I see this Connie Rand I'll let you know."

"Keep this between us, Addie." She was pure mercenary and I knew she wouldn't hesitate to sell Rand or myself out if the chance presented itself and the profit margin was high enough. I still thought it was worth a gamble. Whores had eyes where no lawman ever did.

"Sure, Marshal. I know how to keep a confidence. Part of my work."

"Then I'll say good night to you."

She followed me to the door. "Marshal, you ever want to come by and have coffee and cinnamon cake, you're more than welcome. I don't get many nice gentlemen callers."

"Thanks. I appreciate the invitation."

Her hand rested on the gold doorknob. The lamplight was full on her face; there were lines around her mouth and her eyes, but she was a handsome woman. She wasn't one of those rail-thin consumptive women you often see working the line. She had womanly curves a man could appreciate, and she knew how to carry herself in regal fashion.

She touched my hand, holding me back.

"I'm sincere, Marshal. Most lawmen would have barged in and ordered me around. You didn't push at all. You treated me like I was somebody and not a rag cowboys wipe their peckers on. You don't know how that makes me feel." She gave my arm a final squeeze. "My offer of coffee and cake stands."

"I won't forget. You don't forget what I said, either. Good night."

"Good night, Marshal."

As I turned down the lane I looked back. Her slim figure was silhouetted in the rectangular light of the doorway.

I pulled my pocket watch and flipped the dust cover open. Going on eleven. The biggest saloons and dance halls would stay open all night. One last stop, then I would head to the office and start on paperwork for my two prisoners.

I crossed the plaza and turned into the Quarter Moon. I gave the usual talk, abbreviated, because the word was out and my speech had lost a lot of its punch.

August Wicker, who was also a founding member of the Haxan Peace Commission, owned the establishment. He hustled me aside.

"I wish you would shoot a hole in my ceiling, Marshal," he pleaded. He was a pear-shaped man with a smooth voice like croton oil. His side-whiskers were combed out and his eyebrows were thick and heavy, like coal smudged on wrinkled paper. His hair was so full of pomade it looked painted on.

"Maybe I can carve my initials in that piano over there."

"I'm not joking, Marshal. Jonah Hake sold more whiskey tonight than he has in a month. That's hardly fair to me."

"I'll tell you the same thing I told Jonah. If I catch any crooked games I'll shut you down, Wicker."

His lips were wide and rubbery. His eyes were kind of slanted like that of a hungry catfish.

"Marshal, there's no call for that. Look around you. My place is the biggest and the fanciest in town. That diamond-dust mirror cost over a thousand dollars. The oil painting above the bar, the one of the bull snorting flames from his nostrils and the naked girl sleeping on his back? That was commissioned from New York. We've got nice rooms upstairs for the girls. The Quarter Moon isn't like those other horse-traps. Okay, the Sassy Sage has girls swinging over the bar and a parrot that barks like a dog, and meows like a cat. I concede that's a real attraction. But my place has class. You can't buy class."

I watched a roach on the floor nibbling beer-soaked breadcrumbs.

"I can see that," I said.

"Best pay-out roulette tables in town, too. Guaranteed

winners. Any game you want I got. Dice, faro, roulette, chuck-a-luck. You name it, we've got it."

"Same rules go for you, Wicker. No special favours."

"Why, Marshal, that's what the commission wants so that's what I want." He quickly changed the subject. "How about a beer? On the house, to commemorate your first night on the job."

"Okay. Sure."

"Dave, a draft of our finest for our new marshal."

"Coming right up, Mr. Wicker," one of the bartenders replied. He wore a crisp white shirt with a celluloid collar and starched apron. Red garters were snug around each arm. He served the foaming beer with a proud flourish.

Wicker watched me take a drink. "What did I tell you, Marshal? We ice our beer down. We don't put it in a water barrel like those other horse-traps. You get quality service in the Quarter Moon. I pay my saloon girls proper and hardly have to knock them around. Why—"

"I been looking for you all night, lawdog."

You get so you recognize the inflection.

Sometimes they make it clear outright and you have to pull your gun and spin and shoot, leaving your life to chance. This voice wasn't like that. It had the timbre of a man who wanted to seal his reputation, yes. He was standing on the edge of a razor, waiting to see which way he might fall. There are men like that. They work up enough nerve until they push themselves to the brink where they call someone, even a stranger, out.

The really craven ones back-shoot a drunk on the street, or cut the throat of a stray dog at night. Then they pretend they were upholding some semblance of honour. This voice wasn't like that, either. It was just a man who, at this point in life, thought it would be a fine idea to call a U.S. Marshal out. Hell, he might get lucky and kill me. In his mind he associated that luck with fame.

In other words, he didn't give a damn what happened to either of us. These were the most dangerous kind of killers because they were careless with their lives, and the lives of others.

I set my beer down and turned around, slow. People had

already moved aside and cleared a path between us. The smart ones ducked through the bat-wing doors and fled outside.

He stood twenty feet away beside a roulette table. I pegged him as a boy off the farm. Early twenties, with fuzz on his face that he wished would pass for man-whiskers. He wore pants torn at one knee, a sleeveless shirt of coarse homespun, and a white planter's hat with a snap-brim. He didn't sport a rig. He wore his gun, a rusty Navy Colt, thrust through the belt of his pants.

He had probably practiced with it all of one afternoon after hearing there was a new marshal in town. The body of a federal lawman would cement his reputation like nothing else could.

It would make him somebody, instead of a nameless farmhand who hated and feared life and everyone around him.

August Wicker started forward. "My good man, there is no gunplay allowed in this establishment. Why don't you—"

I grabbed Wicker's collar and shoved him aside. "Shut up and get out of the way, Wicker," I growled. Few things made gunfights more dangerous than idiot bystanders who stumbled in your way. They interrupted the rhythm of the challenge and made muscles twitch before they were meant to twitch.

Idiots like that were more dangerous than the man you had to face.

Wicker gawped at me, his fat mouth opening and closing like a fish that couldn't get oxygen.

I kicked my grey duster back with one hand, revealing the bone handle of my Colt Dragoon. "You called me out, boy?"

The air inside the saloon froze into a block of ice. Nobody moved or breathed. Movement meant death. Beer dribbled from an open tap into a metal basin. Even Wicker's rubbery mouth stopped gulping for air.

"I guess I did." The boy swallowed, squared his shoulders. "I'm going to roll a hammer on you, Marshal."

That's when I heard something else deep in his voice. A tiny note of creeping doubt. A shadow scream coiled somewhere inside his brain telling him that maybe this wasn't such a good idea after all. But he had pushed things too far along and had to be taught this wasn't a game. Despite what the sainted philosophers say, living has always been a man's one real trade.

If he moved wrong he was going to die, and he knew it.

"Trust me, son," I said slow. "You don't want this distinction."

"What distinction might that be?"

"Of being the first man I kill in Haxan."

I let him chew that for ten seconds. It dug into him and set a hook in his lower gut.

"But if dying is what you crave, then killing you will serve no great hardship on me."

"Sweet Mary," a card dealer whispered from the crowd, "it's like he doesn't care if he kills that boy or not."

The kid heard it, too. My voice. Not the words, but the meaning they carried. He looked inside me and came face to face with his own mortality.

It's always that way between two men about to cross guns. You become close. You reach an understanding. You become brothers because you're living together in that single moment in time no one can share, and you just might die together in a combined roar of fire and acrid smoke. So you might as well face each other like brothers in the last second you have left in the world.

He glanced down at the crooked gun butt protruding from his belt. He removed it and laid it on a card table. Then he turned and walked through the swing doors and into the warm night.

I picked up the gun from the table and broke the cylinder open. He had loaded it incorrectly. The hammer would have fallen on an empty chamber with his first shot.

August Wicker approached, his round face pale as Blue John milk. "I've never seen anything like it. Aren't you going to arrest him, Marshal?"

"What for? He's a kid drunk on popskull whiskey and witless to boot. With luck he had sense scared into him tonight." I unloaded the Navy Colt and handed it to Wicker, butt first. "A memento. Hang it over the bar and charge an extra ten cents so patrons can see the famous gun."

Before he could reply I turned on my heel and left. I'd had

quite enough of Wicker, and Haxan, for one night.

Outside, the boy sat slumped on the edge of the wooden sidewalk, head buried in his hands. He might have been crying.

"Go home, son," I told him. "No matter how bad it is living is always preferable to dying."

I didn't wait for him to speak. This was a decision he had to make himself. No man could do that for him.

We all grow up in different ways.

The rest of the night wasn't too bad. I broke up several fights, collected more fines, and arrested two more men for public drunkenness. One had his head submerged in a water trough. He had passed out and liked to drowned if I hadn't stopped by in time. The other christened my jail cell by vomiting his supper on the floor.

Later that night, as the saloons were winding down and a glimmer of red appeared on the eastern horizon, two buffalo hunters pulled six-guns on each other in the Double Eagle. They popped a couple of shots at one another, but were too drunk to hit anything. I slammed the barrel of my rifle across the back of one's legs. When he went down it cleared the way for my rifle stock to smash the other's blunt, heavily whiskered face.

The second man was out for the count but the first wanted to open me up. He yanked a hunting knife from his boot and lunged. I took hold of his wrist and used his momentum to slam him into the bar with all my strength. The crash shook the flimsy walls of the saloon. He crumpled and I kicked the knife from his hand. He reached for a Colt Pocket Model inside his coat and found himself with the bore of my Colt Dragoon pressed against his nose so hard it made his eyes water.

I rolled the hammer back so he could hear the click through his drunken haze. He soiled himself and dropped the gun. I confiscated their guns, fined them each fifty dollars, and kicked them out of town after Doc Toland patched them up with iodine and plaster.

"It's been steady all night long, Marshal," he said.

"Glad I could accommodate you, Doc."

"You look beat, John. Best get some sleep."

"Headed that way after I make one more round of the town and finish some paperwork."

An hour later I checked on my prisoners and locked the office up tight. I headed back to the Haxan Hotel at the end of the road. It had been a long day and an even longer night. I was bone-tired. I hoped to snatch a couple hours sleep before riding out where Shiner Larsen was killed. I still wanted to cut those tracks and run that wagon and those horses down.

"Marshal!"

A redheaded boy, eight or nine years old and dressed in drab homespun, ran up the wooden sidewalk toward me. He had to pause and catch his breath. "Mayor Polgar told me to find you, Marshal. There's a fire out at the edge of town. Two men are dead. Mr. Polgar says you'd better get out there fast."

"What's your name, boy?"

"Davie Peake." He threw out his narrow chest. "My friends call me Piebald seeing as how I got this marking on my—"

"Run to the livery stable and get my horse saddled, Piebald. Bring him back to my office."

"You mean Old Sheriff Cawley's place? The one by the feed store?"

"That's right."

"Won't take me long, Marshal. I can run a hole in the wind when I want to."

"Then let's see you do it."

"Yes, sir." He disappeared in a flurry of kicking feet.

I went to the stockroom in the hotel. Magra was asleep. She had turned her Union coat backward, using it as a blanket.

I woke her up.

"Magra. Someone has been out to your place tonight. They burned your house to the ground and killed two men."

"What for?"

"I don't know for sure. I'm headed out there now. Here's your shotgun. You stay awake until I get back."

"Where are you going?"

"I told you, out to Gila Creek. You stay inside my office. Here's the key so you can lock yourself inside. There are prisoners in back, but they won't harm you. I'll be back soon as I can."

After seeing Magra safely away I met Piebald outside with my saddled horse. I swung into the saddle and kicked for Shiner Larsen's place.

CHAPTER 7

When I rounded the bend I saw three men watching the last of the night breeze scatter the remaining embers and sparks from the house fire. Polgar met me as I drew rein, his face creased with worry.

"Good thing you brought that girl back to town last night, John. Whoever did this," he hooked a thumb over his shoulder, "was looking for her."

"Where are the two dead men?"

"Down in that ravine. Shot through the heart, their throats cut like butchered hogs."

"You recognize them, Frank?"

Polgar shook his head. "People always drift through Haxan. Sometimes they don't leave."

"Who found them?"

An older man and his teenage son came forward. "Marshal, we were rounding up stray calves in a slot canyon to the west when we saw the glow of a big fire. We found them two dead men and rode in to tell the mayor there."

Polgar studied the smouldering debris. "They trampled the corn and shot Larsen's pig. Why would a person do a thing like that, John?"

I dismounted and scraped my boot heel across parallel lines in the dirt.

"Buckboard." I scrambled down the crumbling bank of the ravine. I turned the men over and examined their faces.

"Frank."

He slid down the ravine by my side. Loose dirt piled around our boots. "Yeah?"

"These men were dead long before they were shot."

"How do you know?" Polgar asked.

"There's not enough blood on their shirts, even though their throats were cut. Their clothes are burned and singed in one spot from the hot powder of a gun. Which means they were also shot point-blank. I want you to take these bodies back to Doc Toland so he can do an autopsy right away."

"Rex Toland?" Polgar snorted. "Have to sober him up first."

"I've already talked to him about that," I snapped. I took my hat off and ran my fingers through my hair. "Sorry, Frank. I want to know what killed them, that's all."

I stood over the bodies. There was an unusual, yet familiar, odour coming from them. I couldn't place it because the morning air was filled with dust and swirling wood smoke that stung my eyes.

I frowned, my mind working like a lathe while I listened to the doves cooing on the morning air.

"What's wrong, John?"

"These men aren't hired killers."

"How do you know?"

"Because I ran these two buffalo hunters out of Haxan early this morning. They aren't the kind of men who would nail another man to a tree."

"I don't see—"

"These men were killed to throw us off the scent. They were in the wrong place at the wrong time and got cut short. That's all."

"What are you saying?"

My stomach writhed like a ball of snakes. "This was a dodge to get me out here. Connie Rand is going after Magra."

When I reached Haxan I knew the worst had happened. The street outside my office milled with excited people. I rode in among them.

They watched me with stoic faces.

"What happened?" I asked.

An elderly man in the crowd took it upon himself to answer. "They grabbed that little boy, Piebald, and held a Barlow to his throat. Said if Magra didn't come out they would kill the kid. She laid down her gun and then they tried to take her away."

I sat upright in my saddle as if a bolt had gone through me. "What do you mean, 'tried'?"

"This here cowboy pulled his pistol and started firing over their heads." A few hands in the crowd tried to push the man in question out front, but he was reticent. The older man continued telling his story. "They let the little boy loose when everyone started running out of their houses to see what the commotion was about."

"What man are you talking about?"

"I guess'n he means me, Marshal." He stood back in the crowd, wearing striped pants and green suspenders. He held his crumpled sombrero between his hands like a penitent schoolboy.

"I was sleeping behind that cantina over yonder because I didn't have money for a bunk," he explained. "I was washing my face in a trough when I saw them grab that little boy. I didn't know what was happening, so I unloaded over their heads from behind a clump of chaparral. Spooked one of their horses, I guess. The little boy picked up a stone and smacked one of the horses in the flank so it started kicking. The men got scared and rode off when people started coming into the street."

"Maybe they thought they were in a crossfire," another man said. "Sounded like it, what with the echoes bouncing off these false fronts."

The man who fired at Rand pointed down the street. "They rode away down Front Street. I don't know where they turned but they might have gone south toward Las Cruces or Mesilla."

"Wait a minute," I said. "I know you from last night, don't I?"

"That's sure, Marshal. I'm Jake Strop. I was Fancer Bell's pard."

"Were his pard, Mr. Strop?"

"He's headed back to Texas. He's had enough of Haxan. I

don't have money so I'm stuck here for now."

"Where's Magra Snowberry, Mr. Strop? And Piebald?"

"Once't those outlaws let her go, the Indian girl, she carried Piebald up to Doc's. He had a bad cut on his neck. Lost blood. I guess they left 'bout five minutes ago."

"While this was going on, what were the rest of you doing?" I swept my eyes over the gathering.

Their empty faces stared back.

"Why should we take a bullet for a half-breed squaw?" another man remarked. "She ain't kin to us. Anyway, her father was crazy, so it more 'n likely runs in her blood, too."

I swung out of my saddle and walked up on him. The crowd pulled away to give us elbowroom. He did his level best to hold my stare.

"I'm not armed, Marshal." He swallowed audibly. "I got no truck with you."

One of the women put a hand to her breast. "Look at his eyes," she whispered to a friend.

I turned my back in disgust. "Which way did they ride, Mr. Strop?"

"Like I said, they tore hell for leather down Front Street. Didn't see after that."

"They have a buckboard with them? With two men riding a three-point bay and a sorrel mare?"

"Yes, sir, and well-armed. Marshal, I'm no hero like these people make out. When they heard the bullets whizzing over their heads from behind they lit out like scalded cats is all."

"Strop, you've just been deputized for as long as you want the position. I'll see you get paid for this job of work, come what may."

He scratched his head. "I won't lie I could use a job. What do you want me to do?"

"Pick three men and meet Mayor Polgar. He's riding in from Shiner Larsen's shack with a couple of dead buffalo hunters. I want Doc Toland to autopsy them."

"I can do that, Marshal."

I swung into my saddle and took the reins. I leaned over the pommel and glared down at the crowd.

"Don't let me down again," I told them. "Not ever again."

Several men and all the women dropped their eyes. A couple of hard-noses mumbled under their breath, but no one bucked me outright.

"We'll do like you say, Marshal," Strop promised.

"After I see Magra and Piebald and grab some sleep, you stop by my office, Strop. We'll talk about your new appointment."

"I'll be there, Marshal. People call me Jake. Mostly, they do."

"All right, Jake, have it your way. There are two drunks in the right hand cells. Jail key is in the top desk drawer. They've paid their fines. Give them breakfast and let them go after you see Mayor Polgar."

"Yes, sir."

I kicked my horse into a canter down the street and ran up the stairs to Doc Toland's office. Magra stood alongside Piebald in the surgery. Doc was bent over the boy, his long face intent.

"Magra."

She turned around. "Hi, John." She stopped, perhaps wondering if it was right to use my given name under the circumstances. When she found she didn't mind how it sounded on her lips, she pressed ahead with a slight, relieved smile.

"Davie is going to be all right," she said. "Doc says he lost some blood and must rest, but he's going to make out fine."

I looked down at Piebald's white face. "How you feeling, boy?"

"Tell this croaker to let me go, Marshal. I was gonna go fishing today with Smarty Coker after I ditched school."

"Doc, we have a very brave boy here," I said, gravely. "He helped save this young woman's life, and that's fact. I'd be proud to pay the medical bill for his family, personal like."

Doc Toland finished cleaning and bandaging the neck wound. He wiped his hands on a towel. "That won't be necessary, Marshal. He's suffering from shock more than anything else. I'll keep him here. I know his parents well. I'll get word to them."

"My deputy is bringing in two dead men from Gila Creek,

Doc. Can you autopsy them when you have time?"

"Deputy? You have been busy, Marshal."

"Man goes by the name of Jake Strop. He's not a genius, but he's honest."

"That would be a most welcome trait in Haxan. All right, but I've been up all night, no thanks to you. Tell your deputy put the bodies in the dead house. I'll cut them up when I can."

"Fair enough."

I took Magra's hand and led her aside. "How are you feeling? Did they hurt you?"

"I'm sorry," she began in a fluster, "I didn't want them to harm that boy, so I surrendered Papa's shotgun. I know I shouldn't have. I heard shots and there was a lot of pushing and shoving and then Piebald threw that rock. When I had the chance I kicked where Mother told me to kick a man before they could bundle me into that wagon."

"Did you see their faces?"

"They wore bandanas."

I slapped my hat against my leg in frustration. "That figures." It would help if I could pin Connie Rand's description to the bunch that tried to kidnap her. That would be enough to get a dodger out on Rand.

"Did you ride out to Papa's shack?" she asked.

"They burned it all down, Magra. I'm sorry. Killed the hog and trampled the crop. There's nothing left but ashes." Her face was stricken. "You can always rebuild."

She sucked in a shaky breath. "I don't understand why this is happening."

"Neither do I." This whole mystery made very little sense to me as well. People didn't go around causing this kind of death and destruction because they believed a man and his daughter were witches. This was the nineteenth century. Haxan was nothing more than a cattle town in the Territory of New Mexico. It wasn't Salem, Massachusetts, and it wasn't 1692.

There was a deeper hate at work here. A calculating malevolence.

There was nothing supernatural at the core of this problem, that much I knew. Whoever was behind this was all too human. That made him even more dangerous.

The worst kinds of monsters are *always* human.

"John, I want to see Papa's grave before I return to the reservation."

"Not by yourself, you're not."

"Then you will have to come with me. But I am going."

She was a stubborn woman. "Let's check on Piebald and have breakfast first. We'll rent you a horse down at Patch Wallet's stable."

"I can't afford any horse."

"I'll loan you the money."

"No, John." She put her hand on my arm. "You've done enough. Anyway, you need sleep. You're dead on your feet. You can hardly keep your eyes open. We'll ride out together on your horse. I like him. Does he have a name?"

People in the west didn't always name their animals, especially their horses. That was the stuff of dime novels.

"I'll tell you about it someday," I said. "Come on, I'm too tired to argue."

At breakfast Magra ordered buckwheat cakes and sorghum. After filling myself with side meat, peppers fried in oil, corn tortillas, and black coffee, I collapsed in bed for five solid hours. When I awoke I felt most human, except for a headache stabbing like a white-hot poker behind my right eye.

I sought out Magra and we rode for the hackberry tree. She rested her chin on my shoulder. At one point she asked me to stop so she could pick purple sage and Indian paintbrushes for her father's grave.

The blistering sun was high overhead by the time we reached the tree. Magra slipped off my saddle and knelt beside her father's grave. She laid the flowers down while I stood with my hat in my hands. She lifted her palms and sang something in Navajo. It was a soul-shattering wail that filled the desert and open sky.

When she finished the death song she put her ear to the

ground. When she stood she brushed herself off and turned around so I couldn't read her troubled face.

I watched her slender back, not saying a word. I figured she needed time alone. She didn't make a sound as she wrestled with her grief. She stared at the expansive desert, the high grass in Larsen Valley burned yellow by the sun, the silver curve of Broken Bow River miles away, and the blue buttes and red mesas rising like giant chess pieces to the north.

For all its brutality and raw violence, Sangre County was also wild and beautiful, free and open country.

Magra faced back around. I saw she accepted the unavoidable fact her father was gone forever. She was a strong girl. I found myself wishing I had known both her parents. I think I would have liked them.

"My heart is on the ground but you picked a good place to bury my father, John. Even though a very bad thing happened here."

The tree was scarred where I had pulled out the railroad spikes last night. One remained embedded in the trunk, driven deep and caked with dried blood.

"I did what I could for him, Magra. I'm sorry I couldn't do more."

"No, I want to thank you." She squatted beside the grave and rested her brown hands on one of the stones. She looked very small and frail inside her big coat with its jumbled carpetbag patches.

"You did more than enough," she said softly. "When I put my ear to the ground I listened to the desert speak. My mother taught me how to do this. The land is at peace and my father is resting."

"I hope so." I didn't know what else to say.

She regarded me. Her hair was braided tight on either side of her face. "Papa can still night-walk me if he has a mind. Mother did it when I was back east, long after she died on the Long Walk to Fort Sumner. Yet I haven't heard from her in many, many years. Maybe she lost her way in the Everywhere Land and can't find a spiritual path back to our world. It happens sometimes when you night-walk."

"I hope they both visit you soon, Magra."

"I carry much grief inside. I should cut my hair and knife the tip of my little finger off."

"I know it's your custom, and it's not my place to say, but I don't think you should. I don't want you to mutilate yourself. It's not right."

"Papa would not like it, either. He loved Mother, yet he did not believe in all of her ways. So I will continue as he would have wished and not do those things to myself." She sighed. "I am ready to go home now."

I helped her back on my horse. We rode around, looking to see if we could cut the trail of the wagon. We couldn't follow it far. The ground was too hard. As we rode toward town she put her chin back on my shoulder.

We listened to coyotes calling across the flat.

"The season has been very dry," she remarked. "They will come to the ranches and kill cattle if we don't get rain."

"I've heard they already started. What's that big butte off to the north?"

"That's Cottonwood Butte. Many of the largest ranches surround it like spokes on a wheel."

"Ranches like the Lazy X?"

"Yes. John, stop by Papa's old place."

"No." There was nothing for her to see there.

"Please? I want to look around."

I tugged the reins and we set out across flat, weathered stones. We followed a thin, meandering creek between the black boulders and their shining white symbols of mystical power.

I pulled short. Magra stared at the blackened and charred remains of her father's home. Her entire life lay in ruin.

"All right," she said, releasing a pent up breath. "Let's go."

PART 2
GRASS, WATER, SKY

CHAPTER 8

When I reached the office I had to head right back out to deliver government papers to Fort Providence. It was a long, hot ride. When hours later I returned to Haxan I discovered my packages from the mercantile emporium had arrived. I opened them and was putting things where I thought they belonged when Jake sidled through the door, a bundle of mail in his arms.

"Hello, Marshal. How was the ride to Fort Providence?"

"Damned hot and dry."

"We're hurting for rain," he agreed. "While you were gone I thought I would run down to the depot to see if there was mail. Most of this stuff is addressed to Sheriff Cawley—circulars and other letters marked with an official stamp."

"Did you meet Mayor Polgar?"

"Yes, sir, I took care of that. The men are in the dead house."

"Have a seat, Jake, and we'll discuss your appointment."

He doffed his hat and folded himself into a straight-back chair against the 'dobe wall. Sam Beetle owned a feed store next door to us. You could smell it plain.

"You ever done lawman work before?" I asked him.

"No, sir." He had a lopsided grin. "Got chased by a town marshal once for stealing apples as a kid. That's about it."

"Where you from?"

"Austin, Texas, sir."

"You can call me Marshal, Jake. Or Marwood, if you prefer."

"Yes, sir, Mr. Marwood."

"What brought you to Haxan?"

"I was a rider for the Circle C Ranch. We pushed one of the

first big herds up from Brownsville to Haxan. I rode swing."

"At least it wasn't bobtail." That was a thankless job held by the man who watched the cattle while everyone else ate supper.

Jake had a funny way of laughing. It was a series of suppressed sneezes through his hawk-like nose. "I've done that, too. But since I made this run to Haxan twice't I got moved up in job order."

"You've been to Haxan before?"

"Yes, sir. I mean, Mr. Marwood. I ran into a spot of trouble this go. Lost all my wages in a crooked faro game first night in."

He quickly amended, "That was before you took over, Mr. Marwood. I expect they'll watch themselves a sight more closely now."

"I wouldn't bet on that."

"Anyway, I lost all I had but kept enough back to get my horse out of hock. I was thinking I had to pull out of Haxan and look for work before I landed this here job."

"Well, long as you work for the Marshal's office you can keep your horse in the livery stable. The U.S. government will foot the bill."

"I'll go for that. What's the pay?"

"Job pays twenty-two dollars a month."

Jake circled the hat brim through his skinny hands. "I was getting thirty-three with Circle C, sir."

"You'll also receive two dollars for every arrest you make, fifty cents for every stray dog you shoot, and a dime for every rat you kill in town. In a normal month you should be able to bring in another twenty or forty dollars on top of your salary."

"I can make out on that right enough."

"Fine. You can sleep in the office if you want. There's a cot in back. Spread your bedroll there. We'll trade off when we have prisoners, anyway, to give the other man a break."

"Okay, Marshal."

"There are other things I want you to be responsible for, Jake. Grab the mail every morning from the train and stage depots. Send wires to all the big territorial newspapers and have them delivered to our office. I want to read them every day."

"I understand." His face cleared. "That's smart, keeping up on things."

"This is a federal appointment, Jake. Our jurisdiction isn't only local, even though that's what the Haxan Peace Commission expects." I told him about the commission. He didn't know anything about it or appear to care. "Can you read and write?"

"I know most of my alphabet."

"Most?"

"Except for two or three letters near the end. I never use them much when I have to write."

I couldn't help but grin. "Sounds okay." I opened a drawer and tossed him a badge. "I'll submit the paperwork to the Marshal's office in St. Louis, but as of now you're on payroll. Best put that on and we'll make this official."

He pinned the badge to one of his suspenders and I swore him in.

Jake sported a knife with buckhorn handle on his belt and a pistol in a Mexican loop holster. "May I see your gun, Jake?"

Without hesitation he drew it and handed it to me, butt first. It was a Schofield .44-40 top-break revolver.

You can tell a lot about a man by his gun. Jake's six-gun was clean and in good working order. He had the hammer seated on an empty chamber. He was a cautious man and knew basic gun safety.

I handed the weapon back to him. "Brand new Schofield. Where'd you get that?"

"My Uncle Henry got me this here pre-production model."

He was being evasive. I decided not to push it. A lot of men had secrets, big and little, out on the frontier.

"Know how to use it?" I asked.

"I can hit something if I have time to aim."

"Let's go out back and try it out. Do you mind?"

"Not at all, Mr. Marwood. I guess you need to know if I can shoot."

We exited the office through the back door and found

ourselves in an empty sandlot with broken crates, discarded bottles, and wild bunches of purple cactus growing along a ragged fence line made from ocotillo.

"Let's see you plink that tin can." I pointed to a can lying against the fence twenty yards away.

He set himself, pulled his gun from the Mexican holster, and fired. He was much too quick. The bullet ploughed dirt a foot in front of the can.

"This job doesn't call for quick draw tricks, Jake," I cautioned. "The man who keeps his cool and takes his time, even under fire, can beat the faster gun."

"Sorry, Marshal. I guess I was trying to show off." He holstered his gun, relaxed, and pulled iron. He thumbed the hammer back, took careful aim, and fired. The tin can jumped.

I clapped him on the back. "Good enough for government work, Jake."

He flushed at the compliment. I got the idea he wasn't the kind of man who heard a lot of them in his life.

"How about you, Marshal?" he questioned with a glint. "Can you hit it?"

I drew my gun and fired. The can jumped a foot in the air. Jake aimed and kicked it forward once it landed. We knocked it around the yard two or three times until he missed.

"You're awful good, Mr. Marwood," he admitted. His eyes were shining. "Fast, too. Why do you use a cap and ball?"

"Comfortable with the feel of the iron, I guess. Anyway, it's what I got used to when I learned to shoot. Too old a dog to change now."

"I heard Hickok uses a cap and baller."

I knew what he wanted to talk about. You could see the curiosity building in his face. No wonder he lost at cards, with a readable face like that.

"You ever kill a man, Jake?"

He pursed his lips and thought. "Don't rightly know. In Laredo we were set upon by Mexican bandits who had crossed the Bravo. They were out to steal our remuda. Me and my pards fired into them and two men fell into the river. The others ran hell for leather back across the border. I don't know if I killed one of those men or not. I don't like dwelling on it."

"No man does if he's honest."

"I heard about that trouble you cleared up in Montana Territory," he prompted. "Once you hit this town people started talking in whispers. There are other stories, too, about your reputation. They say you ran with a hard bunch in south Texas. There's even stories you spent time with the Mandans up north. I hope you don't mind my asking, Mr. Marwood."

"When your back is against a wall, Jake, you do what you can to get out of it. When it's you or the other man, that's an easy decision."

"Yes, sir," he answered in earnest. "I will remember."

Back inside the office I told him everything I knew about Connie Rand and his gang.

"I want to run this man down, Jake. If Rand is *comanchero* then he might also be the one who killed Breggmann. Keep your eyes and ears open when you move about town. Don't try to take Rand yourself. Come and get me first."

"Yes, sir, Marshal."

We finished setting up the office. Jake tacked the circulars up and put the important ones outside on the flat board.

He came back in. "Marshal, I remembered something I ought should tell you. After I brought Fancer to the Doc's I went back to the Texas Star for another beer."

"Trouble?"

"It was Pate Nichols. He and Coffer Danby liked to crossed guns while you were in one of the other saloons."

"Nichols. I keep hearing that name. He's that big rancher who owns the Lazy X. He's on the commission, too."

"He's sewn up Larsen Valley. They say he's worth half a million if he's worth a dollar."

"Anybody hurt?"

"No, sir. Jonah Hake took a bung starter to them and broke it up before it got serious."

My warning must have made a mark with Hake. "What brought on the argument?"

"Danby came in drunk and accused Nichols of cutting fences and killing his flock."

"Danby doesn't run cattle?"

"No, sheep on Shadow Bend. Nichols swore he didn't do it but claimed Danby was chasing his cattle away from water. You know how dry it's been lately."

"Magra and I heard the coyotes, and maybe a few wolves, wailing out on the flat. Anything else happen between this Danby and Nichols? You seem to know quite a lot about them."

"Only high talk. They say Danby's wife is what they call a 'stunner' back east. Danby promised he'd kill Nichols if he lost more ewes." Jake shook his head in wonder. "You would think in this whole big territory two men could learn to live with one another."

"When you get down to it, it's not human nature, Jake, despite how we like to pretend otherwise. Mayor Polgar told me about Nichols the first day I rode into town. Apparently the man carries some weight around town. Where can I find him?"

"I believe he's staying at the Haxan Hotel. I heard he wanted to have words with the new marshal about Coffer Danby so he's been waiting there."

"And I expect Danby wants to buck me about Nichols." I sighed. "Thanks for the warning."

"Those men are going to keep pushing each other until someone gets hurt. Where are you going?"

"To buy penny candy for Piebald. I want to hire him to help Patch Wallet take care of my horse. He can exercise our animals and brush them down. Stuff like that."

"He'll like that."

"Might keep the kid out of trouble. Acts kind of wild. Hold down the fort, Jake. Tonight we'll patrol the town and I'll show you the ropes."

"I'll make coffee, Marshal. Break in that new pot."

I strode outside. The sun was low, slanting rays across the plaza with a washed-out amber glare.

Right on cue coyotes started howling on the desert flat. It was a keening, plaintive sound. I could smell cooking fires up and down Front Street: mule deer backstrap, chili peppers, and fresh tortillas fried on a clay comal. A snatch of fandango from one of the Mexican cantinas tripped between the weathered boards of the sidewalk and ran back inside to hide.

I was on my way to the Haxan Hotel to scare up Magra when a gaunt man with intense blue eyes and long brown hair blocked my way. His face was drawn, as if the skin was stretched too tight across the bones. His eyes had a distant, lonely gleam to them, like hollow caverns at the edge of a sea.

"Are you Marshal John Marwood?" he asked.

"I am. Help you?"

"I'm Pate Nichols. I suspect you've heard 'bout me. I'm a member of the peace commission. I also own the Lazy X ranch." He made a vague gesture off to the north, which encompassed most of Larsen Valley and the better grassland beyond.

"I've been meaning to have a jaw when you hit town, Marshal," he added.

"I'm on my way to find something to eat."

"I've been waiting for the law to handle my problem. I'm through waiting."

"Can't we talk about this after I've had supper?"

"No, we can't." He interposed his body between the street and me. His hard, whiskered face was closed. He was a man used to having his own way.

"I have life and death business with you," he said. "I'm not waiting another minute."

CHAPTER 9

All right, Nichols, I'm listening. But you should know first off I'm not one to push. What's your business?"

Nichols returned a sharp nod in appreciation. "Neither am I, Marshal," he began. "You don't know me, but ask anyone in town. They will tell you I don't like woolers."

He made a half-hearted attempt at a pacifying motion. "But I can learn to live with my enemies like the good book says. Up until they scare my cattle away from water. You know how dry it's been of late. The upper fork of Gila Creek is the only decent tank water that cuts through my ranch."

"What's your point, Nichols?"

His eyes glittered like spent bullets. "If Coffer Danby runs my cattle off water again I'll kill him. I'm giving the law fair warning so there won't be any misunderstanding when I put a slug through his damn head."

"You do that, Nichols, and you'll hang," I told him. "Danby claims you've cut fences and killed his ewes."

"I know what he's saying and he's a goddamned liar. It ain't me. It's coyotes killing his rams and ewes." He jerked his chin in the direction of the chorus of howls emanating from the desert. They became louder as the sun sank behind the mountains to the west.

"It's like this every night. You can hear them, unless you're deaf. Scarce water makes them pack in large numbers. They'll always murder a sheep before they will a steer. Aside from that, I've lost calves myself but you don't hear me crying about it like Danby. I can't be blamed for what wild coyotes do to his sheep. Rain or no rain."

"Coyotes don't cut fences, Nichols."

"I don't cut fences, either. I don't like the goddamn things but I don't cut them. Until the law says different this territory is free range. I don't take to being closed up by my neighbours, but I don't cut them and I never have."

Nichols hung his thumbs over his gun belt. He wore a Remington Model 1858 in a Mexican holster. His weight rested on his back foot. "I'm warning you, Marshal, I know how to use this gun. If Danby scares my cattle off again, I'll shoot him down like a broke-dick dog."

"Nichols, you kill Danby without giving him a clear call and I'll see you hang for it. I won't tolerate a range war."

"That's what you'll have on your hands if Danby keeps stampeding my thirsty cattle. I've got more than enough men to see this thing through no matter how bloody it gets. I'll hire more out of El Paso and Santa Fe if I have to. I've been a patient man, Marshal. But patience has its limits."

"I'm not going to get into a pissing match with you, Nichols. You let the law handle this problem. That's all."

"Marshal—"

"You're not talking about defending yourself, Nichols. You're talking up murder."

We traded stares. "I'm not one to buck the law," he relented, "but I thought you'd better know where I stand. Far as I'm concerned I've done my civic duty. If the law in this valley won't do anything about Danby, I will."

"Okay, Nichols, we've warned each other. You remember I've got the law on my side. All you have is your pride." I was about to leave when I realized I had an opportunity here. "Now that you've made me late for supper," I said, "I have something to ask since you're a member of the peace commission. I'm searching for a man by the name of Connie Rand. He hired out to your place."

"Rand?"

"That's right. Conrad Rand. People call him Connie. Tall jasper with blond hair. Forties, got a drooping eyelid."

"He hasn't worked for my outfit in more than a month,"

Nichols said. "Leastways, not that I know of. I can ask my ramrod about it. He knows the crew better than I do."

"I'd appreciate your help. Rand is wanted for questioning in the death of Shiner Larsen."

"Yeah, I heard that crazy old coot got himself killed. Well, like I said, I don't mind helping the law so long as they back my play. Good day to you, Marshal."

Nichols started to go, stopped. He faced around, a sharp gleam sparking his eye. He didn't want to leave on amicable terms—that might be considered a reconciliation. He wanted one more dig at me.

"Just so you know, Marshal, I have talked to people in town. Seems you've made an impression with everyone already." An oily smirk whipsawed across his face.

"What are you driving at, Nichols?"

"Between you and me, Marshal, are you really rutting that half-breed on the side? And her father hardly cold in the ground yet."

The coyotes howled at the starry night. It was a cold and lonely sound.

"You're on a tight rein already, Nichols. Don't strangle yourself with the little slack you have left."

"Might touchy, aren't you, Marshal? Don't get riled. Unless I miss my guess she's like any other woman of her kind. You flash enough money under her nose, she'll spread for anyone."

I took one step forward. "I won't say this again, Nichols. Get out of my way before I take you apart."

"Have it your way, Marshal." His eyes and hands remained steady. "You must know next time we cross words I might not be so amenable. I'm not green, sir. Someday I may have to draw on you and take you down a notch."

"Then that's the day you'd better dig your grave first, Nichols."

He laughed, stepped off the sidewalk and ambled down the centre of Front Street, whistling a tuneless song. I watched him mount the stairs to Doc Toland's second-floor office and close the door behind him.

To hell with him. I continued on my way to a restaurant on Avenida de Haxan and found Magra Snowberry waiting.

"Hello, John."

"Magra. Sorry I'm late." My, but it was good to see her again.

A waiter came by with a chalkboard listing the night's menu. I ordered a beefsteak, fried potatoes, and stewed corn. Magra ordered grilled *pollo* and beans.

As the food came her dark eyes searched my face. "You look angry about something."

We hadn't known each other long but she already knew my moods better than most.

I used a silver spoon to ladle mustard from a china boat. "I ran into Pate Nichols on the way. He and Coffer Danby almost killed each other in the Texas Star last night."

I reached across the table and pressed my hand against hers. Her square, brown hand was soft. "But I don't want to talk about them, Magra. I had a long day and it was a hot ride to Fort Providence. I'm hungry. Let's eat."

After coffee I lighted my pipe and we sat and talked. She was pretty under the glimmering lamplight. Her long black hair was brushed and she wore stiff, yellow calico. I had the idea she had dressed this way special for me, but I couldn't prove it.

"I like your dress," I said, fishing.

"It's two years old. I only wear it when I come to stay in town. I can near pass for white when I'm wearing this instead of buckskin and moccasins."

"I see." I frowned. "Magra, you shouldn't be ashamed of who you are."

"Oh, I'm not, but why make things harder than they already are?" She put down her coffee cup. "John, I've made a decision about my future."

I cleaned out my pipe. "Okay. Let's hear it."

"I'm going to sell Papa's land and use the money to buy a new mail-order dress. Then I'm going to serve drinks in the Quarter Moon."

I leaned back in my chair and gave her a long stare.

"That's a big decision, Magra."

"August Wicker, he owns the Quarter Moon. He came to see me while you were in Fort Providence. He said I could earn a lot of money."

"I'm sure he did." She wasn't naive. She knew what the job meant.

"I have to do something, John. Or it's back to Fort Sumner and the reservation."

"Your father wouldn't like this, either, Magra."

"Papa is dead. I have to live."

"I know he's dead. You keep forgetting I'm the one who found him."

She covered my hand with both of hers. "John, you've done enough for me already. Anyway, people are talking and it's going to hurt your reputation and maybe cost you your job."

I remembered how Nichols had smirked and how I wanted to hit him, and keep hitting him, until his face was webbed with blood and the knuckles in my hand were all broken.

"I'm not interested in protecting my reputation if this is the trade I have to make," I told Magra. I gave her a meaningful glance. She knew more about me than anyone in Haxan. More, maybe, than I knew myself, given who her father was.

Her father had believed a man would come to Haxan because it was the centre of things, and a man like me had to be here, in one way or another.

"Magra, your father was a very special man. He was able to see things others couldn't, and it cost him his life. He also saw something in me, and I think he saw something special inside you, too. He had that kind of deep vision."

I waited as the waiter refilled our coffee cups before I continued.

"I told you about my past, Magra, what there is I can remember." I took a contemplative sip of the coffee. "I don't know if those memories are real, or if I pretend they exist so I won't go mad. I'm know I'm sent places, and times, where someone like me is needed. I was sent to Haxan and it's here I must work."

I finished low, "And in this long, dry war, in this never-ending sea of blood and dust and wind, I found someone I can trust."

I held her eyes with mine. Her lips were slightly parted.

"Maybe someone I can love."

She didn't speak. She just stared at the checkered tablecloth, her long hair falling on either side of her face.

"I want you to wait on this Quarter Moon business," I said firmly. "Let's see what happens after I catch the men who killed your father. Then we'll talk more about it. Please?"

She raised her eyes. "Will you walk me back to the hotel?"

"Be proud."

It continued to irk me she couldn't sleep in one of the main rooms. At least Hew Clay had changed out her straw pallet for a worn army cot. But she was still sleeping in a storeroom behind the kitchen. Where the house cat slept.

We strolled outside, her arm linked through mine. It was a fine night. There were many people on the street. The last stage had arrived and the La Posta station master was unloading luggage and mail sacks.

"Trouble out there, Steve?" I asked the teamster.

He shook his head. "Weren't carrying a strongbox so this was a milk run, Marshal. Those coyotes made the horses nervy, though. Never heard such racket."

The yips and yowls were a never-ending chorus. It sounded like Haxan was surrounded.

"There they go again," Magra said. "It's lucky you didn't run into them on your way to Fort Providence, John."

"I didn't scare up anything but a covey of quail."

The howls sounded like they were circling Haxan in an ever-moving ring, closing in. It gave you the crawlies.

Without thinking, I rested my hand on my gun.

It was then the howling stopped, and an uneasy silence filled the night air.

CHAPTER 10

The next morning Jake and I rode out to Coffer Danby's place. He lived west of Cottonwood Butte where the banks of Gila Creek were covered with bluestem grass. The shallow water sparkled clean and clear over round, mossy stones. North of him was Nichols's ranch, a huge sprawling empire of five thousand head that swallowed a quarter of Sangre County. Both places were out a ways and it took us most of the morning to saddle.

A thin wisp of white breakfast smoke rose from the pipe chimney of Danby's house. Jake and I dismounted. I knocked on the cabin door.

Rose Danby answered it.

The talk hardly did her justice. She was one of those striking women who carry her beauty like a knife; if they're not careful, they can cut themselves with it.

"Good morning, ma'am. I'm Marshal Marwood out of Haxan. This is my deputy. I'm here to see your husband."

She knocked back a curl of auburn hair with the back of an ivory hand. She was wearing a blue percale dress with a floral print and neatly trimmed lace collar.

"High time you rode out our way, Marshal," she said, one fist on her hip. "Fine thing when people have to crawl on their bellies to the law for justice."

"Yes, ma'am."

"Well, don't stand there. Come in, both of you. I've got biscuits and coffee is on the boil."

"We don't want to be a bother, Mrs. Danby."

"No bother, Marshal. Coffer is camping in Shadow Bend. He would take it wrongful if I didn't offer you men something to eat.

We take pride in the hospitality of our home."

"Thank you, Mrs. Danby."

She pushed the door open and we stepped through, hats in hand. Rose seated us round a dining table. There were two children, an eight-year-old boy and a small five-year-old girl playing with wooden toys on the floor.

Rose shooed them outside. "You two scamps run along. We have grown up talk to settle. Jessie Anne, you feed those chickens or you'll get the strap."

"Yes, mama." The kids left, slamming the door behind them.

Rose busied herself clinking saucers and pouring coffee. "Please, Marshal, you and your deputy make yourselves to home. Coffer will be back soon, I hope. We had a bad night. Some of our stock got killed again even though we posted guards."

"How many, ma'am?" Jake asked.

"A wether and fourteen ewes."

"Coyotes?" I asked.

She put a coffee cup down in front of me. "Since when do coyotes carry guns, Marshal?"

"You mean they were shot, Mrs. Danby?" Jake watched her put a platter of sourdough biscuits in the centre of the table. "Thanks, kindly, ma'am."

"You're welcome. Of course they were shot, and Pate Nichols shot them."

"You have proof of that, Mrs. Danby?" I asked her.

That made her hesitate. "Not as such. Nothing a court would accept. But he hates my husband with a passion, that's certain enough." She clacked a bowl of fresh butter on the table. "No one else lives around here for miles. Who else could it be?"

"I have already talked with Mr. Nichols," I told her. "He believes your husband is chasing cattle off from water."

"Pate Nichols is a bald-faced liar and you can tell him I said that." She poured herself a modest cup of coffee and sat opposite us.

"Coffer and me work very hard to make this place a home and a success," she explained. "We mind our business. We don't pry into what other people have going on. We're certainly not fool enough to buck a rich cattleman like Pate Nichols for sport. He could crush this family with the change in his pocket."

"Mrs. Danby, I'm trying to prevent a gunfight between those men. Believe me when I say I don't want to see either of them hurt."

"You think I want to see my man dead?" She scowled into her cup. "I appreciate what you're trying to accomplish, Marshal, I do. Coffer isn't much good with a handgun. He will admit that. But when a man is threatened, what can he do if he wants to remain a man?"

"Mrs. Danby, do you know what started this hate between the two of them?"

For the first time she avoided my eyes. She got up and busied herself stacking dirty breakfast dishes on the kitchen sideboard.

"I wouldn't know anything about that," she said. "Do you and your deputy want more coffee?"

"Jake," I said, "Mrs. Danby needs a bucket of well water for her kitchen."

He said around a mouthful of biscuit, "I didn't hear her say—"

"Take your time, Jake."

He looked between Rose Danby and me. "Yes, sir." He cast a longing look at the remaining plate of biscuits and went outside.

Rose Danby leaned against the sideboard. Her arms were folded under her breasts.

"You didn't need to do that, Marshal," she said. "I have got nothing to say to you even in private."

"I hoped you would be more forthcoming if you only had one person to confide in, Mrs. Danby."

"Well, you might be wrong about that, mightn't you?"

"Mrs. Danby, look at me. How long have you been in love with Pate Nichols?"

"Since never." She stacked one or two more dishes. "But he's made his intentions known toward me and that's all I'm going to say."

"He mentioned this in front of your husband?"

"Not in so many words." Her shoulders slumped. "Not like you say. But you know how it is out here. There aren't many women and Nichols has a *lot* of money. He thinks he can buy anything he wants. I told him he can never buy me, and that's the God's truth."

"Have you been seeing Pate Nichols?"

"That's some more of your nosey business, Marshal."

"That's where you're wrong, Mrs. Danby. These men are out to kill one another and I'm sworn to uphold the law, such as it is in these wild parts. If you don't want to see your husband shot down by Nichols, and your children fatherless, then I'm asking you to help me."

She wouldn't look at me. I pushed away from the table and stood in front of her.

"Rose," I said, "if you do nothing it will be like you shot your husband yourself. You'd better think about that and get rid of your stubborn streak. I'm not the enemy. I want to help."

"I . . . I will consider it, Marshal." Her eyes were the colour of green bank moss in summer.

I went outside. Jake sat on the porch with a bucket of well water between his feet. The children were throwing seed corn to the chickens.

"Let's go, Jake," I said.

"Yes, sir."

We rode to Shadow Bend. "Sorry about that back there, Jake," I apologized. "I didn't mean to embarrass you. I thought she would be more open if it was just me to talk to."

"I figured it out after a while, Mr. Marwood. You pry anything out of her?"

"No, but I think Nichols might have asked her to marry him."

"How do you know, sir?"

I remembered what he had said about Magra. "It's how he thinks. A man like that uses his money like a stone club."

Shadow Bend was a wrinkled depression where Gila Creek's banks overflowed during the rainy season. There was a lot of good grass burned hay-yellow by the sun, and trees for shade if you wanted to try your luck fishing.

We spotted a large flock of sheep standing like white clouds on green baize in the distance. There were four riders on guard. One of them, a smallish man with a sun-tanned face, sat a dun gelding. He saw us and perked.

He drew a brass-framed Henry rifle and spurred his horse forward at a gallop. A black and white sheltie followed, bounding through the tall grass. The man whistled and the dog ran back to protect the flock.

He drew rein and lowered the rifle on us. "Who are you?" he demanded.

"Marshal John Marwood. This is my deputy, Jake Strop. I take it you are Coffer Danby?"

"I am."

"Mind booting that rifle before we talk, Danby?"

"Don't know why I should."

"Because I asked you to and I don't like people pointing guns at me."

He thought about it and shoved it back in its leather boot. "What are you doing on my property, Marshal?"

"I spoke to your wife this morning. She said you lost some stock last night."

"That's right. Pate Nichols killed them."

"Anything else?"

"Fences cut," he replied.

"Can I see them?"

"I guess there's no harm in that." We rode side-by-side along the eastern bank of Gila Creek and came upon the torn and mangled bodies of Danby's stock.

"Coyotes got to chewing on them after they was shot," Danby said. "Over there is where the fence was cut."

I dismounted and stalked along the sharp-edged bank. There was a long patch of sticky mud. I found a lot of paw prints jumbled among a single horse track.

"This looks like the work of one man," I said.

"Only takes one man to cut half a mile of wire if he has time," Danby countered.

I looked at the three stone-faced men watching the flock. "I thought you worked this place alone, Danby."

"I rode into Haxan a day or two ago and hired them."

"Gunmen?"

"They know how to shoot."

Danby crossed his hands over his saddle horn. "I'm not going to lose any more sheep, Marshal. I've buried my last ewe. Next time, I'll bury Pate Nichols."

"Danby, I'm here to warn you. If you and Pate Nichols start a range war I'm going to stop it. Anyway I can."

"Not your place to tell me my business," he snapped back. "I'll protect what belongs to me. That's the right of any man."

A breeze rippled the top of the shallow creek water, breaking the sunlight into yellow, dancing lozenges.

"Does that include your wife, Danby?"

Coffer's face turned purple. He sat rigid in his saddle. "What are you trying to insinuate, Marshal?" His voice sounded like he was strangling on his own anger.

"Only this. If you and Nichols start any gunplay I'll see the other man hanged for it, no matter what the cause. I warned Nichols, and now I'm warning you."

"I've got every lawful right to protect my property. That includes everything that belongs to me. Rose is my woman."

I saddled up and collected my reins. "Danby, this trouble between you and Nichols isn't about fences, or thirsty cattle. It's a personal hurt raging out of control like a hay fire."

"Marshal, you've said your piece. Now I'll thank you to get the hell off my land. You show your face around here again I'll like as not shoot you down, along with Pate Nichols."

I walked my horse toward him and pulled up.

"Danby," I said low, "the day you draw on me is the day your wife turns widow. That's all. Let's go, Jake."

We swung our horses around and pulled for town.

CHAPTER 11

We found more coyote tracks riding in. There were bigger prints, too. Jake examined them. "Wolves," he said.

He thought they were concentrated in the area because of the available water.

"I have never seen so many in my life," he confessed. "The ground is covered with scat."

"They are like any other animal that feeds off death, Jake. They smell when an easy killing is to be had."

We hitched our horses outside the jailhouse. "That was an awful hot ride coming back," Jake said, "and it's half past noon already."

"I'll buy you a beer first. Then we can find Magra and have dinner."

"That sounds like a fine idea. Especially about the beer." He used his hat to knock dust off his pants. "Yes, sir, that was some hot ride."

We went into the Texas Bluebonnet. While we were finishing our beers one of the men at the end of the bar approached us. His shirt was stiff with trail dust and caked with rings of dried sweat. He wore batwing chaps and smoke-coloured buckskin gauntlets with dyed porcupine quills on the back. Tall and hard, he was the kind of man who carried the dust and sun with him his whole life.

"You the law in this burg?" he asked.

"I am. Marshal Marwood."

"Glad to meet you. My name is Gideon Short." He shucked one of the gauntlets and we shook hands. Despite the protection of his heavy glove he had rein burns on his wrist.

"Blacksmith said I'd recognize you. Claimed you always wore

a grey duster and carried a Colt Dragoon holstered crossways."

"What can I do for you, Mr. Short?"

"I'm trail boss for a Texas herd we're pushing toward Denver."

"We've got good cattle agents right here in Haxan, Mr. Short. They'll give you a fair price."

"I've got a buyer waiting in Colorado, Marshal. I thank you, though."

"How big's your herd?"

"A little under four thousand head. I've got them camped six miles back on waist-high grama grass. Here's the thing, Marshal. We hit town early this morning. I want to let you know my boys are going to kick their heels a bit tonight before we push north."

"We've got new laws here in Haxan, Mr. Short."

"I've heard. My cowboys aren't much for pistols, Marshal, unless it's killing rattlesnakes and antelope for camp meat." His smile came bright in his weathered face. One of his front teeth was chipped. "They're just good men who are more interested in salt pork and sundown, but they want to see the elephant before we push on north."

"That's fine, Mr. Short. By the way, have you a man named Connie Rand working for your outfit?" Since I was asking everyone I met about Rand I thought I might as well keep the trend going. Maybe someday I would get lucky. "I'm looking for him and I hear he drifts. Thought he might have hooked up with your outfit."

"Funny you should say," Short replied. "There was one drifter who tagged with us from El Paso way. He worked for grub and was good with a handgun. Never saw one better. He dropped out five days ago and rode on for a big spread by the Gila. Lazy X, I think he called it."

"That a fact? What was his name?"

"Called himself Ben Tack. Sounded like a summer name, but I didn't push it. Long as a man does his job I don't ask too many questions."

I felt my hands go cold. "Ben Tack."

"You know him, Mr. Marwood?" Jake asked.

"Uh, no, Jake. I don't think so. Anyway, he might not be the same man."

"He carried a Navy sixer," Short kept on. "Beautiful silver-plated gun with a diamond set and pearl handle. Funny thing, he soaped his holster for a faster draw and had the front sight filed down so it wouldn't snag leather. He even shaved the hammer for an easy trigger pull. Always looking for an edge, a way to get that extra fraction of a second on his draw. Didn't need it. Could hit a bumblebee on the wing and never break stride."

Gideon Short tipped his hat. "Well, gentlemen, nice talking to you. Thanks for your time." He returned to the bar and ordered a bottle of rye.

Jake studied me closely. "Mr. Marwood, are you sure you don't know that man he was talking about?"

"I honestly don't know, Jake." Last I heard Ben Tack was in Pueblo. We had a history that went back a lot further than that, however.

"Come on," I said. "Let's find Magra and have dinner."

We entered the cool lobby of the Haxan Hotel. A woman I took to be Hew's wife, Alma Jean, was working behind the reception desk. She had a mean, pinched face. She was a buxom older woman with hazel-brown eyes, brittle red hair, and a wasp waist.

"Good morning, Marshal," she greeted us. "Mr. Strop, congratulations on your appointment as deputy. I've always said we need more law in Haxan. What can I do special for you two gentlemen today?"

"Is Hew around?" I asked.

"He's away to Las Cruces on business. Can I help you?"

"I'm looking for Magra Snowberry. Thought we might have dinner together."

Alma Jean's face shut down with the finality of a guillotine on a gourd. "Miss Snowberry is in the stockroom. That's where she sleeps." A pale tongue darted and licked her thin lips. "Marshal, how much longer is that half-breed going to sleep in my hotel?"

I held her eyes with mine. The air was thick between us.

"As long as she needs to, Mrs. Clay. I made a deal with your husband."

"I know all about the deal you made with my husband, Marshal Marwood. However, this hotel was contracted by the War Department to provide room and board for a federal lawman, not a dirty squaw who had her shack burned out by outlaws."

"First of all, you wouldn't call her that if you knew what the word meant. No woman would."

"Indians is Indians, Marshal, never you mind about that."

I took a calming breath. I had just met the woman but Alma Jean had a way of getting under your skin like bull nettle.

"You're making her sleep in the stockroom, so you're not out any upstairs bed. Plus, I'm paying for all her meals. You haven't lost one penny in room and board."

"That ain't the point, Marshal. That ain't the point at all." Alma Jean tapped a sharp fingernail against the walnut counter. "I run a respectable establishment. What will my customers think, seeing a Navajo girl running around like she owns the place? And dressing, pretty as you please, in clean calico like she's white."

"Would you be happier if she was dressed in buckskin and leggings?"

"Don't get smart with me, Marshal."

"Mrs. Clay, that girl is under official protection. She's a witness to her father's death." That wasn't true, but I needed an edge against this unwelcome woman. "The men who killed her father might come after her again."

"They already tried once, Mrs. Clay," Jake said.

"More the reason she needs to be out of my hotel, Mr. Strop. I'm sorry about what happened to her father, but I won't risk losing clientele over a breed who doesn't know her place."

I'd had enough. With everything else happening I didn't need this, too.

"Don't buck me, Alma. I haven't been in Haxan long, but I expect you already heard about my reputation. You know the kind of man I am."

I knew it was a mistake the moment I said it. She would take it as an article of war, and nothing else. I couldn't help myself. She was nettle, pure and through.

I hadn't liked what she called Magra.

Alma Jean's tight mouth frowned in a sour moue of distaste. "I'm not skeered of you, Marshal. I'm a woman, not a man. You can't push me around like the drunken cowhands who blow through town."

Her smirk deepened. "My brother-in-law *and* my uncle both live in Washington. I have considerable influence with the federal government, never you mind."

"Maybe you can find out why the War Department hasn't paid me my back wages."

"All I have to do is telegraph them and you and that Indian girl will be out on tomorrow's train."

"Until that happens, I'm still Marshal of this town, this county, and the territory of New Mexico. So, Alma Jean Clay, if you will fetch Miss Magra Snowberry so I, and my deputy, may dine with her, I'd appreciate it."

"Are you asking me?"

"No, that's more along the lines of an order." I was going to show her I could push, too.

"You would order me in my own hotel, Marshal?"

"Just as pretty as you please."

She rocked back on her heels. "You're going to get yours one day, Marshal Marwood. Never you mind. You're going to get what's coming to you. I only hope I'm there to witness it."

She spun and stalked stiff-legged from the lobby.

Jake watched her go with a low whistle. "My stars, that's the most unpleasant woman I've ever seen. I'm afraid you've met your match, Mr. Marwood. She won't budge an inch."

"Alma Jean obviously feels she has the reins against me with Hew away in Las Cruces. Dammit, I was afraid this might happen."

"I don't know why she has it in for Miss Magra."

"Don't you, Jake?"

He mulled it over. "You mean, maybe because Miss Magra is kindly pretty? Compared to Alma Jean, so to speak. But Miss Magra would never set herself up against Alma Jean that way."

I shrugged my own ignorance. "I don't know. People have all kinds of stupid reasons they dislike one another." I was thinking about Nichols and Danby.

Jake waggled his head. "Seems an awful thin reach to hate someone."

"Hate doesn't need a reason, Jake. It might look that way to you because of where you're from and how you were raised."

I had been lots of places. So many they were jumbled in my mind like lathes of silver. It was hard not to think of them sometimes. What little I could remember. But it was not remembering, knowing there was more to my past than I could ever recall, that nagged the most.

"Mr. Marwood, I'm from Texas. Not much there but starved cattle and chiggers." He blew a few sneezing laughs through his nose. "They say Texas is hard on women and dogs. I can promise it ain't no easier for men and cattle."

He continued to laugh at his own joke, pulling his sparse chin whiskers between thumb and forefinger. "No, sir, there's something else behind Alma Jean's meanness, I'll warrant. I'll continue to study on it and let you know what I come up with."

"You do that." I had already forgotten Alma Jean. "Here comes Magra."

After dinner Jake excused himself. Magra and I were at our usual table in the corner, talking low over coffee.

"I've caused you trouble again, John," she sighed. "You just say the word and I'll go back to the agency."

"You do and I'll fetch you right back, Magra Snowberry."

I paid for the meal and we walked back to the office.

Magra lifted her hands and let them fall against the stiff front of her calico skirt. "Well, I can't go back to Papa's place. It's all burned out and I don't have money to rebuild."

"We'll think of something." I tried to keep my voice light.

"I don't want you to get in trouble over me, John. You've already taken your fair share of knocks for me, by my count."

"That's my worry."

She stopped, disconcerted. "That's where you're wrong. No, now you listen to me, John Marwood." Her waist-length black hair shone in the sun. Her broad face watched mine as her red-brown hands picked at her white apron. "John, what happens if you have to go against someone, and because of the weight of me on your mind, your gun hand slows down?"

The sky was deep blue. It pressed down on me like a fresh branding iron.

The heavy Sharps rifle was cradled in the crook of my arm. "Belike I'll do what I need to, Magra. I always have before."

"You're like Papa before he died. Single-minded to a fault. That's not necessarily a desirable trait in a man."

I grunted. "I guess this is my day for women to point out my limitations."

"Whatever do you mean by that?"

"It's nothing important."

We turned together and walked side by side, our boots and shoes clopping against the weathered boardwalk.

"My father carried something around with him, too, John. He told me parts of it. I never understood everything, but I believed he thought it was real. I guess I do, too. Mostly."

We go where we're sent. We have names and we stand against that which must be faced.

I was one. Ben Tack was another.

"I did learn one thing about my father, though," Magra continued. "Sometimes a man carries a hurt around until he has to give it voice. I think that hurt somehow killed Papa. You're the same kind of man, John, but in a deeper way than Papa ever was. I think it will kill you, too. One day."

I didn't have anything to say. There was a lot of truth in what she said.

HAXAN

The trick in life, any life, was staying alive long enough to beat the odds. Some men were better at it than others.

People like me. Other people like Ben Tack.

We all have different names. I had mine, and Ben had his. His name was deeper. It carried more fire than mine did.

I don't know why he had come to Haxan, but whatever the reason, I knew I was going to have to stand in front of it.

Or die in the attempt.

CHAPTER 12

The red and green parrot barked like a dog when I walked through the swing doors of the Sassy Sage.

"Hell and damnation. I was for sure that bird would meow that time," groused a six-foot bullwhacker with a flaming red beard and a long ragged coat. "That's five dollars I owe, right?"

"That's the tally," the man at the bar said. He was lean and spare with a profile cut from sheet metal. His eyebrows were long and straight, and his hair razored short. He wore a Navy six leathered high on his hip. Despite what the dime novelists like Ned Buntline say, it's the high gun that gives the faster draw, not iron strapped low on your thigh.

"How about we go double or nothing?" the bullwhacker suggested. He gripped his Colt Peacemaker and glared at the parrot bobbing up and down on a metal perch. "If that damned bird doesn't meow I'll drop a hammer on him."

"You've got a bet." He was dressed in black jeans and blue shirt that matched the burning intensity of his eyes. His boots were polished to a high shine, with fancy Spanish heels. He wore a black Spanish hat with a low flat crown. He had no rings on his fingers, or gloves. Gunmen like him never do. They want full palm contact with the butt of the gun because the weapon itself becomes an extension of their reach, their sense of self.

The parrot was perched on a metal T-bar in the corner of the barroom. He hopped back and forth on both feet, ducked his head, ruffled his feathers, and barked.

"Blast that bird to hell." The bullwhacker grudgingly dug through his leather *mochilla* and paid up what he owed. "Well, that cleans me out. Gawd, busted out by a damn bird. I'll never live this down if my partners hear about it."

The other man at his side laughed in an easy, relaxed way. "Hang around. I hear the girls start smoking cigarettes and swing over the bar when the sun goes down." There were two big wooden hoop swings festooned with bright, gay ribbons hanging over the expansive bar. "I'll buy you a drink while we wait."

"I'd like to see that view, mister, especially from down here at this angle. I have to catch the night stage to Albuquerque. Thanks for the offer." The bullwhacker quit the saloon, cutting daggers with his eyes at the parrot.

The parrot flapped its wings and meowed at his passing.

"Hell and damnation," the bullwhacker thundered as he left the saloon.

"Is that all that parrot does?" I asked. I was standing in the doorway with the light streaming behind.

The man with the sheet-metal profile turned. His smile faded when he saw me. Then it returned with intensity.

"Hello, John. Fancy meeting you here."

"Ben. Heard you were in town."

"Have a drink?"

"Let's get a table first."

He motioned ahead. "One over there." The table he picked was flush against the wall and farthest from any window.

"Sure."

He reached the table first, lowering his lean body into a chair so his gun hand was unencumbered. I had to take the opposite side with my gun hand restricted between the wall and table.

It was a neat trick on his part. He hadn't done it on purpose—these tactics were instinctual with him, like breathing.

"I see you're still carrying that bull cannon," he remarked.

I shrugged. "I can hit with it."

"How about that drink, John?"

"Beer is good enough for me."

"Bartender," he shouted, "two beers. Make them cold this time."

"Right up, Mr. Tack."

Ben swung his attention back on me. "How have you been, John? Long time since we've seen one another."

"Going on ten years, my reckoning."

"By other reckonings, even longer," he said.

I shrugged. "If you say so."

"I do." There was no apparent malice in his voice. He was merely stating fact. By other reckonings it had been longer than a decade. Whole lifetimes.

The bartender served our drinks and retreated to wipe down tables on the far side of the room. I picked up the beer with my left hand and took a pull. Ben followed suit.

His right gun hand rested casually on the lip of the table, ready to drop like a hawk with folded wings out of the sky. The pearl handle of his gun was set a quarter turn out of the holster.

"I see you're still being careful," I said.

He brushed aside the observation. "Clumsy men don't live long in this world or any other. How have you been getting by, John?"

"You know how it is, Ben."

We were tiptoeing, mindful of the bear traps half-hidden under thin straw, their gleaming jaws ready to snap shut.

Ben cracked a wide smile, crinkling his eyes and wrinkling the bridge of his nose. "I sure do."

"What happened to you after Sand Creek?" I sipped my beer, watching him over the bevelled glass rim. "You dropped out of sight."

"Thought it best to keep low so I hid out in the Nations."

This was territory north where the Five Civilized Tribes were quartered. The Cherokee, Choctaw, Creek, Seminole, and Chickasaw were all from southeastern states. They had been forced by federal mandate to relocate. It was also a refuge for outlaws and people who wanted to disappear. The federal government had no legal authority, and no way to extradite a man, from the Nations. Those lawmen foolish enough to enter Indian Territory got no help whatsoever from the Indian tribes imprisoned there.

In the Nations, everyone hated the United States government. The rule of law was an unknown concept in that raw and brutal territory.

"You lived in the Nations ten years?" I asked in disbelief.

"No. I kicked around some. Went down to New Orleans and took a steamer up the Mississippi to Cairo. Bounced around and did some gambling."

He was deliberately vague. "How about you, John? I heard you had trouble with John Chivington after Sand Creek."

"A few of his supporters hired two gunmen. They said I had sullied his good name and they wanted to teach me a lesson."

Ben laughed. "Since you're sitting in front of me I won't ask you what happened to those gunmen." He paused. "Someone told me you got an honourable discharge. Something must have worked out right in your favour."

"When Chivington discovered I couldn't be buffaloed he didn't have many options left. Yeah, I got an honourable discharge. I don't miss the Army, though. After I left I never looked back. That's when I started lawing."

The memory of Sand Creek was an open wound in my recent past that had never healed. Ben, dredging it all up again, brought it back afresh.

Ten years ago, Colonel John Chivington, commander of the Third Colorado Volunteers, ordered a surprise attack on Cheyenne women and children in Sand Creek at the behest of the governor.

I was a lieutenant at the time. Chivington ordered four howitzers to fire upon the sleeping village. Soldiers raped and shot women, scalped children, and cut the throats of newborn babies. During the confusion I found the peace chief, Black Kettle, and helped him escape.

What I had accomplished didn't mean anything in the long run. Four years later, Black Kettle and his wife were shot in the back by Custer on the Washita River.

There was talk of a court-martial following Sand Creek. Not Chivington's, mine. Congress got involved and the investigation knocked a lot of starch out of Chivington. No one liked what I had done, but they understood my motives, if not my actions. To sweep everything under the rug I was given an honourable discharge and Chivington got his wrist slapped.

But Chivington's political supporters hadn't liked the fact I had acted so brazenly. They scraped enough money together and hired a pair of ex-Pinkertons out of San Francisco.

The two men never made it back to California. Chivington's backers didn't have the grit, or the remaining funds, to mount another assassination attempt.

Sometimes, when we stand, we not only stand for ourselves, but for others. People like Black Kettle and Shiner Larsen.

Or Magra Snowberry.

We have no choice but to go where we are called. It is the pact we make. We stand against that which must be faced.

People like me. People like Ben.

"Chivington was a bastard," Ben proclaimed. "I remember in Fort Lyon when you tried to persuade him not to attack the next morning. Remember what he said? 'Nits make lice.' I near liked to have shot him myself right there."

"Yet you participated in the attack," I said. "How many women and children did you kill that day, Ben?"

He gave me a long look bristling with needles. "Still high-minded as ever, aren't you?"

"I call it being practical."

"Best watch yourself, John." His smile was thin enough to cut paper. "One day that practicality will be your downfall."

"When I took this job I made up my mind I was going to die from it someday."

He opened his mouth as if he were about to speak. Maybe he wanted to ask me about my marshalling job. Or maybe he knew I was talking about something else entirely.

We were knife fighters looking for an opening that never presented itself.

"Why are you here, Ben?" I asked.

"Same as you. I go where I'm sent."

"And you've been sent to Haxan."

He didn't say anything. That was response enough.

"You sure someone didn't buy your gun?"

"If he did I wouldn't tell you, John." His smile widened, showing teeth, but no warmth.

"I don't want trouble, Ben. You start trouble and I'm apt to forget we were ever friends."

"Why would I want you to forget that, John?" he asked without rancour. "Haxan is the new boom town on the *frontera*. A smart man can make his mark in a place like this."

"Is that what you aim to do, Ben? Make your mark?"

"Haven't I always?" He rose up from the table in one liquid move. He was whipcord lean. The sun pouring through the window nailed his stark shadow to a nearby plaster wall.

"Don't crowd me, John," he said evenly. "I'll take so much crowding from any man. Even you."

"That supposed to be a friendly warning?"

"It's the only one you'll ever get from me, friendly or not." He began to leave. "By the way, don't go thinking we were ever friends. I wouldn't want to see a look of disappointment on your face if we crossed guns and you thought us being friends would save your life." He touched the brim of his hat in a mock salute. "Be seeing you soon, Marshal."

He knocked through the bat-wing doors and strode into the bright desert sunshine.

CHAPTER 13

Work had piled on my desk. Like all government jobs paperwork was the great equalizer. It took most of my afternoon to wade through it. After I posted my last letter I tugged on my hat and mounted the stairs to Doc Toland's office.

"Doc, you get those autopsies finished on those buffalo hunters?"

He was boiling instruments in a pan of water. He used tongs to retrieve them and place them, gleaming, on a white towel.

"Yes, I have, but I can't submit an official report until all the tests are complete."

This stopped me cold. "I thought it was pretty simple, Doc. Their throats were cut like hogs and they were shot point-blank."

"Yes, John, their throats were cut, but that's not what killed them, as you yourself pointed out. They didn't bleed to death because they were already dead."

"Correct. So what killed them, Doc?"

"When I cut them open I discovered an unknown substance inside their stomachs and their lungs. It wasn't water or whiskey. I sent samples to Santa Fe for further analysis. It may take a while, John. That stuff was mixed with stomach acids, which may affect results."

He noticed the disappointment on my face. "I'm sorry, Marshal. I know you want this to stay official. I can't render a professional judgement on what killed those men until I get the results back."

"Do you do believe they were poisoned?"

"I'd bet on it, but it's not a poison I'm familiar with. Not an alkaloid, which you see a lot in this country. They didn't have any of the usual symptoms associated with that."

I gave a sigh of disappointment. "All right, Doc. Thanks for your help."

He saw me to the door. "I hope to have those test results within a couple of weeks, John, if we're lucky. Santa Fe is notoriously slow when it comes to scientific work like this. In fact, they may not have the proper resources to determine the exact nature of the poison. They might send it forward to experts in Denver or Chicago. We may not get word for a month, or more."

"You're saying I shouldn't hang my hat on this."

"Not if you're looking for a conviction."

"Thanks, Doc. I know you did your best."

"I'm sorry I couldn't do more, John. I really am."

As I descended the steps I felt as if I was reaching my last chance to figure out who killed Shiner Larsen. I hadn't any clue where Connie Rand was, or if he was even involved in Larsen's murder or Magra's attempted kidnapping. I was working with shadow and supposition. Not a smart combination for scientific police work, or a watertight case to nail a ruthless killer.

Certainly nothing I could approach a circuit court judge like Samuel Creighton with.

Some lawman I was. I had three murders on my hands and not a single clue who was behind them all. Not to mention a range war about to blow up in my face.

I made plans with Jake to do the rounds that night and ordered a slice of pie in a Mexican cantina calling itself the Cactus Rose. A hand-painted sign above the door read "SOPAIPILLAS." You could smell them frying in lard through the Indian blanket that served as the kitchen door. It was dark inside, and blessedly quiet. I preferred it to the raucous places with their jangling piano music, clink of money, and drunken shrieks of laughter.

I took a table beside a window framed with drying racks of red chili peppers. I was far enough back to keep an eye on things outside without being seen.

"You will come to the paseo tomorrow night, Marshal?" a dark-skinned Mexican girl asked as she set the pie down with my coffee. She had blue-black hair and smoke-dark eyes. Her wine-red skirt brushed the table.

"Paseo?"

"*Sì*. An old custom. Men and women, they walk in circles different to one another in the plaza." She drew opposite circles in the air with her slim fingers. "It is a way for a young lady to show how pretty she is, dressed in her finery, and a man to show he is much interested. You will come, yes?"

"I might." Maybe I could bring Magra.

After washing the pie down with black piñon coffee I crossed the plaza to the Haxan Hotel. The sun was falling behind the mountains. Only their crowns were lighted. The whole sky was aglow with orange fire and jagged bands of red and pink.

I was relieved to see Hew Clay behind the desk.

"Hew. How was your trip to Las Cruces?"

"Profitable, Marshal. Very profitable. I made a great deal on new bedroom furniture from New Orleans. Real fancy iron-lacework. How was your day?"

"Fair." I decided not to tell him about the run in I had had with his wife. There was nothing he could do anyway. "Have you seen Magra around?"

"Not since I got back. She left north on foot. Said she had family business to attend to. I didn't think it was my place to stop her. Anything wrong, Marshal?"

"Not sure." I had a pretty good idea where she was headed. I would be able to catch up to her if she was on foot. "Pate Nichols still have a room here?"

"Yes, sir. Paid up through tonight."

"What room is he in?"

"Sixteen. It's a suite, end of the first hallway and to the right." His face went pale. "There's not going to be trouble in my hotel, is there, Marshal?"

"I hope not but stay here just in case."

He watched me climb the narrow wooden steps, my hand on my gun. I found the right door and thumped it with my fist. Nichols answered.

He was alone in the room. His Remington revolver hung on a wooden peg beside the mirror.

"Marshal. Come in. Saves me the trouble of trying to scare you up."

"You leaving, Nichols?"

"In the morning. I'd like for you to ride back with me so you can see what I've been putting up with at the ranch."

A hot breeze stirred the fancy curtains at his window.

"Mr. Nichols, you may not be leaving after all. I'm here on official business. Did you hire a gunman by the name of Ben Tack?"

His eyes narrowed to slits. "Not sure I understand."

"It's clear enough. A gunman by that name was seen riding to your place five days ago. Since then, fences have been cut and Danby's livestock killed. In all that time, you've been sitting in this hotel room like a guilty man working on an alibi."

He became ruffled. "What are you trying to say, Marshal?"

"I'm saying it, Nichols, only you're not listening. It's awfully suspicious a cowman worried about his thirsty livestock would sit in a hotel room instead of being where he can watch everything."

"Perhaps you can tell me my reason?"

"Like I said, you're cementing an alibi for whatever might happen to Coffer Danby."

His face became hard. The skin across his cheekbones was so tight you could see tiny blood vessels.

"Marshal, you can't prove your allegations. Not one lick. If Danby is stupid enough to get himself in a gunfight with a stranger that ain't my blame."

"It is if you hired Ben Tack to kill him."

"That would be hard proving, Marshal. Mighty hard proving."

"Maybe." I still wanted to hit him, but standing alone with Nichols and his deeply haunted eyes forced me to put a few ideas together.

"Nichols, Tack was seen by another trail boss riding out to your place. Danby started losing livestock. Your cattle are being driven off from water. You see the connection?"

His eyebrows came together. "I'm not sure how you mean."

"Maybe Tack is playing you for a fool. Might be he wants the same thing you're after."

"What might that be?"

"Rose Danby."

Nichols got mad but brought himself under control with immense effort. Then he did something unexpected: he collapsed on the side of the bed and lowered his clasped hands between his knees.

When he looked up again his eyes were more haunted, more cavernous, than ever before. With the light from the lamp his whole face possessed a scarred and ravaged look.

"Did Rose tell you that?" he asked, blinking with nervous tension.

"She hinted she rebuffed your advances. That's why Danby is really out to kill you, isn't it? He knows you've been sniffing after his wife." I could tell from his reaction I was right.

"Rose is a fine woman," he said in a hoarse whisper. The knuckles of his clenched hands were bone-white. "I can give her better than Coffer. Better than any man can."

"Belike she loves her husband, or she would have already left him," I suggested. "She doesn't strike me as the kind of woman who dilly-dallies about such decisions. Unless you know something I don't."

Nichols didn't respond. At first, I thought the possibility of Rose loving her husband more than Nichols jarred him. But that didn't make sense. A man like Pate Nichols, rich and land powerful, wouldn't be afraid of losing Rose's affection. If she could be trusted, her affection was something Nichols never had in the first place.

So why was he moping about something that was never his to begin with?

"Nichols. I thought this animosity between you and Danby was over water. It goes deeper, doesn't it? Deeper than you loving Rose and her not loving you in return."

Nichols drew in a ragged breath. The bed springs squeaked as he pushed himself back to his feet. He stood before the room mirror hanging on a wire over the dresser.

"I look at myself, and I don't recognize who I am," he said. It was the loneliest voice in the world.

He looked over his shoulder at me. "You never knew me

before you came to Haxan, Marshal. I used to carry a lot more weight on my frame. My face was filled out. These days I can't hardly walk I'm so tired. I'm going downhill fast and there's nothing anyone can do to stop it."

I recollected watching him climb the stairs to Doc Toland's office the morning before.

"You bad sick?"

He nodded. "Cancer in the bones. Got another year, Doc Toland says, if I'm real lucky. That's why I want Rose as my wife, Marshal. I want a son to leave what I've built with these two hands."

He gave a single, ironic laugh. "These hands. Look at them. Sometimes I can't stop the shaking. Marshal, I don't want what I've built to disappear in the wind, and me never remembered by anyone."

"Nichols, there are lots of women who would be proud to carry on your legacy. Rose Danby isn't the only woman in the territory."

"No, but she's the best. I always thought so."

He propped one elbow on top of the polished dresser and cupped his chin in his palm. "You know how it is, when you see something and it digs straight to your heart, and you have to possess it, or die trying. Well, I'm dying. I figure I might as well do everything I can to get what I want in the few months I have left. I've got plenty of money—why not use it to my advantage? That is, I felt this way until you walked in here and told me Rose might be playing me false. Even so, when you've walked the road of death as far as I have, you have to see a thing through, or you don't feel straight up a man."

His hand dropped with a light thump on top of the dresser. "If that means killing Coffer Danby that's what it will come out to be. There ain't no stopping it, Marshal. Rose or no Rose."

"Nichols, this is your final warning. If you hired Ben Tack to do murder I'll throw you in jail. I won't have you, or anyone else, deciding the law in Haxan."

Despite everything else, he was shaken Ben Tack might have manoeuvred unseen behind his back. A proud man like Pate

Nichols would never stand to be made a fool of.

If nothing else I had given him something to think about. Maybe it would be enough to save a few lives in the bargain.

"Nichols? Are you listening to me?"

"You're straightforward enough, Marshal. You may not believe this, but I am grateful you stopped by to tell me these things."

He caught me at the door. "Oh, one more thing, Marshal," he said. "My foreman rides into town every afternoon. He keeps me apprised how things are out at the ranch. He said this man Connie Rand has hired with us off and on over the last three months. Jenks, that's my foreman, he claims Rand is a good worker but has a mean streak. He cut up a man in the bunkhouse over a card game 'bout a month ago. The boys said the guy had it coming because he was dealing seconds off the bottom."

"Tells me something about how Rand reacts. Is he out at the Lazy X now?"

"No. Jenks hasn't seen Rand since he left our employ. He's known to partner with another drifter name of Silas Foote. Jenks heard Foote fell into trouble with the law in Kansas. We get a lot of men like that. You know this country. Long as a man does his work, and don't cause too much trouble, we don't ask questions about his past."

"What does Silas Foote look like?"

"Average-sized gomer with straggly black, greasy hair. The bones of his face look like glass pushing through lambskin. Got a strawberry red birthmark on his neck. Good line rider, though. One of the best. Likes his solitude."

"A line rider would have to. Any idea where I can find these men?"

"Foote had to ride into Haxan for a toothache a couple or three weeks ago, Jenks heard. My foreman doesn't know any more than that."

"All right, Nichols, thanks for the information. Any way I can talk to this foreman myself?"

"You ride out to my place with me tomorrow and you can see him. That's where I'll be, Marshal."

Nichols paused with significance. "I'm going home to die."

I took my leave. I was eager to get back to the office. Maybe there was paper on Silas Foote. It was the first real lead I'd had in a long time, and I wanted to bird dog it to the end.

Hew was relieved there had been no gunplay upstairs. He almost pushed me out the door. "Come back anytime, Marshal."

I met Jake at the office. "Go through these circulars and the ones in the filing cabinet. Go back at least five years. We're looking for a man named Silas Foote." I relayed the description Nichols had given. "There could be paper on him. I'll wire the lawmen in Kansas and see what they know about Foote. It's worth a gamble."

"Yes, sir, I'll get right on it."

"Also, find Piebald. If he's up to it, have my horse saddled and brought on over. I'm going for a ride."

"You want company, Marshal?"

"No." I checked the loads in my gun. "Not for this."

"Yes, sir. Here's your Sharps, in case you need it."

Within fifteen minutes I was riding out of Haxan toward the south fork of Gila creek.

CHAPTER 14

I followed the south fork until it took a bend through a jumble of sun-baked boulders. When I came to Larsen's burned out jacal I drew rein.

There wasn't anything left of the shack except the charred posts that continued to stand ghost-like in the late afternoon haze. Magra stood in the middle of the black destruction, her hands out to her sides. The hot breeze lifted her raven hair like a cape and tugged her calico dress against her legs.

"Magra."

She lowered her arms. Her broad face streamed tears.

"Magra, you shouldn't come here by yourself. It's much too dangerous."

"Papa won't talk to me anymore, John," she said. "I thought I would try one last time. He always night-walked to me whenever I needed his advice before." She made a helpless gesture. "Now he's not there."

She took in the charred timbers that stood like a cage around her. She shook her head with sadness.

"There's nothing to remind me of him, except his old shotgun in your office. I have nothing left."

I dismounted and walked toward her. She looked warm and vulnerable. "I think your father knew he could leave safe when I came, Magra," I said in a low voice.

"I went into a general store today and paged through their mail order catalogue. They have some awful pretty dresses, John, but I didn't buy one. Like I said before, I suppose I could always go back to the reservation and teach."

"Or you could stay in Haxan."

"And cause you more trouble. I heard about that set-to you

had with Alma Jean. John, things like that are only going to get worse if I stay."

"Magra, compared to what I have to put up with on a daily basis in that town, any trouble you cause me would be most welcome."

That made her smile a little and it warmed my heart to see it.

"You're a difficult man to convince of the truth, John Marwood."

"Funny. I was thinking the same about you."

The corners of her mouth turned up a little more. We walked around and through the blackened ruins for half an hour.

"You never told me the name of your horse," she said. I think she was trying to find something else to talk about other than the broken pieces of her own life.

"I didn't name him," I said, "and I don't use it very often, but he has a name. He's called Acheron."

Magra smiled. "I like it," she admitted. Perhaps because I had shared something she started to tell me about the desert and what her life was like as a little girl, playing way out here, all alone.

"After Mama died Papa was often away riding shotgun for Wells Fargo. Papa always took the most dangerous jobs, when they transported gold or a cash box, because they paid more. I was by myself but I never felt lonely. Before she died Mama taught me lots of things about the desert and how to listen to it."

"Did she night-walk with you?"

"*Ai*, often. Especially after she died. Then she stopped and I had Papa all to myself. Now I don't have him. I don't understand it." She dropped her head, raised it again. "I'm sorry. It sounds as if I'm ungrateful for everything you've done."

She looked up at me. "I'm not, John. I want you to know that is not the case."

"I know."

"Please, be honest with me. Will you ever catch Papa's killers?"

"No," I admitted. "Not unless they make a mistake. Every day that passes the trail grows colder. I'll tell you a secret only lawmen out here know: most criminals never get caught. That's a solid fact."

We stood beside my horse. "I can make you this promise, Magra Snowberry. I'll never stop trying. Come hell or high water, if there's the slightest chance to find Conrad Rand and make him pay, I'll do it."

We rode slow back to town. I dropped Magra off at the hotel and continued down Front Street. I came to a recessed door with a wooden shingle proclaiming: "JOSIAH HARTLEBY: DENTIST" burned into it with a hot iron. I stepped out of leather and went through the door.

The office was small and stuffy and lined with piñon wood, but it looked reasonably clean. There was a framed diploma from the Baltimore College of Dental Surgery hanging on the wall and a colour chart showing the many parts of a tooth.

"Afternoon," the spare little man with a long chin and pale, freckled hands welcomed. "How can I help you?"

"You Doctor Hartleby? My name's Marwood. I'm the new marshal here and I'm trying to run down a man by the name of Silas Foote."

"How am I supposed to know this Mr. Foote, Marshal?"

"Pate Nichols's foreman, man by the name of Jenks, believes Silas Foote came to your office for a bad tooth one day."

Hartleby held one long finger across his lips. "Hm. Let's check my record book. Perhaps it can be of help."

He bustled around a mahogany desk and flipped the yellow pages of a book where he had itemized all his transactions. "Foote. Foote. Ah, yes, here we are," he said with excitement. "Two weeks ago, almost to the day. Had an impacted molar he said hurt like a sumbitch. I pulled the tooth and charged him five dollars. He paid his bill and that was the last I saw of him."

"Can you give me a description of this man, Doctor?"

He scratched his head. "I tend to remember a person's mouth, not his face," he admitted. "Part of the trade, you might say. Speaking of which, I don't get much trade to speak of as is. Even with the trail herds, and the population explosion, and that little silver strike we had a year or two back. With all that, and Haxan being a new boomtown and all, there's not much call for a dentist in these parts. Isn't that something? I came all the way from Maryland. That's why I'm thinking of pulling up stakes and heading to California. I hear a man can make his meat out there."

I felt sorry for his troubles, but I wished he would get on with what he knew about Silas Foote. I was trying to catch a cold-blooded murderer and he was sobbing his life story out to me.

Hartleby detected my impatience. He fidgeted and hurried on with his tale.

"This man, yes, I do remember him, Marshal. He had a pockmarked face with a very wide jaw and black greasy hair that straggled down his temples. I remember the hair because I was bent over him to pull the tooth and it stank. Don't remember much else, I'm afraid. His mouth was rather small so the bottom teeth were impacted. I guess that's not much help to you."

"As a matter of fact, Mr. Hartleby, it fits the description I already have for the man. Can you remember anything else?"

"I had a terrible time extracting the tooth, as I recall. He yelped like a dog but said he felt better afterward."

"He have a partner? Man with white-blond hair and a droopy left eye. Runs by the name of Rand—Conrad or Connie Rand."

The dentist shook his head. "Nope. Didn't have anyone like that with him. Foote came alone into my office and left alone."

"All right, Doctor. Thank you for your help. If you remember anything else I'd appreciate if you would stop by my office to let me know."

"Is that Sheriff Cawley's old office?" he asked.

"It's my office now."

"Of course, Marshal, I didn't mean offense."

"No offense taken, Mr. Hartleby. Thanks again for your time."

After stabling my horse I helped Jake leaf through the circulars and warrants. We had just begun when a man and woman bustled through the door of the office. The man's right hand and forearm were heavily bandaged. He had a long-barrelled shotgun cradled in his left arm.

"We're looking for the town marshal," he said.

"I'm the U.S. Marshal."

"My name is Ambrose Watkins. This is my wife, Hester. We were riding home in our wagon when the blamed axle froze up. I guess I forgot to grease it proper. My fault. Anyway, we figured we would overnight in Haxan since it wasn't much of a walk." He got more and more worked up as he told his story. "Well, it's them coyotes and wolves, Marshal. They set upon us and killed both our horses. Then they liked to chase us down and take *us* for meat."

"It's getting bad out there, Marshal," the woman said, her voice quavering. She was a bone-thin scarecrow dressed in frayed gingham and high-button shoes. "Something must be done about them."

I pointed at her husband's arm. "They take a nip out of you, Mr. Ambrose?"

"Sure did, the yellow-eyed bastards. I had to see Doc Toland. He sewed me up with boiled horsehair and told me to keep the sutures clean with alcohol."

"That means you splash it on the wound, Ambrose," his wife said, "not drink it down."

"I know that, Hester. Hell, what do you take me for?"

She ignored him and spoke to me. "It was a frightening experience, Marshal. I have never seen coyotes act that way and run with wolves. They're hunger-crazed. Their eyes are all yellow and fierce and those red tongues." She shuddered. "When we made it to the city they backed off like they was scared of the lamplight."

The sun was going down fast. We could hear them now howling at the darkening sky. It was near a scream of madness as anything I'd ever heard.

"There they go," Hester said with another shudder. "It's enough to spook a body into a premature grave."

"Well, Marshal," Watkins said, preparatory to leaving, "we thought you should know. People are starting to lock their doors at night. Many are downright spooked. I don't mind saying I'm one of them. Come on, Hester."

After they left Jake commented, "We may have to bait traps and hire wolfers to hunt them down, Mr. Marwood. Killing livestock is one thing but now they're attacking people."

"A hard rain would go a long way to fixing things," I said. "Since we can't make it rain we'll have to do what you suggest."

I glanced at the clock on the wall and set my pocket watch to it. "We'd best start our rounds. Nervous people do funny things. This will be another long night." However, for a Friday night the saloons weren't doing much business. People were staying home.

It was close to ten when I sent Jake off to bed. I had helped him make two arrests and showed him how to fill out the paperwork. Then I put in another hour talking to the cowmen gathered around the cattle pens. They were waiting for the morning train to freight their stock.

"Look at 'em," one of the men said, nodding at the enclosed herd. "Everyone one of 'em so nervous you can see 'em getting thinner alla time. It will be a wonder if they don't stampede before daybreak."

I stayed with them and we talked about the war. Someone passed around a jug of corn. By one o'clock I was beat tired and trudging for the Haxan Hotel. The town was shut down. No one wanted to be out tonight.

I was passing Slattery's sawmill when someone fired a shot at me from an alley.

I dropped behind a water trough, my gun out. I listened to quick feet running fast in the opposite direction.

I went after the shooter, but he knew the alleys better than I did. I must have made a wrong turn because I ended up in a dead end between two stone buildings. There was a trash barrel lying on its side, empty. I had lost him.

The following morning I told Jake what happened.

"I want you to keep an eye ready, Jake. If this person feels pushed he might take a shot at you, too."

"You think it was that boy you faced down the first night, Mr. Marwood?"

I had almost forgotten about him. "I don't think so," I said doubtfully. "He didn't strike me as the type who would try and shoot me in the back. He was more the fatalistic type."

Of course, this sort of thing wasn't unheard of at all. Lawmen all over the country were shot at, or gunned down, from alleyways or through windows at night. Someone tried it on Bill Hickok in Abilene. Few lawmen ever died face to face with their killer.

It's always easy for a coward to kill.

After loading my gun I ate a late breakfast. I met with Mayor Polgar and relayed the news about Ambrose and his wife. He said he would look into hiring wolfers to handle the problem before it got out of control. I returned to my office and started work on those circulars with Jake.

I didn't know Sheriff Cawley, but he had built a superb filing system over the years. He had warrants going back seven years from all over the territory. We spent most of a good morning checking every one. Jake found who we were looking for along about noon.

He sat up in his chair abruptly as if a bee had stung him. "Yeow! Got him, Mr. Marwood. Silas Foote. Photograph matches the description, too."

He read the particulars in a slow, halting voice. "Wanted for armed rob-robbery in Wichita, Kansas. Five hundred dollar re-reward offered by Wells Fargo. Known *comanchero*. Whereabouts unknown."

Jake pushed the flier across my desk. "Guess they never caught up to him if he's still our man today."

"I'll wire the sheriff in Wichita and see what he has to say about Mr. Foote." I clapped Jake on the shoulder. "That's top flight police work, Jake. Come on, dinner is on me."

It was the first real break I'd had in the Shiner Larsen murder and I was anxious to tell Magra about it.

After collecting fines from our prisoners we locked up the office and wired Wichita. We decided on the Haxan Hotel for dinner. Before we arrived Hew Clay ran out on the porch, his face white as marble dust and eyes round as saucers.

"Marshal," he skidded to a stop, winded. "I was about to come get you. Coffer Danby burned powder on Mr. Nichols up in his room. Put a pillow over his head to muffle the shot, but Alma Jean heard it from downstairs."

"You sure it was Danby?"

"I saw Danby run out of the hotel with my own eyes. He shot him, Marshal. Shot him dead."

CHAPTER 15

Three men carried Nichols down the steep stairs. His head was wrapped in a bloody towel. Blood rained from his body and spattered the Oriental rugs in the lobby.

"He walked right past me," Alma Jean said, "not saying a word to my hello. He stared straight ahead. I heard the shot and was going to go call Hew when Mr. Danby came back down the stairs. His face was cold, frozen. I saw the smoking gun in his hand. I was afraid he was going to shoot me, too."

She was trembling. Hew placed his arm around her and she laid her head on his shoulder.

"It's all right, Alma Jean," he said in a comforting way, his face pressed close to hers. "It's all over now."

Still shaking, she burst into tears.

"Alma Jean," I asked, "did you see which way Danby went?"

"No, Marshal. He jumped on his horse and rode away in a cloud of dust."

I turned to Jake. "Last time we saw Danby he was sitting a dun gelding. Saddle our horses while I finish questioning the witnesses. Make sure you grab my Sharps rifle from the office. Get a Winchester for yourself, too, and plenty of shells."

"Yes, sir."

Before long Jake and I were riding hard. It was impossible to tell which tracks were Danby's on the main road out of town. But when we turned off the trail and struck for his place we hit a sandy stretch spotted with twisted piñon trees.

I dismounted and examined the fresh tracks. "He came and went this way. He's not hurrying at all. Oh well, at least they're headed in the right direction." I swung my arm to show the way. "Off toward his place. Gotta be him."

"I guess he shot Nichols and figures his work was finished," Jake said. "From what Alma Jean said, he was sure workmanlike in doing it."

That had me worried. Jake was green and untested for this kind of lawing. All he had done so far was make a couple of arrests with my assistance.

With a man like Danby on the prowl, there was only one way this was going to end.

"Jake," I cautioned, "if it comes down to it, don't hesitate. Shoot to kill. An angry man can sometimes be talked out of his gun. Or taken because his anger gets in the way of his ability to think. A man like Coffer Danby, cold and focused, is the most dangerous kind of all. Understand?"

"Yes, sir."

"All right, let's ride."

As we kicked for Danby's place I tried to remember the lay of the land. If he kept on in this direction he would have to cross through Shadow Bend, where his sheep had been killed.

"Jake, maybe we can shortcut him if we break through that mesquite and cholla to our left. It's worth a chance."

"Better than riding slap into an ambush," he agreed.

We weren't wearing chaps. We got ourselves and our horses torn up, but we emerged on the other side to see Danby crossing the lower end of Shadow Bend a hundred yards away.

I pulled rein and drew the Sharps from its scabbard. I spurred my horse to close the distance. Jake followed, his pistol drawn.

Danby saw us topping the grass rise from his right quarter. He reined his horse around and came flying at us with his pistol drawn. He popped a shot in our direction, gun smoke torn by the wind, but there was no way he could hit anything on horseback at that distance.

I drew rein hard, jolting upright in my saddle. I sighted along the rifle and cut his horse out from under him.

Danby went down clumsy and hard, tangled in the saddle and reins. When we walked up on him he was holding a broken knee, his face yellow sick with pain.

I kicked the pistol out of his hand.

"Why'd you do it, Coffer?" I asked. "Why did you have to go and kill Pate Nichols?"

The horse screamed in pain. Thrashing the grass and soil with its hooves, it strained its head for the open sky.

"Jake."

"Yes, sir." He walked over and shot the dun with his Schofield pistol.

"Answer my question, Danby."

"Couldn't take no more of it, Marshal," he said, squeezing tears of pain from his eyes. His lips were skinned back from his gritted teeth. "Had to finish it quick."

"Quick? What the hell are you talking about?"

"You ain't seen my home? You ain't been there?"

"Of course I haven't," I said. "Not since yesterday."

"Ride up, Marshal, and you'll see. You'll know why I had to do it quick."

"Danby, you're not making a lick of sense," Jake said.

"He got them all." Danby looked like he was about to cry. "I was out alone and they didn't come back from breakfast. He got them all."

Jake handcuffed Danby to a shattered mesquite stump. I left him a waterskin.

"We'll be back to get you later, Danby."

"You won't be back, Marshal," he said. "Not if he's still there."

We mounted up and rode off. "You think it's all right to leave him alone, Mr. Marwood?" Jake asked.

"He's not going anywhere with that busted leg. And between you and me, Jake, if the coyotes get him, then good riddance."

We rode on and found the bodies lying in the tall grass and dirt. Smoke from a dying kitchen fire threaded from the pipe chimney. The late-afternoon sky was so blue it hurt my eyes.

"Mr. Marwood, those are the three guns Danby hired. Their horses are in the corral."

"Yeah. They must have come in for breakfast and were ambushed right here."

"Not a one has his gun drawn." Jake's voice was hushed. He was scared.

I was, too.

He had a deeper name than mine.

"Let's see if we can find the others, Jake."

We stepped out of leather and walked around the outside of the house. I found the boy lying under an empty hayrick. I stood so my shadow was on his face, thinking maybe it was only right to keep the sun off him even though he couldn't feel it. I removed my duster and covered him. I felt empty, crouched beside his small, lifeless body.

I discovered Jake on the other side of the house. The girl was lying at his feet. She was drenched with water.

"I found her in this rain barrel, Mr. Marwood," he said. His voice was hollow.

"It's okay, Jake."

We wiped his eyes on his sleeve. "I'm sorry, Mr. Marwood. I'm no good to you like this."

I took his shoulder. In a time like this, especially as a lawman who always sees the darkest room of the human heart, it's good to feel another live human being close by. It helps remind you you're not alone, and if it comes to it, you won't die that way, either.

The ground around the half-empty rain barrel was mud-socked. There was no doubting the footprints were those of a woman.

"You take your time," I told Jake. "I'll check inside the house."

I went in with my gun drawn. No one was inside. I checked all four rooms. I went back outside and stood under the cruel desert sun with death all around me.

Jake came from around the side of the house. "I put the little girl with her brother," he said. He returned my duster. "I figured it was right they be together. Was Mrs. Danby inside?"

"No. The house was empty."

"They took her, I guess."

"I don't think so, Jake. You saw the footprints by the rain barrel same as I did." My voice sounded hollow and strange, even to my own ears. I didn't want to believe it. But there it was, and there was no escaping it.

Jake checked over his shoulder at the hayrick. "Coffer must have rode up on this scene and went plumb loco, then."

"Yeah. I expect so."

"We going to bury them, Mr. Marwood?"

I had picked out a single track in the dust. I followed it. Someone had ridden all around the house, looking for more victims. But when he left, another horse from the corral went with him.

"I want to find this man, Jake. I want to take him."

I really could not recognize my own voice.

"Yes, sir," Jake said, "I understand."

The day was drawing to a close. We put all the bodies inside the house so the coyotes wouldn't bother them, and locked the door.

As we were riding away Jake glanced over his shoulder one last time.

"They drowned that little girl," he said. "My stars. Rose Danby drowned her own little girl."

CHAPTER 16

The sun was drawing down fast. Right on cue the coyotes in the thorn and bush howled with one voice. The whole sky, and the entire desert, echoed their mournful sound. It made me go bitter cold. Colder than I'd ever felt.

I could tell Coffer Danby was dead before we got close. You learn so you know how a dead man lies from the way his legs are twisted, his body small and deflated like.

He had worked a Barlow knife from his jeans and sliced his wrists open to white bone. I guess he figured he didn't have anything left to live for.

After coming from his house I can't say I blamed him for the choice he had made.

Jake's eyes were haunted as he took in the blood-soaked ground, the man's clothes splashed with spilled blood.

"This is a bad day, Mr. Marwood," he said.

"We have to find the man who did this, Jake."

"You know who it was?"

"I do." My name carried, too. It was why I had come to Haxan, called by a dead man. Not as much as Ben's, but it carried.

"It was Ben Tack," I said.

"That feller Gideon Short told us about?"

"That's right."

"You knew him after all. I thought so."

"I hoped I was wrong. I won't make the same mistake twice."

"You think it was him who shot at you from the alley?"

"No. Ben would never shoot anyone in the back. He's good enough with a gun, he doesn't have to."

The sky purpled in the east. Jake didn't say anything as we

rode on, but I could tell he was getting worked up more than was good for his nerves.

Finally, he pulled his horse to a stop. I brought my horse around and reined so we were side by side, facing one another.

"Marshal," he started, "a man like this Ben Tack, you think you can take him?"

"Have to try."

"Do you think you can take him?"

There was no sense lying to him. Or myself.

"No," I said.

"I don't mind dying," Jake said, "if it means that boy and that girl will rest easier for us trying."

"There's not much else we can hope for, Jake."

"He's that good, Mr. Marwood?"

"Ben Tack? Yes. He's that good."

Jake picked up the reins in his rough hands and straightened in his saddle.

"I'll ride with you, sir," he said.

We cut their trail on the south side of Gila Creek, where the grass was thin and brown. They had broken trail straight through and it was easy to follow.

As we rode, night came on, dropping like a blanket. The coyotes got louder the closer we got to Haxan. The ears of my horse started to flick back and forth alternately. A sure sign wolves were close about.

Soon I could see them slipping through the brush like grey smoke. Coyotes, too. Our horses were skittish and it took a strong hand to keep them under rein.

"Maybe we should shoot at them," Jake suggested. "Or stop and build a fire."

"There's no way we'd hit anything in this light," I said. "If we stop we'll be surrounded and never get out. Remember Ambrose and his wife."

"Guess you're right. Look at them, Mr. Marwood. They're herding us toward Haxan. I ain't never seen anything like it."

"Tracks we're following lead the same direction, Jake. Haxan is over that next hill. Let's whip for town."

We did and the coyotes came on like a thundercloud. Their long, lithe shapes flowed over the ground like pale shadows. The large, dark bodies of wolves were also running with them. They leaped over rocks and slipped through clumps of high grass with deadly, liquid ease.

The eyes of our horses were round with fear. They could smell death snapping at their heels. We rode hard, raking their flanks with our spurs. Jake leaned over his horse so his body presented less of a sail to the wind. His hat blew off his head.

"They're gaining." He drew his gun, but common sense prevailed and he checked his fire.

If we stopped to fight we would be swarmed beneath their snapping teeth and blinding fur.

I remembered what Ambrose had said. "They'll back off when we hit the town lights." I hoped.

We thundered past the first ramshackle buildings on the outskirts of Haxan and jumped Potato Road. We had come a long way already and our horses were blowing hard and lathered.

"Cut this way, Jake, through this alley. It will narrow down their numbers if they choose to follow."

We turned in, our horses rearing at the sudden change of direction. I held tight and gripped the saddle with my knees so I wouldn't fall. We galloped through the narrow passage before coming out on the central plaza.

The coyotes remained in the mouth of the alley, boiling over themselves in a mass of flesh and fur, yipping and snarling. Their eyes glowed with red and yellow hate, but they would not enter the lighted plaza.

Two people waited at the east end of the plaza, under the cottonwood trees. The streets of Haxan were deserted. A few people left from the paseo were running indoors, slamming doors and windows behind them when they saw the coyotes.

I got off my horse and Jake followed suit. I handed him the reins.

"Take the horses away, Jake."

"Let me stand with you, Mr. Marwood. You can't face him alone."

"Do as I say."

He hesitated. At first I thought he was going to give me an argument but he relented.

"Yes, sir," he said in a broken way. He led our horses toward the jailhouse.

I walked up alone toward the two people at the end of the plaza. "I'm here to take you, Ben."

"You're not going to arrest me, John?"

"No."

He grinned. He had a good, strong face, but his eyes in this light resembled black stones pressed in putty. His manicured hands were long and brown. His .36-calibre Navy revolver was holstered with a quarter turn.

"I knew you'd see the truth sooner or later, John," he said. "You always were one to see right to the centre of a problem. I forgot you were a good chess player."

"Nichols hired you to push Danby, didn't he? But you decided you wanted Rose for yourself and started running his cattle off, too. Yes, Ben, you always were one to play both ends against the middle. Just like Sand Creek. Facing Chivington down one night and then killing innocent women and children the next morning."

"That's right, John. Just like Sand Creek. And it usually works. Did this time, anyway."

"Why did you come here?"

"The plaza?"

"You know what I'm talking about."

"Oh, Haxan. Like I said before. I go where I'm sent."

I picked out the figure standing beside him. "Mrs. Danby, your husband is dead."

She wore a blue dress with red cuffs and a yoke collar. One side of her face was lighted from a coal oil lamp in a cantina behind her. The lamp was behind a red muslin curtain and it drowned her face in blood.

"I made the decision I had to make, Marshal," she said.

"I saw the consequences of your decision."

"I won't back away from it," she told me. "I love this man. He came to me when I needed him most. If Coffer really loved me he would have shot Pate Nichols the day he propositioned me to marry him. That's all there is for you to know."

"Rose, if you don't step aside I'll shoot you down, too, for what you did."

"You'd kill a defenceless woman, Marshal?" she asked.

My voice sounded like flint striking sparks on stone. I didn't recognize it. Something cold and ancient dark was coming awake inside me.

"I'd kill you and never think twice about it," I told her.

Ben pushed her away with a stiff arm without taking his eyes off me.

"Step aside, Rose. This is between him and me. You got no part to play in this. You're not important anymore."

She rocked back. "Not important?" It was like a scream of outrage. "How can you say that after we—" She swallowed hard. She resembled a cold knife rising out of the white sand.

"You used me," she hissed. Her hair was Medusa-wild around her face. Her green eyes were dark with mistrust. "You used me to get him here, didn't you?"

"I said go." His words dripped ice. Rose Danby looked like she'd been kicked in the stomach. She clutched both hands to her throat like she was going to be sick and drew back behind a wooden post on the sidewalk. She bent her head and began to cry. It was a wracking, forlorn sound.

The coyotes continued to yip and moil over one another at the edge of the plaza.

"I want you to leave Haxan, Ben," I said.

"Can't." His iron grin deepened, pulling the lineaments of his face taut like wires. "Won't."

"This is my town."

"I like what I see. Might want to put down a stake. Caught a glimpse of that little Snow Berry, too. Maybe I'll make her my lost cause."

I took a deep breath, let it out slow. "I'll kill you, Ben."

"You can't do for me, John. You're not fast enough and you know it."

"I'm giving you a call."

He stopped grinning and stepped out a pace or two. We were bathed in a circle of light. In a weird way the stars above us stopped shining.

"It's your play," he said. "You deal the cards, Marshal."

I went for my gun. His first shot hit me between the ribs. His second went through my left thigh as I was going down in a helpless spin. All the breath slammed out of my body when I hit the ground.

I never cleared my holster.

He approached. I watched him come. There was nothing I could do. Gun smoke drifted across the empty plaza in a tangled cloud. I saw my hand scrabbling the plaza dirt, trying to hold onto life.

"Sorry, John. I had to do it." Ben raised his pistol. "And this."

"Mister, you twitch one hair and I'll fire both barrels into your back."

It was Jake. He had gone to the office, grabbed Magra's old scattergun, and circled up from behind, coming onto the plaza through the cantina.

Ben never gave him a chance. He dropped and spun, firing his Navy Colt. When Jake fell, the butt of the shotgun hit the edge of a water trough. The buckshot from both barrels cut Rose Danby in half. She fell without a sound, like a marionette with the strings cut.

Ben watched it all unfold without a blink or a word. He had his back to me, admiring both his luck and his handwork at dropping Jake so neatly.

But when Rose went down his body stiffened with shock.

I knew him. Despite everything else he wasn't without human feeling. Maybe Rose meant something to him after all.

Maybe that's what made him forget.

He took a single step toward her body.

"Ben."

He turned. His head was silhouetted against the red light from the cantina lamp. My Colt Dragoon kicked once in my hand.

But once was all I needed.

HAXAN

I let my gun hand fall. Someone ran across the plaza toward me, screaming my name. It was Magra.

The stars began to shine again.

CHAPTER 17

My eyes fluttered open. Magra sat beside my bed. Her braided hair fell across one shoulder as she bent forward and laid a hand against my forehead.

"You're in Doc's surgery," she whispered. "It's been three days since you were shot. You had a fever."

"Jake?" I rasped. Last I saw, he was reeling backward with a lot of blood on his back.

"The bullet skinned under his left arm and went through the muscle of his back. He hit his head against the windowsill and got a concussion, but he's going to be all right. No, John, you must lie still."

I tried to sit up. Big mistake. My head felt like it was full of jelly. Waves of leaden fatigue sloshed through my limbs, deadening my hands and feet.

"You had two bullets in you," Magra said. "You got an infection and almost died. But you're out of it now." She squeezed my hand, hard.

Someone drummed on the window and eaves with muffled sticks. "What's that noise?" I asked, confused.

"Rain."

I stared at the ceiling and tried to count the vigas. My brain was too tired. I closed my eyes.

"Magra."

Her voice drifted out of the darkness. "I'll be here when you wake. You sleep now."

Ten days later I could hobble around pretty good. I could even stand for an hour without my knees wobbling.

Magra took me for walks up and down Front Street like I was a crippled dog. I sat on the bench in the plaza to show the badge while Jake made his rounds and read the territorial newspapers. There was other news besides the normal political shenanigans. A businessman named Levi Strauss had filed a patent for blue pants with copper rivets. He wanted to sell them for $13.50 a dozen, which sounded expensive to me.

All in all, the exercise, sun, and fresh air went a long way to bringing me back to the land of the living.

One morning, after loading my gun, Magra and I sat in the sun before breakfast. I had slept the entire night without too much pain and felt almost human. The morning sky was burnt orange. The San Andres Mountains were blue and stark. The long black shadows under the mesquite trees were filled with mystery. Mourning doves cooed to one another across the *acequia*, their voices carrying like soft music.

Sitting here was beneficial to me in many other ways. Magra explained who the people were when they walked or rode past on business. It was good information for a new lawman to know.

"That's Mr. Slattery. He owns the sawmill. Widow Fowler has four children. She fries tortillas for the cowhands. Moses Spielman is the editor of *The Iron Cauldron*, our local newspaper. He said the issue describing your gunfight with Ben Tack sold more copies than all the other newspapers in the territory put together. Charlie Kizzle lost his foot in a hunting accident five years ago. His wife ran off with a whiskey drummer. That's our undertaker, Ezekiel March. He's nice, but doesn't smile often."

"Goes with the job," I observed.

"Like a certain lawman I know," Magra said.

"Who's that pretty blonde girl drawing water? The one on the piebald mare."

"You can't make me jealous. That's Phaedra Finch. She lives with her husband and stepson up in the mountains. She comes to Haxan to buy sugar and flour and whatnot. They're not very prosperous. They keep to themselves."

An undercurrent in her voice alerted me. "Who blames them for doing that?"

Magra shrugged. "People say it's a sinful family. No one speaks about it openly in public. They only whisper."

"Why?"

"Mr. Finch beats Phaedra. And word is she's more in love with the stepson than the father. I don't know about that part. People in Haxan gossip." She eyed me with speculation. "Like they do about us."

"I have told you what I think of the good people of Haxan and their damnable gossip."

"Doesn't stop it from happening, John."

"I don't care to argue about it. This is a nice day and I like sitting here with you. Let's talk about something else. Tell me about your father. How did he come to America?"

"He was born in Stockholm on All Hallows' Eve. There was a famine when he took ship to America. He came with my Aunt Tea. She found a husband in Chicago, but Papa kept moving west. Papa was like that. He let the wind blow him."

"That's not true." I nodded at the town around us. "He settled here. How did he meet your mother?"

"Black Sky was the daughter of a Navajo war chief. She believed the things my father said about hidden voices in the rocks and sky and grass. You see, at first everyone lived in Coldwater off to the east. It was even voted the county seat. But when silver was found Haxan took off. The silver didn't last but by then people had moved here because there was more money to be made. Many of the rich businessmen who made money in the sliver strike promoted the Santa Fe railroad to lay down a spur. The train didn't come every day, but the population exploded. When that happened Papa moved us farther into the desert. He never liked crowds and he liked the people of Haxan less. He said the clamour of their voices drowned out the real voices of the desert. Plus, he didn't like their obsession with money."

"What was it like growing up?" I asked. "Were you bored?"

Magra hugged her knees and rocked back and forth. "Mother

taught me everything I needed to know. She showed me how to use the stars and sun so I would never get lost, and how to tell time by them. I can find water by watching which way a bird flies in the morning. I could trap and track any animal as well as a man by the time I was five. Mother taught me how to skin and tan hides, dry meat on a sun rack, and cook bread in a beehive oven. I had a pet rattlesnake. Don't laugh—it's true. One night he slithered through a knothole in the floor and coiled in the corner of my room. I fed him desert mice. Papa said that wasn't a proper pet and bought me a puppy for my birthday. That made the snake sad."

"How so?" I couldn't tell if she was greening me or not.

"He crawled away and I never saw him again. Maybe he thought I didn't love him because I had the puppy. I had lots of pets like that, though. Mother taught me how to tame most animals. Any animal can be tamed, John, except man."

"Thank goodness, or I would be out of a job. You said something about Pennsylvania once, if I recall."

"I hated it there." She made a face as the old memories came flooding back. "Everything revolved around a clock. They ate by the clock and slept by the clock. For all I know they made babies by a clock. I know Papa came from that world, but he didn't live that way."

"It doesn't sound like you were a good student."

She laughed at this and said with a bit of pride, "I was often in trouble. The nuns used to whomp me good and make me kneel on rice and say prayers of contrition. That made me hate them all the more. I learned how to read and write, though. They had a lot of history books."

"When did your mother die?"

She became quiet. "It was on the Long Walk. That was in 1864 when the Army forced the Navajo onto reservation. Mother was married to a European, so legally she didn't have to go. But she wanted to stay with her people. Papa said he understood."

"How did she die?"

"Mescalero raid. She was protecting two women who were

with child. Later, an official from the agency said Mother died of consumption. We will never know the truth. Mother never said."

"You mean when she night-walked you."

"That's right. I was back east, remember? She came to me in my dreams and told me she had crossed over. That's when I decided to run away and come home to Papa. But he sent for me before I could do that. Later, I asked him why. He said Mother told him that same night it was time for me to come home. Papa always listened to what Mother said. He respected her spirit magic and he put great store in her intuition."

I recalled my past—what little of it I could remember.

"Magra, do you really believe in spirit magic? Rattles and beads and such not."

She was indifferent to my scepticism. "I don't know how else you can explain the mysteries of the world. I'm not talking about things like how big the moon is or why people grow old and die. I mean what is inside the human heart. No one can ever measure that. At least, not yet they can't. But it does exist."

She looked around with furtive eyes to make sure no one was watching and put both her hands on mine. "You're proof of that, John Marwood."

"Me? I'm afraid you caught me short."

She leaned back and cocked an eyebrow.

"Papa called you here, didn't he?"

Thing was, I couldn't gainsay what she said. I had memories, sure. There were aspects of my life I knew to be true, like I had explained the first night we met. But there were also gaps in my past I couldn't explain to anyone. Even to myself.

Sometimes, late at night, I dreamed of towering cities that had long ago vanished under blood and dust and time.

I couldn't shake the feeling that one day those memories would come flooding back in a monstrous wave.

And when that happened it would be time for me to leave Haxan.

A week later I was well enough to head for the jailhouse. I had little choice. The biggest news around town was that a day or so ago Navajo braves had started jumping reservation. No one knew why.

"They're mostly peaceful and don't have much call to fight," I said, reading an army telegram from Fort Providence. "Something's got them stirred up."

"Bad news if true." Jake unbuttoned his shirt pocket. "I've been keeping this on ice for you, Marshal. Thought you would like to read it once you got back on the job full time."

"What is it?"

"A wire from the town marshal in Dallas. He heard you were on the prod for Silas Foote. He said Foote and two other men came through town and camped on the Trinity River. By the time the sheriff rode out they had moved on. One of the men matched the description of Connie Rand."

"This is the best news I've had in weeks." I tapped the telegram with a fingernail. "He thinks Rand and his gang pulled west. Mayhap they're returning to Haxan."

"Thought that would interest you, sir."

I felt my blood rise. I was getting stronger every day. With luck I'd run these *comancheros* to ground and be shed of them.

Jake poured himself a cup of strong coffee. "If they accepted money to kill Shiner Larsen then it stands they took money to kill Miss Magra, too. Otherwise, there's no reason they would burn her place down or try and kidnap her."

"That's how I've got it figured, too," I admitted. "She hasn't gone back to her father's place since I've been sick, has she, Jake?"

"Oh, no, sir. I've seen to that. She wanted to put a tent out there and move out, but I wouldn't let her. She kicked about it, but you know how she is. She was more concerned about your health. We all were."

"What about you, Jake? How are you holding up?"

"My back creaks me at the end of the day. Doc gave me some liniment. It helps a tad."

"Magra has a mind of her own about many things, Jake. But I don't want her where we can't protect her. If Rand is headed this way mayhap he's decided to tie up loose ends and earn the money he was paid."

"I agree, Mr. Marwood. Rand will like as not try for Miss Magra next. As far as I can tell, she has taken up residence in Haxan. If truth be told, she's been a help while you were down."

"How so?"

"Since you were shot she comes to the office every morning to sweep out and boil fresh coffee."

"I wonder why."

"Maybe she feels she owes it to you. Some Indians is like that. They're better than most white people in that regard. Thing is, she came in this morning and then rushed out for some unknown reason." He picked up a fistful of paper and dropped it. "The paperwork has piled up on your desk something awful, Mr. Marwood."

"Hang the paperwork." My voice was hard and brittle. "I want my hands around Rand's scrawny neck." I made a twisting motion in the air.

"That works for me," Jake said. "Oh, this also came for you early this morning by wire. Where did I put it?" He dug through the mess of papers on my desk. "Here it is. The county sheriff in Mesilla wants us to pick up a prisoner he's holding."

The door to the office opened before I could answer. Frank Polgar rushed in. He was grim and flustered.

"Marshal," he opened with a curt nod, "I heard you were back on the job. Good thing, too. We've got bad trouble."

"Morning, Frank. What can I do for you?"

"A hide hunter rode into town half an hour ago. He came across Pat Wheedle's spread. That's on the other side of Broken Bow about fifteen miles out. Well, this hide hunter, he claims Wheedle's place was torched to the ground and everyone killed."

CHAPTER 18

I walked between the bodies. Everyone was dead. Horses. Dogs. Men.

The smoke from the burning wagons towered like black pillars against the blue, un-winking sky. Broad canvas from the canopy ribs snapped and tore in flaming shreds. Sometimes the wind moaned through the broken wheel spokes like a ghost trying to find its way home.

There were a lot of ghosts here.

We had been riding to Pat Wheedle's farm when we happened upon the wagon train.

Jake tipped his hat and leaned back in his saddle. "I don't know why we live here, Mr. Marwood. The desert . . . it kills people."

A young woman, all of sixteen, lay at my feet. Her green dress was ripped and torn.

"The desert didn't do this, Jake," I said.

"Apache?" He shook his head in sad wonder at the mutilation. "Savage enough. And they didn't just count coup, neither."

I studied the arrow in the back of a man. He was face down, one arm around the girl. He had tried to protect her with his last breath. Father, maybe, or an older brother.

"They didn't take the horses, either, like they are wont to do." Jake was disgusted. "Just plain murder."

"I know. That bothers me, too." Indians always took horses in a raid. So did white men posing as Indians, which happened more often than people cared to admit.

Whoever did this wanted to kill every living thing in sight. Like they were trying to scrub everything alive out of the territory.

I put my boot against the dead man, took hold of the shaft and pulled it loose. "Look at this point, Jake, and the fletching. That's not Apache."

"Navajo." He tossed the bloody arrow away. "That fits with what we've heard about war parties jumping the reservation. But this isn't like them." He meant the wanton slaughter. "They're mostly peaceful folk, as I reckon."

"Something made them mad. We'd better find out what." I took the reins from Jake and swung into my saddle. I grimaced at the twinge of pain that lanced through my side.

Jake eyed me with grave concern. "You up to this riding, Mr. Marwood?"

"Don't suppose I have a choice anymore, Jake."

"We still have to ride to Mesilla and pick up that prisoner. Sheriff Olton is waiting with transfer papers."

"He can hold that man a while longer. If renegades jumped the Bosque Redondo they might hit Haxan next. They're headed in the right direction. We can't let that happen."

For a lot of reasons. I had come a long way through time and wind and dust to make sure something like that *never* happened. Either to the town, or to *her*.

Like it or not, this forced me to put my hunt for Connie Rand on a back burner as well.

We followed the unshod pony tracks. It was hard to judge in the packed earth, but it looked like twenty or thirty horses were in this war party.

"A fair sized group, Jake, and moving fast. The way they always do when they're on rampage."

"Lucky thing we were skirting Crooked Mesa back a ways or we'd have never found that wagon train." He pursed his lips in contemplation. "Six wagons and they didn't have time to circle up and defend themselves proper."

I pointed to a bare hillock in the distance. "From the tracks it looks like the war party came over that rise. Let's ride that way and investigate."

Jake pulled his Winchester from the scabbard. The desert was quiet all around us. We were holding our breaths, too.

I was thinking about the dead girl. Her hair was long and black. Like Magra's.

"My stars, can you imagine what it was like?" Jake's voice was hushed. "Thirty men on war ponies screaming out of the sun. It's enough to frost your liver."

"That's enough, Jake."

"Yes, sir."

We crested the rise. The wind was in our faces. We could smell smoke. "Oh no. . . ."

A cabin nestled in a canyon a quarter mile away was wreathed in dying flames. There were more people on the ground. All the livestock were dead.

All men are born of blood. We die that way, too.

It is the blood of our family and friends that ties us together. Makes us human. Gives us enemies.

I cannot remember how long I have travelled or from what depths I arose. I only know I am here now, brought to stand against that which must be overcome.

As all my people are.

"I wired Fort Sumner before the lines were cut. The agency claims a war party of fifty braves jumped the reservation two days ago, and another one, a smaller one, yesterday. Two more parties jumped this morning. Something's got them stirred up like a hornet's nest."

Mayor Polgar and Doc Toland stood in my office, over strung and unsure of themselves. Jake sat beside the potbellied stove oiling a Winchester.

Polgar's face was drawn and yellow in the desert morning light that streamed through an open window. "Who's in command there?" he asked.

"Colonel William Colorow," I answered. "I've dealt with him before in another capacity. He's competent enough. They've got a troop trying to run this first war party down, the big one, somewhere along the El Camino Real. No luck, so far."

"What do you think we should do, Marshal?"

"People are safe if they remain in town," I said. "It looks like this southern party is hitting up and down the territory, restricting their terror to Sangre County. From what I can gather they're bypassing towns like Haxan and Glaze and Coldwater.

"Are these random attacks, John?" Doc Toland asked. On this morning he looked more grizzled than ever. His black frock coat had the ever-present dusty cuffs and chemical stains.

"No, Doc, more like they're searching for something. Or someone."

The two men exchanged swift glances. "Say again, Marshal?"

I used the map of Sangre County behind my desk. "Here's where they hit the wagon train Jake and I found. This is the cabin where Flat Bush Creek hits the rise. This is Wheedle's farm beside it."

I picked up another telegram from my desk. "An hour ago I got a report from a whiskey drummer who had his mule train attacked yesterday. It's scattered all over the county, Frank. Back and forth along a line between Crooked Mesa and Coldwater."

"That covers a hell of a lot of territory, Marshal."

"The attacks are concentrated there. The first party that jumped the rez, well, if you ask me, it was a feint to give this second one time to gather and attack in force."

"If they're raiding up and down like you say, then we'll never stop them short of all out war."

I shook my head. "This isn't an ordinary raiding party, Frank. Jake and I saw that for ourselves."

"Right enough we did," Jake broke in.

"The wagons were fired and broken, but they weren't ransacked. They didn't even steal the horses, Frank. Nothing was stolen, except for maybe guns and ammunition, which you would expect. Same thing on the farms. Everybody was just . . . dead."

"Scalped?" Doc Toland asked.

"They were dead, Doc. Leave it at that."

Jake put the Winchester down and loaded Magra's old shotgun with buckshot. He clicked the breech shut and handed it to me. "Ready when you are, Mr. Marwood."

Jake had come a long way since the night we faced Ben Tack together. He was still green, but I trusted him more than any man I knew to watch my back.

He was faithful to a fault. You gave him an order and he would carry it out, even if it meant his death. He had proved that in the plaza.

Polgar gaped in amazement at us. "Where are you two going?" He and Doc Toland followed us onto Front Street. "You must stay and protect this town, Marshal," Polgar said.

I lashed the shotgun to my saddle. "No, Mayor. I told you these renegades are skirting big settlements. They're not on a suicide mission. They're roaming the countryside and that's where we need to be. Maybe we can run them down and learn what this is all about."

"This is an Army problem," Doc Toland put forth. "Let the Army handle it. We must look after our own interests."

"I'm a U.S. Marshal, which makes this federal business, Doc. Fort Providence is helping Sumner chase that big group up north. Like or not, this small war party is our problem."

"I don't support this decision, John," Polgar said, scowling. He grabbed my arm and turned me around. "You were brought here by the Haxan Peace Commission to protect our town."

"That's where you're wrong, Frank." I had known this was going to happen. When a city pulls strings to get a federal lawman they always think they own him.

"I was sent by the War Department in Washington to uphold the law, and that's what I aim to do." I made sure my saddle was cinched tight. "Look, I don't like this any better than you. But I must handle this problem the way I see fit."

"What do you want us to do while you're away?" Doc asked.

"Keep everyone inside. No one will get hurt."

"Be very careful out there, John," Toland said.

"We will. Come on, Jake."

I mounted my blue roan and he kicked a little. He was always able to smell blood coming.

I addressed the two men from my saddle. "I mean it, Frank." He was glowering. "I don't want armed posses forming up without my knowledge. I won't stand for it. You want me to protect this town. Okay, that's what I aim to do, but I'll work it my way. Doc, you help the mayor keep a lid on things while I'm gone."

He waved back his understanding.

Polgar hung onto the bridle of my horse. "John, you're taking an awful risk going out there alone."

"Maybe. Like I said, I prefer to handle this my way."

"How, may I ask, do you plan to do that?"

"I'm headed for Magra Snowberry's place. She's part Navajo, but as far as I know they've always trusted her because of who her mother was. Mayhap she has an idea what this is all about. Can't hurt to ask."

"Then why are you riding? She's staying at the Haxan Hotel."

A cold grin crept like ivy across my face. "You don't know Magra the way I do. I'm sure she's heard about this trouble by now. That girl has her own way of doing things, no matter what anyone says."

Jake and I rode hard for Shiner Larsen's place. As we rode through town shopkeepers called from their doorways, begging us to stay. The plaza was abandoned. People were worried and I couldn't blame them. We followed the main road out and cut across country to save time.

Magra's place—everyone continued to call it the Shiner Larsen place after her father—was on a small rise. I followed Gila Creek through the familiar field of boulders. I had been out here so many times the trail was becoming worn.

Jake and I rounded the last big boulder covered with magic symbols when we reined our horses hard enough to cause them to stumble and snort.

"My . . . *stars*," Jake choked with awe.

Navajo braves mounted on sleek, painted ponies surrounded the blackened remnants of Magra's cabin. There must have been twenty or more and they all wore war paint.

"Ride easy, Jake," I said under my breath. "Keep your hands in sight or we'll both end up as a smear spot on the desert floor."

"You think they're holding Miss Magra hostage?"

As we approached I saw someone had tied buffalo hides to the blackened posts left standing so as to create a small enclosure.

"I don't know. I don't see her anywhere around."

We rode slow. Hard faces watched us come nearer. We pulled short ten yards away.

"Now what?" Jake wondered aloud.

"Let them make the first move. They hold the cards."

A flap to the hastily constructed shelter opened and a tall Navajo wearing breechclout, moccasins, and an imposing war headdress emerged. His face was marked by the New Mexican desert and wind, his shoulders burned red from the blistering sun. He had a single white feather tied in his hair.

Magra emerged after him, unharmed. She wore buckskin instead of her in-town calico, perhaps as a concession to her people. Her hair was tied back and braided, Indian fashion.

Addressing the war chief standing at her side, she pointed at me.

"That's him," she said. "That's the man known as Long Blood."

CHAPTER 19

Thermopylae. Masada. Agincourt.

And now Haxan, New Mexico.

We have many different names, we who come. Some are unpronounceable. Even we don't know them all. I don't think we're supposed to because it would be too overwhelming. But we all have names and some are bigger than others.

We go where we are needed.

I have a name. Lots of them. So did Ben Tack. When I am called I must stand against that which must be faced. I have done it since the beginning of time.

You see, there is a thing inside me, coiled in wintry sleep. Rarely does it awaken. But when it does I let it have full voice.

It's who I am. It's my Name.

"I am White Hawk," the war chief said.

I had a name in his tongue, too, but he probably wouldn't believe it. "My name is John Marwood. I'm a U.S. Marshal for this territory. This is my deputy."

"My people know you as Long Blood. I will call you that. We will talk between us, Long Blood. I have much to say and I will listen to you as well."

"I think that's a fine idea, White Hawk."

"We will speak inside Magra's lodge. She is the daughter of Black Sky. Her words and her heart are made straight."

"I think so, too."

"We will sit as White Men so you will know my words have serious meaning. We will sit inside a circle, which is important to my people."

"I appreciate that, White Hawk." It was a big concession on his behalf. I wondered why he was making it. "Jake, stay here. White Hawk's men won't hurt you. Magra. . . ."

She smiled at me. It always made me feel good when she smiled. "I'm all right, John," she assured me. "I'll remain with Jake. Go and listen to what White Hawk has to say. I . . . I hope you can help him."

I nodded and followed the other man inside. We sat on either side of an upended stump that served as a table, hands crossed before us. We studied one another for several moments before White Hawk began to speak in slow, measured words.

"The roof of Magra's lodge is open to the sky." He meant this was a place we could trust one another. He didn't want there to be any half-truths between us.

"It's a good place for men to talk straight," I agreed.

"I have killed many Whites these past days. I will kill many more."

"It has to stop, White Hawk."

"I cannot stop, Long Blood." His sadness sounded genuine. "I must keep killing until I find that which our people have lost."

"What did you lose?"

I had pushed him too hard. His pride and his culture would not allow him to be so direct with a stranger. Even among his own people he would be more circumspect.

"My great-grandfather, Crooked Tent, told me stories how it was before the Many Whites came," he said. "He taught me our people believe all things are living in this world, so we should not be surprised there are other men who also live. But over the years I have learned the White does not believe all things are alive. To him, all things are dead. Even other men who are living are dead in their eyes. This makes their hearts hard and they have no reverence for those who are truly dead. This saddens me as a human being. Men should live together in peace. When they do not we must fight. This is the way of all men. I have spoken. I ask you to remember my words."

"I think you're right, White Hawk. You shouldn't have to

apologize for who you are, and what you believe."

White Hawk stared down at the "table." He was moved by his own words, and my willingness to agree to them.

"We have allowed our nation to be put on land that is not ours," he confessed. "By doing this we have let the hearts of our ancient fathers be cut from our memory."

He made a cutting gesture with his hand.

"But it is not my hand that broke the treaty. We are not the ones who forgot the words on paper. I am White Hawk. I speak straight."

"I know you do." His talk about reverence for those who are dead had me thinking. "Listen. Did something happen on one of your burial grounds?"

He returned a solemn nod but didn't pursue it further. Now I understood why he was reticent, why it was such an internal battle to reveal what was bothering him. It wasn't the topic itself, but the cultural embarrassment mixed with righteous anger.

"We are in Magra's house," I reminded him, "a place of friendship between men who can confide in one another. Like you said, her roof is open to the sky. Tell me what happened, White Hawk. Magra, the daughter of Black Sky, thinks I can help."

The mention of Magra's mother at last swayed his decision. Apparently, her name carried great weight among his people. It was something to remember in case I had need of it again.

The stoic man began to speak. At first he had to push the words out one by one, but then they came more easily.

"You know something of our medicine, Long Blood. Our burial grounds are sacred. Last week men dug holes in the earth and put the bodies of our dead in them. They said their own spirit words from the book they lean upon like a crutch. Then they went away after violating the quiet medicine of that place."

That was bad enough, the way he explained it, but there was more.

There was always more when whites were concerned.

"When the moon was yellow a Navajo maiden died of sleep fever. Her name was Morning Star. Her passing cut the heart from my body forever and made me lose my memory. I have forgotten who I am. I will not remember until I find her again."

He made a motion with his hands to signify the pain he felt and passed them across his eyes to show his spiritual blindness.

"She was brought to the burial grounds in the tradition of my people so her body could cross into the spirit world. When those men came she was not put into the ground with the others. Morning Star was stolen."

I couldn't believe what I was hearing. All too often settlers moving through the territory, who didn't know any better, precipitated cultural clashes with various Indian tribes. I had never heard of anything like this. No wonder the entire Navajo Nation was up in arms.

"Who did this, White Hawk?"

"One of the Great Wheels that bruises the ground and makes the buffalo stampede." The wagon trains moving along the El Camino Real. The Navajo, and other native people, had less cause to fear the great cattle herds that trailed north. That was something they could understand, even if they didn't particularly like it. Mechanical wagons ferrying armed settlers in numbers hitherto unimaginable to them, as were the stars, was downright frightening and incomprehensible.

"Why did they steal Morning Star's body?" There had to be a reason. Despite what White Hawk believed white men didn't do anything without reason. Their intentions might be misguided, but there had to be a reason for it.

"Morning Star was beautiful even in her death," he said. "She was dressed in white and wore beads, and her hair was braided in the fashion of our dead. Too, it is not uncommon for men of your race to steal totems and fetishes from our burial grounds and sell them to people in the east. We know this happens. I have heard Whites sell our scalps in a place called Lon-Don across the Great Eastern Water. They put these totems and fetishes in their lodges and make themselves feel superior to people whose shoulders are burned red from the desert sun."

"White Hawk, I'm sure you have taken badges of honour from enemies yourself."

"Yes, Long Blood, you speak a truth." His face was impassive.

"But I honour the enemies whose lives I have taken. There is no honour in what the White Man does. His eye is focused on the money he makes, not the sacrifice a fallen enemy gives in battle."

It was a damning condemnation.

"Mayhap you are right," I conceded.

He released a long, slow breath. I think he was relieved now that he had unburdened himself of part of his pain.

"After Morning Star was stolen I didn't know what to do. My mind was swallowed with immeasurable grief. I went riding and the power of my memory returned. I remembered Snow Berry, daughter of Black Sky. How it was said in the old stories and medicine visions a man of blood and violence would one day come to this desert. I sent a night bird to speak these words to Magra. She told me a man known to care for a half-white Navajo girl was someone I could have faith in."

"I hope so."

"Too, Magra is the daughter of Black Sky, a woman of great Earth power in our nation. This will never be forgotten."

"It won't be, I promise."

"This is my story, Marshal Who is Long Blood." His voice was deep and measured . . . and full of conviction. "My words are straight. I will not turn away from them."

"I know you will not, White Hawk."

He crossed his arms to show how serious he was in this matter.

"They stole Morning Star's body," he went on. "Now I kill Whites. And I will keep killing until her body is returned to my people."

CHAPTER 20

I rode with White Hawk for five days along the El Camino Real. I never knew there were so many people on the move, but this was spring, the season for travel. We came upon camps and river sites and way stations, searching for a wagon train that had passed through Indian burial grounds in the Bosque Redondo when the moon was yellow.

We had a fair idea where the train could be found. After all, wagons can only roll so many miles a day under the best of conditions. Given the relation of the burial ground, and the fact wagons stick to well-marked trails, it should have been easy.

But there was an awful lot of territory for two men to cover.

The Navajo Nation was standing down for the moment. It hadn't been an easy armistice to arrange. White Hawk reminded me if I helped find Morning Star before the next moon he would call off the slaughter. It was a huge concession on his part, but that didn't leave much time. On the other hand, President Grant, a man not known for leniency, particularly with American Indians, ordered the Army to stand down. He understood if this thing got out of hand all the Nations of North America might rise up together. No one, White or Red, wanted that.

It was enough to put anyone off their feed.

Meanwhile, despite the truce, the Army sharpened their sabres and the Navajo braves sang their death songs, preparing for war.

One thing stood in our favour. The entire countryside was talking about this, which both helped and hindered our search. Most people were supportive, understanding the nature of White Hawk's shame, while others on both sides were downright hostile and wanted to hurry the war along. It felt like we were riding through a powder keg. Every day the fuse sputtered closer to detonation.

With two days remaining before the new moon we found the wagon train in a wooded draw. It was twenty miles south of Santa Fe. There were four wagons in the train: one boat-shaped Conestoga with faded red and blue paint, and three smaller prairie schooners. One of the schooners had broken its whiffletree and they had stopped to carve a new one. If the wagon hadn't broken down it was likely White Hawk and I would have missed them by hours.

Like I said, we go where we're sent. Yet, sometimes it seemed those who sent us were also looking out for us. I didn't actually believe that. But it was nice to think it could be true.

It was dipping on toward evening. The western sky was a cauldron of bright fire.

The people we were looking for had a small central campfire blazing with the wagons circled. White Hawk and I let the horses browse while we walked out of the gathering dark.

I warned White Hawk to let me do the talking. His noncommittal grunt didn't fill me with much optimism. His eyes glared with hate.

"Hello in the camp," I called.

I heard the sharp click of a gun. I put an arm across White Hawk's chest to hold him back. He would have kept walking right into the gunfire. He was that angry and blind with hate.

"Who is it?" Gruff voice. Challenging. And more than a little frightened.

"My name is John T. Marwood. I'm a federal officer out of Haxan." I opened my grey duster so he could see the glint of my badge. "I'm a United States Marshal duly appointed by the government. Mind if we share your fire?"

"Who is with you, Marshal?"

"You know damn well who it is," I said.

"Let me hear him say it," the hidden voice demanded.

"I am White Hawk. I have come for the woman you stole."

"Let them in, Paul." This second voice was measured, with a fair hint of culture and education behind it. "We can't run forever."

"Come easy," Paul warned, "both of you."

We walked between two wagons and into the flickering firelight. Two adult men stood to one side of the central fire. One held a 12-gauge double-barrelled shotgun with hammers rolled back. He had a round, bearded face, wind-blistered neck, and heavy shoulders. His partner was lean and clean-shaven with a wide-brimmed hat, fancy striped waistcoat, and silver watch chain.

There were a dozen other people, keeping to the relative safety of their wagons—families holding their grubby children close, all of them with fearful desperation burning in their eyes.

Everyone was staring but the stares weren't fixed upon me. It was likely they had never seen an Indian up close. All they knew were stories from penny dreadfuls and tall tales heard around a drunken campfire.

The lean man broke the silence once we had taken our measure of each other.

"Marshal," he started, "my name is Dr. Robert Carver Graves. This is Mr. Paul Hickle, my personal bodyguard. I hired him for protection while travelling west. Put down your gun, Paul. Marshal, I want you to know we never meant any harm."

"Where is she, Graves?" I asked. "Morning Star."

"In that wagon." One wagon stood a little apart from the others. "She's wrapped in canvas and packed in a barrel of salt and charcoal."

White Hawk started beside me. "I want to see," he told me. I nodded for him to go ahead. I couldn't have held him back anyway, not without getting a knife in my gut. The settlers between him and the wagon moved aside to clear the way. He crawled into the back of the wagon and disappeared under canvas.

I turned to face Graves. "What for?"

"What? Oh, so the body will be preserved, Marshal. We were going to ship it east by rail." He lifted his hands out to his sides, let them fall back in futility. "But once word got out we thought it prudent to keep low until the brush fire burned itself out. If you get my meaning." He tossed a knowing smile. When I didn't respond in kind he wiped it off quick.

Paul Hickle decided to chime in. "This here is an important man from Washington, Marshal. You would do well to treat Professor Graves with respect."

"Is that why he hides dead Indian maidens in freight wagons and hires a melon head like you to protect him?"

Hickle's face closed like a gate. His hand tightened on the stock of the gun. "There's no call for rude talk, Marshal. We ain't done nothing bad wrong. We gave those people a proper Christian burial. Only a godless savage would leave them to rot in the sun and rain like that."

"Gentlemen, please." Graves glanced with concern at the wagon in question. He cleared his throat as if he we were about to give a lecture. "Now look here, Marshal, let me explain a few things. I'm a natural history curator for the Smithsonian Institution and a founding member of the Megatherium Club. Though that guild disbanded in 1866 many of us continue to work exclusively for the museum. I collect and classify anthropological specimens. My particular expertise is primitive cultures, documenting them as they become extinct in our time. From a scientific point of view we must have a record of these cultures that are disappearing from the west as they are supplanted by a superior one. Therefore, you can realize the cultural importance of—"

"You can stop now."

"What's that, Marshal?"

"Talking. You can stop."

"Why, Marshal, I'm only trying to explain—"

"I said shut up."

"You can't speak to Professor Graves that way," Hickle bristled.

I met his eyes. "That's where you're wrong."

One of the women pioneers screamed. White Hawk emerged from the wagon with a long canvas-wrapped body doubled up in his arms.

I could not describe his face as he stood in the firelight. Words like that simply did not exist in any language.

"Where does he think he's going?" Graves blustered. "That's a very valuable artefact."

White Hawk approached me. His face was stone. "I will need fire, Long Blood."

"I understand." I had spent enough time with this man to know what was churning inside him. I motioned to the settlers standing around and gawking. "You people, start gathering wood for a bonfire."

Graves rushed forward, waving his hands. "Wait one blessed minute. You can't order these people around. I'm in charge of this expedition."

The men and women, for their part, remained uncertain. "Do what I told you," I told them. They looked at me and Graves and started stacking fresh wood in the clearing.

Graves pushed through the working throng and confronted me, his face choleric with rage. "I protest this outrage to the highest degree, Marshal. I'll telegraph Washington and have your badge pulled. I am trying to preserve the memory of this declining culture. How can I make you understand that?"

"Graves, if you say one more word I'm going to shoot you."

He opened his mouth to protest and found himself staring down the iron barrel of my Colt Dragoon. Sweat glistened on his wide forehead.

"Easy there, Marshal," Hickle burred. "I've got this shotgun trained on your back. Put the gun back in your holster."

"Don't be a damn fool, Hickle. You kill me and you, and all these people, will never see the sun rise."

"You don't bluff me, Marshal. I'm the original bluffer. Anyway, I'm the one holding the shotgun."

"Look around you, Hickle."

"All I see is you about to be cut in two squirming halves. I'm the man who can do it."

"No, melon head, *around* you. Through those wagons over yonder and up to my right. Now you see what I'm talking about?"

"Oh my God. . . ."

The others looked, too. Some screamed and fell over themselves, flinging firewood in the air and crowding like sheep toward the centre of the wagon ring.

There were hundreds of Navajo braves dressed in war paint and standing in the enclosing dark. They were armed. They drew closer. The dim light from the campfire played over their features and limbs.

"Put your shotgun down, Hickle," I said. "Do it slow. That's right. Maybe we'll live after all."

I guess when you came down to it he wasn't as stupid as I thought. "All right, professor, or whatever you call yourself, back up against that wagon there. The rest of you settlers, keep stacking firewood. Go on, do as I say. These braves won't hurt you. They want to go home to their families as much as you do."

With reluctance, and then renewed energy because there was nothing else for them to do, the settlers gathered the remaining firewood and carried it toward the clearing. All the while White Hawk stood with Morning Star cradled in his arms. He did not move. He did not speak.

While they were getting the bonfire prepared I walked over to the wagon White Hawk had searched. I peered inside. It was stacked with crates and barrels and hundreds of glass bottles. More specimens. I pulled aside one of the men who was helping to build the bonfire.

"Whose wagon is this?"

"It belongs to Dr. Graves," he explained. "We met him in St. Louis and he asked if he and his bodyguard could come along. We thought there would be safety in numbers. We never knew anything like this was going to happen, Marshal. We thought we were doing the right thing burying those exposed bodies. That part is true, we never meant any harm."

"Go on."

He licked his lips. "Then we started hearing stories how Indians were on the warpath because a burial site had been desecrated. We knew we were responsible and wanted to admit our fault. That man Graves," he jerked his chin toward him, "he said the furor would die down if we laid low. He said stone-age cultures always overreacted because they were ruled by superstition and not science. Hickle backed him up with his shotgun. We're just families trying to find a place to live. We have guns, but we're not hard like Hickle. We sure didn't mean to cause trouble."

"What's your name, mister?"

"Joyce. Caspar Joyce."

"Where are you headed, Mr. Joyce?"

He lighted a hand rolled cigarette. His hands were steady enough. Most men would not be under the circumstances.

"The Territory of Wyoming." He watched the braves and picked a fleck of tobacco off his lip. "I have a wife and two small children, Marshal. I hope we get out of this with a whole skin."

"You're not going to be hurt, Joyce. These people will go home once they finish what they have to do here."

"Maybe so." He took a long drag on his cigarette and watched me through the tangled smoke. "Marshal, there's something I don't understand."

"What's that?"

He leaned against the wagon's lazy board. "Well, sir, doesn't this land belong to whoever can hold it?"

It was a dark night. All the world was dark, maybe. I guess it's always that way when human beings talk.

"I'm not sure I understand you, Mr. Joyce."

He made tiny circles in the air with his cigarette as he searched for words. "The Indians had this land for a long time. Hell, they took it from each other. Killed each other for it, time and again. Now it belongs to us. Our people. One day, someone will push us off our claim. That's how life works, Marshal. May not be fair, but no one ever said life was fair."

"Better get back to work, Mr. Joyce. They're almost done."

"Yes, sir." He ground the cigarette under his boot heel. I joined White Hawk.

"No one is going to stop you," I addressed him under my breath. Graves stood off by himself. "Don't worry. I'll keep an eye on him."

"I want to thank you, Long Blood," White Hawk said. He had been holding Morning Star all this time and showed no sign of fatigue.

He regarded the white bundle in his arms. "Morning Star's spirit also wishes to thank you. Now she will cross to the other side and have me as a guide to make sure she won't get lost again. She will rest in the morning sky where she belongs, thanks to you."

"Goodbye, White Hawk."

"Goodbye, Long Blood." He started to go. "Magra was right. You are a man who can also be a brother."

Everyone drew back, leaving White Hawk to himself. He placed the body of Morning Star on the pyre and raised his face to the starry heavens. There was a little night breeze that ruffled Morning Star's hair, which had escaped its tight wrappings.

White Hawk lifted his hands and began to sing. Tears fell from his eyes into his open mouth.

When he finished he raised a flaming brand from the small fire and lighted the base of the dry wood. It caught easily. He stepped into the smoke and flame and stretched out beside Morning Star.

The flames leaped higher, whirling around their bodies like a tornado. They burned for a long time. After a while the wood beneath them collapsed and they fell into the spirit world forever.

When it was over the remaining Navajo braves melted back into the night without a word. By the time the fire died down the sky toward the east was tinged with pink.

There wasn't much left of the pyre. I picked up a smouldering brand and walked toward the far wagon.

Graves threw himself at me, his face wild and livid. "No, you can't. I won't let you."

Hickle grabbed the older man's shirt and wrenched him back. "Dr. Graves, those Indians are still out there. We have no other choice. We have to do it or we won't live out the day."

"Out of the way, Graves." I elbowed him aside and pitched the lighted brand into the rear of the wagon. There must have been loose straw or something back there because it caught fast.

The other settlers were packing their wagons in a hurry and getting ready to pull out in the grey morning. Hickle wrestled with Graves until the latter suddenly lost any fight he had left in him. Graves watched his specimens and artefacts literally go up in smoke and crackling flame.

He turned on me. "Does this give you satisfaction, Marshal?"

"As a matter of fact, Graves, it doesn't. But I don't expect you to understand that."

I put my back to him and walked out of the circle of wagons to find my horse.

"You must realize you haven't changed anything," Graves shouted behind me. His voice sounded thin in the wide-open prairie.

"The west will die," he said, "and the Indian culture will die, and nothing you or I or anyone can do will ever change that. Marshal! All you did was destroy the memory and record of that change. All you did was destroy yourself."

A half hour later I caught my horse and rode along the spine of a hogback. Half a mile away three covered wagons creaked west. A tiny dot followed on foot.

I watched them disappear in the desert haze.

Magra. She had long hair tied back Indian fashion and it smelled clean and crisp. I wanted to see her.

I turned my horse toward a bright star rising with the morning and rode straight into it.

CHAPTER 21

That same morning I rode into Santa Fe and wired Fort Sumner. I also wired Washington. Telegrams flew thick and fast over the next four days. I had to remain in Santa Fe to help coordinate everything. Tensions were running high, but it looked like things were going to stand down. The Navajo came back on reservation, reluctantly. There could have been reprisals on the part of the Army, but cooler heads prevailed. For once, people on both sides recognized they had dodged a deadly bullet. Best not push their luck.

On my last night in Santa Fe I checked into La Fonda, had a hot bath, and caught up on sleep. I awoke early, looking over the central plaza from my high bedroom window. I thought of Magra and wondered what she was doing.

That morning I attended a meeting at the Governor's Palace and had a late dinner with Judge Creighton. We talked about the Rand case.

By midday I started the long ride back to Haxan. I spent the dark nights in country staring at the stars and thinking of White Hawk. I had spent a lot of time alone with the man. I understood the lengths he had gone to restore the pride of his people, and the woman he loved.

White Hawk had called me Long Blood. That Old Indian Grandfather in the tent city had called me the same thing. I wondered what it meant, and what they knew about me that I didn't know myself.

Magra might have answers to that, I reasoned. I looked forward to seeing her again.

Haxan didn't look too much different than when I had left. Some of the windows were still boarded up from the Indian scare, but they were coming down.

HAXAN

Jake had done an admirable job in my absence. I found Magra waiting for me outside the Haxan Hotel. The sun was in her face. I didn't care who was looking or what people might say. I took her in my arms and held her close.

"Are you okay?" She touched my face with gentle fingers.

"I am glad to be home."

But this was Haxan. Nothing ever stayed the same for long.

I was walking out of the hotel early the next morning on the way to the jailhouse after a rough night keeping peace and filing the cells with drunks and spoilers, when I saw Phaedra Finch riding into town.

It was first time I saw her up close. The last time I saw her, she had a gun pointed at me.

She rode across the empty plaza on her piebald mare, dragging a mesquite travois that left parallel tracks in the sand drifts.

Lashed to the frame was the body of a man, a red blanket swathed about his face.

I ran up and caught the rope bridle of her horse. Phaedra's head was down, her blank eyes fixed on the pommel horn. She wore tattered tent canvas around her shoulders like a Mexican serape. Her feet were bare and dirty, and her red, blistered hands hung limp at her sides.

"You're Phaedra, aren't you? What happened to you?"

She blinked as if coming out of a long sleep. Her disarrayed hair was white-blonde and needed a curry comb, but her lips were red as pokeberry juice. She looked older than her twenty-five years. I wasn't surprised. From what Magra had told me, and hearing the whispered gossip, living with a man like Abel Finch on a mean plot of land above the timberline for six years would sap the youth out of any woman.

"Phaedra. Can you hear me?"

"It's Abel, Marshal. My husband. He's dead." Her voice dribbled like tired water over worn stones. The morning sun was in her face. She fought hard to swallow back tears. "I brought him to Haxan to be buried. He never thought we had a real home, even though I tried to make one. I guess I was never much of a wife, anyway."

"How did he die, Phaedra?"

"He went riding. Yesterday, it was. Came on a rattlesnake, I guess. His horse threw him and his foot caught in the stirrup. The horse dragged him and his head hit a rock."

I didn't say anything for a long time. "Are you the one who found him?"

"Clayton did." Clayton Finch, as I recalled, was her stepson.

"Where is Clayton?"

"Up at the homestead. He doesn't care to see his daddy buried. I had to come do it myself."

"Come down off that horse, Phaedra. I'm going to take you to Doc Toland."

"I don't need a doctor, Marshal. I want to bury Abel."

I took her arm and said soft, "Come on, Phaedra. You need help."

She slid off the saddle without a fight, half falling into my arms. She felt more like bones than girl under that canvas.

"What happened to your hands? They're all blistered."

"I don't remember," she murmured.

I helped her limp across the wide plaza. "My horse," she said, trying to turn out of my arms. "Abel."

"I'll have my deputy take care of them. Don't worry."

Doc Toland's office was only two doors down from mine. I had to carry Phaedra up the steep steps. I propped her against the wall and banged on the door with my fist. "Doc," I cried.

The door opened. Rex Toland was in shirtsleeves instead of his usual black frock, and his hair was tousled.

"John Marwood, why are you hammering on my door at this ungodly hour?" He saw Phaedra limp against the outside wall. Her face was stoic. Only her tears left tracks on her dusty cheeks.

Doc Toland sighed heavily. "Oh. Well, I guess it's been a long time coming. All right, Marshal, bring her inside. I'll see what I can do."

I left Phaedra with Doc and went down to the office. Magra was sweeping the floor while Jake poured fresh coffee.

"Good morning, Marshal," he said with a bright smile. "Care for a cup?"

Magra stood her broom aside. "Hello, John." She waited a beat for my answer. When one wasn't forthcoming her face changed. "John. What is wrong?"

"Trouble. There's always trouble in Haxan." I felt like kicking one of the chairs. Or hitting somebody. But there was nobody good to hit. Even the prisoners I had in back had taken their lumps last night when they decided they wanted to continue their drunken brawl with me using a saloon chair. The barrel of my Colt cracked across their skulls had changed their minds quick enough. We even had Sheriff Olton's prisoner waiting on transportation to Hays City. Olton had sent the man on a stage under guard when he learned I was out country helping White Hawk.

"John?"

"Phaedra Finch rode into town a few minutes ago. Her dead husband is strapped to a mesquite drag. Jake, get the body and hold it for Doc Toland. He'll have to autopsy it."

"Where's the girl, Mr. Marwood?"

"She's up there with Doc. He's examining her."

Both Jake and Magra fell silent. I had learned in the past people often turned quiet when Phaedra's name was mentioned in polite company.

"Better see to it now, Jake. With her in town there's no telling how this will break."

He put down his coffee cup with exaggerated care. "Yes, sir. Morning mail is on your desk."

"Thanks." I didn't care about that right now. If Conrad Rand were to walk through the front door I would not have been aware.

Jake hurried out of the office. I watched his broad back and green suspenders pass beyond the window and out of sight.

I sat behind my desk. Collapsed was more like it. What with the Ben Tack shooting, chasing that idiot Graves all over the desert, and last night's arrests, I was done in.

I sat there feeling used up. I wasn't looking at anything. I didn't want to.

"John." Magra, again.

"Yeah."

"It's not your fault."

I looked her way. I had come a long way to love Magra Snowberry. We never talked about it much. We didn't have to. Maybe it was because she knew who I was and why I had come to Haxan. Or maybe because when two people cared about each other they didn't have to speak a lot of words.

I can't explain it. I don't understand everything about the world. I just know it was that morning, with me sitting behind my desk and the sun pouring in through the grimy windows, that I knew I loved her more than anything else in my life. It didn't matter one whit that she was half-Navajo and all-desert wild.

"People are going to say Phaedra got what she deserved." My voice sounded prickly to my ears. It ran up the walls and got stuck in the corners of the room.

"John." Magra's voice was sharp with reproach.

"I'm not saying I believe that. It's what the people of Haxan are going to think."

Magra moved closer to me. "Since when do you care what the people of Haxan think, John Marwood?"

I put an arm around her waist. It wasn't proper conduct for a government office, but I didn't care.

"This is going to be bad," I told her. "The townspeople of Haxan aren't going to stand having Phaedra in town, even for burying her husband. Especially for that. Not with Clayton Finch waiting back at the mountain for her to return. All open like, if you know what I mean."

"What Phaedra and Clayton do is their own private business," Magra said. "Abel learned to live with it in his way. Everyone else should, too."

The world was often basic to her. She lived in the desert. Her roots went deep that way. For her people the desert was simple. It was sun and wind, food and hunger, life and death and love. There wasn't much else, except survival, thrown into the mix. It sounded like a pretty nice way to live.

"Yeah, private." My chair creaked as I got up and went for the door. "But the people of Haxan aren't going to see it that way, Magra. You know that's true."

I returned to Doc Toland and met Jake coming the other way. He waved at me and loped across the plaza. His back still stiffened on him after a night's sleep and he always had to work the kinks out by favouring his off leg.

"I put her horse in the livery stable, Mr. Marwood. Abel Finch is lying in the empty grain warehouse. I thought I would try and hide him in there rather than the dead house. But a couple of people saw me carry him inside." He made a helpless gesture. "They're already starting their talk."

"That's fine, Jake. You see Magra back to the hotel, will you?" Most days she and I had breakfast together. There wouldn't be time for breakfast. Not today.

"Yes, sir, I will. I'll see the prisoners are fed, too. You want me to hang around after?" He meant to look after Magra.

"No, she'll be all right." If Rand were truly headed for Haxan he would be here soon. But I didn't think he would try anything in broad daylight. So far as I could tell he didn't like operating in the open.

"Once you see her to the hotel come back here. I'll likely need you before the day is out."

He watched the shuttered windows of Doc Toland's office. "Yes, sir, I figure so. See you later, sir."

"Keep your eyes open, Jake."

I ascended the wooden stairs to Doc's office and entered without knocking. The examining room was in back but he was out front behind his desk, writing in a big black book.

"Hello, John," he said without raising his eyes. "I guess you want to know how my patient is doing."

"That's right. I guess we'd better make it official."

"Well, she's in a bad way. A very bad way." He put the ink pen aside and sat back, his hands thrust into his trouser pockets. He pursed his lips. "She's been hurt, John. Badly hurt in both mind and body. I guess you know why. Most people have heard the rumours."

"I know something about it. This seems to have been a dark secret in Haxan for many years. What can you do for her, Doc?"

"First, I'm going to ask you a personal favour, Marshal."

"'Course. Anything."

"I'm going to need that bottle of laudanum." He quickly amended, "Not for my own use, but for my patient. I put salve on her wounds. Tried to get her to sleep. It's like her mind is racing in a thousand directions now that she's free of Abel Finch."

"I understand, Doc. I'll bring it over, no problem."

He scratched a lucifer across the sandpaper block and lighted one of his black cigars. "She told me how her husband died." His eyes found mine and settled. "I just let her talk. I didn't pay it no heed."

"Yeah. But I have to, Doc. I don't have a choice."

"I don't envy you in that regard, Marshal." It didn't escape either of us that he had addressed me by my official title. But he meant what he said and I was glad for the sentiment.

"Can I talk to her, Doc?"

"Won't do any harm. Not any more than Abel Finch has already done." He looked like he wanted to slam his fist down. I realized I wasn't the only man in town who wanted to kick a chair that morning.

I had never seen him this angry. He always struck me as genial and easy going. It most surprised me, this degree of passion.

"Doc, did she say how she got those blisters on her hands?"

"She was boiling water for the wash and it slopped on her."

"You believe that stupid story?"

"I'm telling you what she said, Marshal Marwood." His forced professional tone let me know I wasn't going to find a sympathetic ear. Not with this. There was a hurt life in that back room and he was committed to saving it. As far as he was concerned nothing was more important, not even the law.

Unfortunately, I didn't have the luxury to think that way.

"Doc, I don't want to fight you on this. Listen, Abel Finch is lying dead in the grain warehouse. Can you examine him for me?"

"I'll do it right now if you'll stay with Phaedra. She shouldn't be left alone, John." At least we were back on a first name basis. "Not for one minute."

"I'll wait until you get back. Here's the key to my hotel room. You can pick up the bottle of laudanum while you're out. It's in the bottom drawer of my dresser."

"Thank you for your trouble. I'll be back directly."

After Doc Toland left I stepped through the curtain divide into the examining room. Phaedra was lying in bed, her blonde hair spread across a tasselled muslin pillow. Her eyes were fixed on an open window. A hot breeze scraped the curtain back and forth.

"Hello, Marshal."

"Phaedra. We need to talk."

"I know. I knowed all morning this was coming. But I had to bring him to Haxan to be buried, Marshal. It's what he wanted. He never liked this town much, which is why we lived in the mountains. But he hated that homestead and he hated me and Clayton more for what we done behind his back."

"Phaedra, there's no way to get around this. You're in a lot of trouble."

"Maybe you measure trouble by a different yardstick than I do, Marshal." She turned her face away and pressed it into the pillow. "I'm sorry. I don't mean to joke about it."

I couldn't say anything. She wiped her face with the palms of her hands and then held a fist against her mouth. When she spoke her words were real and had frightening weight to them.

"My husband beat me, Marshal. He beat me hard. For five years Abel Finch beat me. When I was pregnant I lost that baby because of him." She squeezed her eyes shut, trying to hold back the tears. Maybe the bad memories, too. "But now he's dead. He ain't going to beat me no more. Not ever again. And I'm not sorry for that even if I hang."

"Phaedra, did you kill Abel Finch?"

"No. But he got killed and that's fine with me."

"It's not fine with the law, Phaedra. I can't turn a blind eye to murder. Your story how he got killed is too pat. You couldn't possibly know all those little details if you weren't there."

"It don't matter now."

"That's where you're wrong. It matters to the law and it's going to matter to Judge Creighton when he's due to ride through in a couple of days. Now tell me how your husband died."

She wouldn't say anything else. She lay there, watching the curtains move back and forth.

I gave up and returned to the front office. Doc had left his record book open. I read the entry he had written for the Phaedra Finch case. There was a list of bruises over her entire body and an old fracture he found in her left wrist that had never healed properly. When she lost the baby she wasn't able to have any more. Beside the entry Doc had prescribed laudanum to rest her mind and body, and sunflower salve and cold packs for her bruises. Underlined was a single word: REST.

The door creaked open. It was Doc. "That didn't take long," I said.

He shelved the bottle of laudanum. "How is she?" he asked.

"Resting. I couldn't get anything out of her." I watched him move about the room. "What did you find when you examined Abel?"

He rummaged through his medicine cabinet. "About what you would expect. Abel Finch's face is a parboiled mess. The skin is hanging off his bones."

My stomach felt hollow. "Like he was held down in a pot of boiling water?"

"That's correct. I also found a lump on the back of his head where someone struck him." He touched his own scalp behind his right ear to show me the spot. "It's likely he was hit from behind by a right-handed person. While he was unconscious, or too groggy to fight back, he was drowned. A messy way to die, John."

"I don't know a good way yet, Doc."

"You may be right."

He didn't have the shutters open in this part of the office and it was way too hot in the room. "Doc, do you think Phaedra could have killed her husband?"

Doc Toland studied me with his watery eyes. "After what she suffered? I'm surprised it took her five years to do it."

"But Abel was a heavy, grown man and she's no bigger than a fence rail."

"Doesn't matter. Anyone, pushed to that limit, can find the strength needed to do murder. John, you don't understand murder the way I do. You view it through the intractable lens of the law. A dividing line between right and wrong. I see murder as a human response to uncontrollable stress factors. When those stresses get to be too much anyone is capable of killing. Even a broken girl like that one."

"All right, Doc. Thanks for your help." I made to go.

"What are you going to do about this, John?"

I paused, my hand on the doorknob. "I don't have much choice. I'll ride out to the Finch place and talk to Clayton. See what he says. Then I'll arrest Phaedra for murder."

"I don't envy you that task."

"Yeah. You said that already, Doc."

I slammed the door when I left.

CHAPTER 22

I wasn't halfway down the stairs when four men from the Haxan Peace Commission marched across Front Street in my direction.

That didn't take long at all, I thought with a sinking feeling.

"Marshal," one of them called out. It was August Wicker. "We must talk."

I waited for them to walk to me. No reason to meet them halfway in any sense of the word. I already knew what they wanted and I was determined to kick as hard as I could against it.

I propped one shoulder on a wooden post, letting my grey duster fall open so I could reach the Colt Dragoon. These men weren't armed and they weren't looking for that kind of trouble. But I might have to open up their heads with the gun barrel to make my position clear.

They stopped lined abreast on the street. Wicker gaped at me with his catfish mouth. The other three were Hew Clay, Micah Slattery, and Seth Choate, the banker. All were reasonable businessmen. Or so I thought.

"Pleasant morning, gentlemen."

"Uh, morning, Marshal." August Wicker was chosen, or knowing him, had chosen himself to act as their spokesman. He hooked his thick thumbs under his navy blue silk vest. "Marshal Marwood, I'll get down to brass tacks. We know Phaedra Finch is upstairs in Doc Toland's office."

"That's no secret."

"We want her run out of town. We've got no truck for the likes of her."

I didn't say anything. I was doing everything I could not to punch his smarmy face. I hadn't forgotten how he tried to get Magra to come work for him, and had gotten in my way the night that stupid kid tried to face me down with a gun set to misfire.

Yeah, hit his face with a straight right. Throw my shoulder behind it, too. Then maybe stomp his head against the wooden boardwalk to make my morning just that much sweeter. I liked the idea a whole lot. It was hard to fight down the impulse to carry it through.

When I had myself under control I said slow, "You listen to me, Wicker. That woman is sick. She's under Doc Toland's personal care. I don't want her bothered."

"A woman like that mars the moral probity of this town," Wicker shot back.

I would have laughed if the situation weren't so serious. "What do you do for a living, Mr. Wicker?"

His face was pinched. "You know damn well I own the Quarter Moon. But that's no reason to disparage me."

"How many soiled doves do you employ? How many girls do you slap around every night when they don't carve enough whisky money off the drunken trail hands?"

His face reddened. But for the moment I had him backed into a chute and the gate closed.

"Marshal," Seth Choate said in a reasonable voice. "I'm a family man. We all are. It's not good to have a girl like that in our town. Haxan has enough of a bad reputation already. This commission is trying to rectify that. This looks doubly bad after what she's done. I'm not talking about killing Abel Finch, either."

"Nothing has been proven in a court of law, Mr. Choate."

"Oh, come now, Marshal, we're not stupid," another of the men shot back.

"You could have fooled me, Mr. Slattery. Anyway, she hasn't been arrested."

I was disappointed to see Hew Clay with these men. I had counted on him as something of a friend. I guess what they say is true about the world. If a man wants a friend he should buy a dog. And then shoot the dog before he bites you.

"You haven't arrested her? Then what are you waiting for?" Hew asked, incredulous. "Marshal, we have wives." The men nodded in unison. "They don't cotton to the idea of someone like Phaedra, who's done what she's done, being around our families."

"I don't know that she'd be around your family, Hew. Unless you invited her over to dinner."

"Don't make light of our concerns, Marshal." Wicker had discovered his voice once more. "A man like you wouldn't understand the concerns we have. That much is plainly evident."

"Why is that, Mr. Wicker?"

"Now who's being naive?" His sleek catfish smile was meant to wound. "Everyone knows you bundle with that Navajo slut every chance you get."

The other men lapsed into uncomfortable silence. Hew stared at his shoes in an embarrassed way. He had gone out of his way to help Magra. Nevertheless, this was a road they weren't prepared to walk shank's mare unless I forced them to.

"Come again, Wicker?" My words were filled with black ice.

"You don't scare me, Marshal," Wicker challenged. "You may have these other gentlemen buffaloed, but not me. I haven't forgotten how you went traipsing off with that murdering White Hawk while our town needed protection. Not to mention your heavy-handed ways in keeping the peace. Why, you threaten good honest folk as much as the drunken rabble that dusts through our town. No, Marshal, I'm not afraid of you. I'll write Washington and complain."

"Make sure you ask them about owing me two weeks back pay. I still haven't seen that money."

"I won't be bucked and thrown by a common civil servant, Marshal Marwood. I don't care if you are federal. Our commission hired you and by God we'll get what we paid for. We're respectable citizens. We demand to be treated with respect by the man we employ to protect us."

"Mr. Wicker, you're wrong on all counts. No matter what you say, I work for the United States government, not some cobbled together 'peace commission' you and these other jaspers pulled out of your ass. I'm a licensed federal officer and I'm making it as clear as I can: I won't have you interfering in government business."

"Perhaps we will hire a sheriff to come in and take over those local responsibilities you find too difficult to perform," Wicker threatened.

"Go ahead," I said. "Then I can get a full night's sleep for once."

"Marshal," Mr. Choate added, "we're not trying to fight you. We're concerned about our town."

"Gentlemen, that woman in Doc's office is government business. You get in the way of this investigation and I'll throw you all in jail and have you on bread and water for a week. Count on it."

I stepped off the boardwalk, slow. The men backed up the same number of paces. I singled out Wicker and they moved aside. They were leaving him alone to me.

"One thing more, Wicker. You'd better take this to heart." I tapped the badge on my vest. "I don't have to wear this tin to kick the hell out of you. Say what you will about me. But don't ever believe it applies to Magra Snowberry. Do you understand me, you possum-lick sonofabitch?"

His quick tongue stabbed a fleck of saliva from the corner of his rubbery lips. "Are you threatening me, Marshal?"

This could go a dozen different ways. I was half-surprised I didn't care which way it broke.

"Yeah. I guess I am."

"Well, my good man, you've gone too far." Now he wanted to play the victim. People of his ilk always do. They eschew any personal responsibility for their words and actions, and when it comes back to bite them on the foot they immediately begin to wallow in self-pity.

Wicker attempted to gather the remaining shreds of his dignity. "I will write Washington and lodge a formal complaint against you. I will not be pushed around in my own town by the law. Your days in Haxan are numbered, Marshal."

"Get out of my way, Wicker. I've got important work to do." He didn't budge. I didn't raise my voice. I just told him again in a low growl:

"I said get out of my way. Or I'll move you myself."

He opened his mouth, thought better of it, and closed it fast. "Your time will come, Marshal. Come on, men, we were wrong. We can't reason with him at all."

They turned and walked down Front Street toward their various businesses and establishments. I watched them go. They weren't bad men. Hell, even Wicker wasn't all bad. They were scared because of what Phaedra represented. How she flaunted the things they believed in, or pretended to believe in.

I started for my office when Jake slipped out of the alley between the icehouse and a dry goods store. "I heard it all, Mr. Marwood," he said. "I thought I should hang back unless you really needed me, though."

"You did right, Jake. Too much loose powder can be set off with a single spark." My heart was hammering. I hadn't liked what Wicker had said about Magra. He didn't know how close he came to dying.

I admit it scared me a little.

I was supposed to be the law here.

Jake grinned that easy grin he had when a tight situation turned out for the better. "They backed down quick enough. Not much spleen for a real fight."

We walked side by side. The town was quiet. Not much was happening in the plaza other than Alma Jean Clay buying an armload of Indian paintbrushes off a blind Mexican woman.

"Those men didn't want to fight," I told Jake. "They just needed to blow steam so they could feel better about themselves. Once I recognized that I thought it best to let them do it."

I watched Alma Jean collect her flowers and head with a purpose toward the livery stable.

I cut a glance at Jake. "Did you see Magra to the hotel without any trouble?"

"Oh yes, sir. She's safe and sound."

"Good." On top of everything else I didn't want Magra dealing with Alma Jean. What was she doing with those flowers? She whipped a horse-drawn Texas buggy past us. She was wrapped in a knitted shawl and headed out of Haxan. Strange.

We clomped into my office. I lifted my Sharps from the gun rack. "I'm riding out to the Finch place, Jake. You stay close to Doc while I'm gone. Keep an eye on things. I don't think those men will cause any further trouble but you never know. They may decide different. If they do, you will have to handle it alone."

"I'll stay awake. What about the prisoners? The Haxan Peace Commission always wants us to release them after collecting fines so they can keep spending what money they have left."

"To hell with the Haxan Peace Commission. We're here to uphold the law. That's what I aim to do."

"Yes, sir."

I stopped. This wasn't helping. I was venting my frustration on men who had paid their fines and their jail time. "Never mind me, Jake. I'm steaming over Wicker. Give the prisoners breakfast and let 'em go. If the stage comes for Olton's prisoner release him under custody, too."

"Yes, sir. I thought that's what you would decide, Mr. Marwood. I was only checking."

I saddled my horse at the livery stable while Piebald looked on with curious eyes. That kid hung around the stable more than he did at home or school. Couldn't blame him, though. Aside from the saloons the livery stable was the one place in town you could always pick up news.

"You going after someone, Marshal?" he asked.

I cinched a strap tight. "That's right, Piebald."

"Going to gun him down?" He cocked his thumb and finger and took aim on a skinny brown rat rustling through the straw.

"That's not my intention, son."

"What kind of lawman are you?"

"A smart one, I hope." I chucked him under the chin and swung into the saddle. "Keep an eye on things while I'm gone."

"Don't I always, Marshal?"

I rode west and hit the foothills before dinnertime. By late afternoon I was working my way high in the San Andres Mountains.

The mountain range lay between the arc of the sun and me. It was getting dark fast by the time I rode onto Abel Finch's property. It wasn't much to be proud of, if truth be told. There was a wooden cabin built around a natural rock chimney that also served as a fireplace. They had a makeshift corral and lean-to for Phaedra's mare, but no other animals were on the property.

At least there was water. It dribbled from a crack twenty feet up and pooled in a rock basin as large as a pool table. It wasn't much, but it provided moisture for a few large scrubs and one or two scrag trees bent and twisted by the ever-present wind. There were also signs rain sheeted down the side with so much force that it splintered rock. Other than that there wasn't much in the way of green about the place, or material prosperity.

I knew Abel made what little money he needed from hunting and trapping. Though what he found to hunt and trap in these barren mountains was beyond me. It was by all accounts a cold, mean place for any man to live.

I dismounted and ground-tied my horse. I stood on a narrow rock ledge. Far below me the lights of Haxan glittered white and yellow. I was so high up their tiny pinpricks twinkled like stars. It made me feel there was a distance there I could never traverse.

I had come to Haxan. But I would never be part of it.

I felt a shiver ripple through me. I didn't like this mountain. It had a bad feel that scraped your soul like a dull skinning knife. How many nights had Abel Finch stood on this rock ledge hating the glittering town below?

The cold desert wind ruffed my hair and flared my grey duster.

How many nights had the lights of Haxan, that Gomorrah of the desert, twinkled into the night like a lost constellation while Phaedra was being beaten?

How often were her screams scrubbed by the cold wind until only the impassive mountains remained?

I turned from the view, and my tumultuous thoughts, and advanced on the squat, dark cabin. In the middle of the yard was a big iron pot of water. Beside it lay a galvanized washtub. The coal and ash in the fire bed was dead. Rumpled clothes lay on the ground as if they had been thrown aside and forgotten.

The high wind moaned across the broken mouth of the rock chimney. There wasn't a porch or any place to sit outside where you could enjoy the sweep of the land and sky. This wasn't a home. It was a place to hide while fear scrabbled like a rat around the edges of your soul.

The cabin door was unlocked. I hit the latch hard and went inside.

I froze when I smelled the gun oil. I stood rooted, letting my eyes adjust, waiting for my pulse to drop back to normal.

"I could shoot you now," the boy said with calm deliberation, "and never bat an eye."

CHAPTER 23

I tried to tell myself if Clayton Finch wanted to kill me he would have already done it. I had given him plenty of opportunity while I poked around outside—my back had been toward him more than once, and I had made it a point to hit the door latch hard so he wouldn't be taken unawares.

A man like that, waiting and all alone, gets jumpy and starts busting caps at the least little noise. I had wanted Clayton to know I was coming inside the house so he could think things through a bit. It was a huge risk on my part. But if you don't want to stake your life on risk you'd better never pin on a badge.

"I thought you were hiding up here," I said to the figure half-hidden in the dark room. "Phaedra said you were."

"You talked to her?"

"Of course I did. What do you think?"

He was seated behind a table. I couldn't make out much detail other than a formless grey shape against other geometrical objects that might have been a bench, a cabinet, a churn, a flour mill. The ceiling was low. I had to watch I didn't crack my head on the rough-hewn rafters.

"Take a chair, Marshal. You're outlined good against the open door. I won't miss."

I sat at the table, moving slow.

"Phaedra took Pa to Haxan, didn't she." It wasn't a question. I got the impression he was trying to find out where he fit in the world now that both of them were gone.

"Your father will be buried on Boot Hill."

"Better to burn his carcass and feed the charred remains to rabid dogs."

"Clayton, put that gun down."

"Got no reason to do that, Marshal. I have no intention of going back to stand on a gallows. Besides, I don't want to see my father, and I don't want to see her."

"I thought you loved Phaedra." The quiet yawned between us like a bottomless gorge. "That's what people say."

"I guess I did once." His chair made a small sound when he shifted position. "She was pretty when Pa brought her to live with us," he said.

I couldn't tell if he was talking to himself or me.

"We were alone after my real Ma died of the cholera. But this mountain ain't a fit place for any woman. Especially one as young and pretty as Phaedra. Hell, it's barely liveable for a man. I watched this mountain sap all that was good from her. All that was saveable, you might say. I couldn't stop what happened, Marshal. I want you to believe that. When you're trapped like we were you look for an escape. We found it in each other. When Pa found out, well, he went a mite crazy. He didn't have far to go. He never did walk down the centre of a rail long as I knew him."

"Don't you have a light, Clayton? Candles or a lamp?" I wanted to get a look at him. His voice sounded familiar but I couldn't place it.

"No. Pa figured a man should live by the natural rhythm of the day. Oh, sometimes he would light a tiny fire in the chimney, or light a grease-burning Betty lamp, and Phaedra would read from the Bible. She had another book, too. Old stories about the ancient Greeks and the gods they used to believe in. I liked them. She read those stories good. She made them come alive with her voice, almost like we was living it."

Clayton fell silent. When he spoke again his voice was full of wistful longing. "She was so pretty, sitting there with the red glow of the fire in her hair and the light dancing happy on her face. She was nice, Marshal. Nicer than Pa or me ever deserved. That's fact."

"Why didn't you leave, Clayton, if things were as bad as all that?"

And it was then, with that simple question, when I realized whom I was dealing with.

"Phaedra wouldn't quit on Pa no matter how rough he treated her. Even after she and me . . ." I could hear his throat click when he swallowed. "Even after she lost the baby she felt she owed Pa her life. In a way she was right. Her family was dirt starved in Texas when Pa bought her as his bride. I remember the day we rode down to Haxan to meet her on the stage. She was so fragile, with nothing but a worn carpet handbag clasped to her breast. We had apple pie and sarsaparilla at the Haxan Hotel. Then we rode into these here mountains and never left. Marshal, it was most like something out of a storybook."

He didn't say anything more. He was talked out.

"I have to take you in, Clayton."

"I will never leave this mountain."

"You have to stand trial for killing your father." I paused. I had to find a way to reach him. I didn't want to kill him. There had been enough killing in this family.

"Phaedra would want you to do the right thing," I said. "That girl you remember, and once loved, sitting by the fire reading those old stories you liked."

I couldn't tell if the sound he made was a sob or a snort of derision. Perhaps both. "Pa hit her, Marshal. He hit her alla time and she took it. I never could understand that. I asked her 'bout it. She said she was more afeared of going back to Texas than to die in these cold and bitter mountains. Taking a beating every day wasn't so bad, she told me, compared to what she suffered in Texas. She was a little girl when the war ended. They had to eat raw cactus pulp and lizards what they could catch, when they had anything to eat at all."

He made that sound again. This time it sounded like a cry for help.

"Marshal, is Doc Toland looking after her proper?"

"Yes."

"I told her not to do it. After I killed Pa she shoved her hands in that boiling water afore I could stop her. She said she didn't want to see me hang and so she was giving me an alibi. I suppose I got a little crawly myself. Pa was about to go after her with an axe handle, you see. I wrestled him and pushed his face down in the boiling pot. I held a wooden lathe across the top of his shoulders to keep his head down in that hot steam. When I knew he was dead I took off. I was free, Marshal. It felt good, like when you see a sun hawk falling out of the sky on a cottontail. I was falling, too. I ran all over the face of this mountain. When I got back Phaedra was gone. That little girl got on her horse and rode down to Haxan all by herself. Took her most of the night, I reckon."

"Who built the mesquite drag? Who put your father on it? She couldn't have done that herself. Not with burned hands."

"Huh." He was taken aback by my question. "I guess I did those things. I don't remember none too clear, Marshal. Maybe I came back after I ran that first time and then took off again. I can't see it straight in my head. I only see spots and fragments that rise from the bottom and disappear like pond scum. You know, like when a lake turns itself over in the fall."

"I can't leave you here alone, Clayton."

"Ain't going nowhere with you, Marshal. You forgot I got the drop on you."

"Clayton, hear me out. It's dark in here and you can't see, but my gun is out of its holster and under this table. You shoot me, I promise I'll gut shoot you if it's the last thing I do. You'll scream every last inch of your life away. That's as bad a way to die as life ever made. And every time you scream Phaedra will hear you."

I couldn't tell if I was reaching him. "Do you really want to do that to her, Clayton?"

He didn't say anything. I think he was weeping, silently.

"Hasn't she suffered enough?"

"All right, Marshal. You win." His gun thumped on the table. I drew it toward me. It was a single-action Colt Peacemaker, one of the civilian models with a five and a half-inch barrel. The hammer was cocked. A few ounces of pressure on the trigger and I would have been stone dead.

When you see something like that the crawl starts in your

hands and feet. Then it draws toward the centre of your body like a worm crisping on hot metal.

I rolled all six of the .45-calibre centre fire cartridges out of the cylinder. They clacked and skittered on top of the pine table. I stuck the gun in my belt and got up.

I don't know where he got the gun, but it was in better shape than the old Navy Colt he had wanted to use that night in the Quarter Moon.

"All right, Clayton, you're under arrest. It's time to go."

He used his arms to push his body away from the table. I followed him outside. There was more light out here. The stars were shining deep and a slice of white moon was rocking the world to sleep.

Clayton passed my blue roan and kept on walking. He called over his shoulder, "I want you to tell Phaedra I loved her, Marshal."

"Stop, Clayton. Stop."

I pulled my gun but it wasn't going to do any good. He was standing on the ledge. He turned around. He was dressed in the same torn pants and sleeveless shirt he wore the night he called me out in the Quarter Moon. He had lost his snap-brimmed planter's hat somewhere along the way.

The light from the moon and stars was on his face. It was still a good face, confused and bewildered by life.

"I loved her bad," he told me.

He stepped into space and disappeared.

There wasn't any sound afterward. I walked to the edge but there was nothing but blackness. The wind from the abyss sheered off the side of the mountain and hit me square in the face.

There was no use trying to find his body. The mountain and the night had swallowed him whole.

"Clayton's dead, isn't he?" Phaedra asked.

It was the next morning. It had taken me most of the night to get back down the mountain without breaking a leg, or my horse's leg, on a spall or a chuckhole. I was exhausted. It had been a long twenty-four hours. More, if you counted the previous day somewhere in there.

"I'm sorry," I told her. I meant it. "I tried to bring him back alive."

"I know you did, Marshal. I'm sorry, too. I know he confessed everything. That's the kind of boy he was." She tried on a tired smile. "He was always trying to save me."

She stood beside an open window. Her blistered hands looked ugly in the orange light shining from a coal oil lamp on top of the dresser.

"We have to go, Phaedra. You're under arrest for aiding and abetting the murder of Abel Finch. The Territory isn't going to hang a woman. But I expect you're going to do time."

"I'm ready."

We walked into the front room where Doc and Jake waited. "I don't want you to worry, Phaedra," I was saying. "I'll speak on your behalf at the trial. I'll do everything I can to help you get clear of this trouble."

"I know you will look after me, Marshal."

Something about the way she said it should have alerted me. If I weren't so beat I would have been. She couldn't hide a thing like that in her face. Few people could.

I blame myself. I am responsible.

We were moving for the door. Doc Toland held it open when Phaedra backed up causing us to crowd together in the doorway. Phaedra grabbed Jake's pistol from his Mexican holster and bolted down the wooden steps, her bare feet kicking white under the dirty hem of her homespun dress.

"Mr. Marwood, I'm sorry, I never thought—"

"Out of the way, Jake." I ran down the stairs after her. Fool girl. I was more angry than surprised. She should know she couldn't escape.

When I reached the bottom she was already halfway across the plaza.

"Phaedra!"

She skidded to a stop. Good. At least she had some sense left. She raised the gun in my direction.

"I know you will look after me, Marshal."

I stopped. My mouth was cotton dry. "Put the gun down, Phaedra."

"I know I can count on you."

She smiled. Her lips were red as pokeberry juice and her hair was like spun gold spilling soft on her shoulders in the morning sun.

"No man can do what you'll do for me."

She cocked the hammer. She had to use both hands. "You'll help me, Marshal. We both know that."

I felt the thing inside me stir awake and lift its head.

"Phaedra, no." My hand was already moving for my gun. I couldn't stop it. If that was Magra standing across from me I couldn't have stopped it.

"You go and help me now." She fired. Wild shot, but my nerves were working on their own accord and my gun cleared leather, thumb rolling the hammer back with one motion.

She had her pistol cocked again. She snap fired. The bullet fried the air beside my head.

My first shot hit her in the centre of the breastbone and my second was three inches to the right of that. She went down on her knees, dropping the heavy pistol in the dust. Then she folded back with her legs trapped beneath her body.

I ran toward her and knelt swiftly.

"Phaedra."

Her eyelids fluttered. The front of her dress pumped blood. "Clayton."

I took her blistered hand in mine.

"I love you," she said. "I love you bad."

"Phaedra."

She was gone.

I got up and remained alone in the middle of the plaza for a long time. When I walked out of there I was aware a lot of people had amassed in the street, watching me, amazed they had been alive to witness such a thing. Someone touched my arm in sympathy.

"Marshal," Wicker said, "that was a bad thing. No man . . . I'm sorry for what I said earlier. All of us were wrong about what we said."

I went into my office and closed the door. Later, I heard a stray dog was licking the white sand soaked with her blood. Little kids threw rocks and chased it away, laughing.

That afternoon four men buried Phaedra next to Abel Finch on Boot Hill.

I never did see the grave.

CHAPTER 24

The inquest was the hellish affair I expected it to be. I had to relive the whole thing over again. As if I hadn't been doing that since the shooting.

Throughout the legal proceedings I sneaked glances at my hand. I didn't recognize it as being part of me.

I shot her. Without thinking. That coiled, wintry thing deep inside had awakened and I let it have full throat.

But—and I knew this to be true—if I didn't have that thing inside me I never would have been sent to Haxan in the first place.

Nevertheless, it didn't make me feel any better about what had happened.

I had done the unforgivable. I shot a woman.

The inquest was held in the Sassy Sage saloon, much to August Wicker's dismay. He claimed the chairs "were wobbly in that saloon."

Prior the inquest, Mayor Polgar apprised me of the political war being waged inside the commission. We discussed it over drinks in his freight office late one night.

"They don't like you anymore, John," he said, pouring a glass of rye, "but they're making a profit so they're willing to hold back their fire on you."

"What's got them backed up?" I waited until he poured himself one and we drank.

"They're afraid if they push too hard you'll put the deadline back. No one wants that. It would force the saloons to move out of the plaza. They're the ones with the real voting power in the commission."

"I suppose Wicker is one of those who wants me gone," I said.

Polgar viewed me funny, like I should know better.

"As a matter of fact, August is one of your strongest supporters." Polgar swirled the glass of brown rye in his hand. "He doesn't like you, but he knows which side his bread is buttered on. Besides, it was only one or two men who were drumming for your removal. They lost interest quick enough."

"What brought that about?"

He sipped his rye. "I'm not at liberty to say."

"Come on, Frank."

"Outside pressures," he said. He wouldn't elaborate when I pressed him for further details.

I had to wait for the judge to make his way to Haxan. Samuel Creighton wasn't a bad judge. He was nicknamed the "Iron Hammer" and had sent his share of men to the gallows. Twenty-three by last count. Nevertheless, he wasn't without compassion, though you saw little evidence of it in his courtroom. Given a choice, he would sooner send a man to prison for the sake of expediency than give him a second chance to put a foot wrong.

A lottery was held to see which saloon would provide the venue for the inquest. When the Sassy Sage won it gave away free drinks and then sold tickets to the inquest for ten dollars apiece. The owner, Henry Gumm, made a killing.

Even August Wicker grudgingly admitted that it had been a sharp business move.

On the morning of the inquest the Sassy Sage was crowded. Men sat shoulder to shoulder. Judge Creighton was dressed in a coal grey suit and black string tie. His snow-white hair was immaculately combed and his face scrubbed pink.

I sat up front, along with the other witnesses. Following my testimony, and that of Doc Toland and Jake, Judge Creighton ruled.

"Marshal Marwood acted in the only responsible fashion

left open to him," he pronounced from the bench—the rich mahogany bar that ran along one entire wall. The swings above the bar had been taken down in deference to the gravity of the judicial proceedings, and the parrot was locked in an upstairs room belonging to one of the girls.

Judge Creighton led us step-by-step through the reasons behind his decision. "Marshal Marwood could not knock a gun out of a crazed woman's hand, or incapacitate her with a .44-calibre bullet, while she was intent on killing him. That is the stuff of dime novels. It has been suggested in this court Phaedra Finch used Marshal Marwood to commit suicide. I find no evidence of this. While I have little doubt Miss Finch was mentally unbalanced due to certain factors in her life, I find no reason to believe she used the Marshal to kill herself. And, even if true, this would have no bearing on the fact that the life of a federally appointed officer was in danger and, under these hazardous circumstances, he had every right to protect himself along with the citizenry of Haxan."

I thought it was a long-winded way to say she had deserved to be shot. It sure as hell didn't make me feel any better.

Judge Creighton regarded the packed spectators. The oil lamps above his head gave out a cider glow. The thinning crown of his bald head gleamed in response.

"Therefore, it is the ruling of this court Phaedra Finch was fleeing a charge of first-degree murder when she was forcibly, though the court admits, regrettably, brought down by lawful force. She was a dangerous suspect fleeing justice. This shooting is not only justified, deadly force was essential. Further shots from Miss Finch's gun could have wounded or killed innocent bystanders, or claimed the life of the only federally-appointed marshal in this territory."

He gathered his papers and books together. Those citizens who had been most voluble in wanting my badge pulled held their tongues. I could feel their eyes weighing on me.

They could afford to wait. Creighton would leave Haxan and they would start bending their political power against me.

Letters to Washington, more editorials written against my harsh methods. Whatever it took.

Judge Creighton picked up his brassbound gavel. "My ruling stands. I hereby declare this inquest closed."

He slammed the gavel down. Men bolted from their seats and rushed the bar, clamouring for drinks.

"I'm sorry this had to happen, John," Creighton said, preparatory to leaving. "You can expect a firestorm. People aren't going to like you shooting a woman, no matter what the provocation or how I tried to cover for you."

"I know." They had been happy enough to sing my praises when I faced Ben Tack. "I'm surprised you didn't pull my badge, Judge."

"What the hell good would that do?" he fired back.

I helped load his travelling bag and stack of leather-bound law books into a black Concord buggy.

"I've been in law enforcement a long time. Maybe it's time I find a different line of work."

"Problem is," Creighton said, "you don't know how to do anything else."

Judge Creighton never minced words. That was more damning than anything else he could have said.

He climbed into the buggy and settled his bulk. He lifted the leather reins in a red, meaty fist.

"John, you need to shake yourself out of this. This isn't the east where everything is civilized with ice cream parlours and indoor plumbing."

He glared with belligerence at the 'dobe houses, the saloons, and the dance halls fashioned from ripsawed lumber.

"Helldorado," he said. "That's all this shithole will ever be. Someday the desert will open its maw and swallow it whole. No one will remember it existed."

He swung his attention back to me. "We live on the border

of a new world, John. A true *frontera*. This may be the last time it happens in the history of our country. Maybe the world. Therefore, it's incumbent on us to see that the people who come after will build something of lasting value. They can't do that if they don't have a solid foundation. That's why we're here. That's why the *law* is here."

"Perhaps."

He peered over the rims of his tortoiseshell glasses that he used for driving. "You know I'm right. I am truly sorry for what happened. It comes down to this, John. You're on thin ice. I can only do so much to protect you. If you want to keep your job you will have to bring in Conrad Rand."

He lifted his fat chin, ever a signal he was ready to change the topic. "Speaking of which, any word on that outlaw you're trying to run down? You told me in Santa Fe you had promising leads."

"Doc Toland mailed samples of the poison off to be analyzed. Santa Fe shipped them east for further tests. I hope to get results soon."

Creighton pulled a face. "Hell, I don't give a tinker's damn about the poison," he groused. "There's enough evidence to hang Rand already. We've got warrants out for murder, arson, and attempted kidnapping. That's for starters. You bring Rand into my court, Marshal. I'll see he gets what is coming to him."

"Yes, sir." I understood Judge Creighton's desire to wrap this up. Rand and his gang had run loose long enough, flaunting the law. He wanted to make an example of them.

But that wouldn't solve the reason behind Shiner Larsen's murder, or help me discover who had set Rand upon this path. This wasn't happening by itself. Someone had set these events, and Conrad Rand, into motion.

I wanted Rand. I also wanted the man who was bankrolling Rand.

Creighton released the brake on his buggy. "You did an admirable job with that Indian uprising, John. Could have turned out a lot worse. Very important people in the War Department sat up and took notice of the man I have working for me out here.

What I'm saying is, you've got spending capital." He offered me a broad hand. "Just see you don't spend it too fast."

"All right, judge." I didn't know what to say. When it came to politics I was often lost at sea.

He fixed his blue-grey eyes on the horizon. "Heh. And maybe a guardian angel to boot."

"I don't get you, Judge."

Creighton tipped his flat-crowned hat to shade the sun. "You've got a very good friend in town, Marshal." He lifted his hand in farewell and whipped the reins. "Be seeing you, John."

"S'long, Judge."

He trundled out of town in a rising cloud of dust. I watched him round the far bend of Potato Road and disappear from sight.

I released a pent up breath and walked to the office. Jake was waiting with mail from the morning train.

"How'd the inquest go, Mr. Marwood?" he asked, eager for news. After giving his testimony Jake had come back to guard our prisoners.

"I still have a job. There may be political hell to pay later on, if I don't bring in Rand."

"For my money Creighton made the right decision." Jake was much relieved. "I mean, about you keeping your job."

"Perhaps." I was trying to grasp how I felt about this now that it was over.

It wasn't the first time I had killed someone. Far from it. In this line of work it's often you or them. I had told Jake as much when I swore him in. At any rate I vowed long ago to make sure it was never me.

Fact is, from my days in Montana Territory, and the time spent in Haxan, I had built quite a raw and woolly reputation. But a reputation, like a politician, was a two-sided knife. Nevertheless, I was certain I had never killed anyone who didn't, in one way or another, deserve it.

I knew people might argue with me on the *degree* of deserving. That was human nature. As I worked at my desk that morning, reflecting back, I'd have shot Rose Danby and never thought twice on it. I would have called it just, ignored any civil repercussions, and gone ahead with my life.

Phaedra was different. There was an air of Greek tragedy surrounding her death. I had made a fundamental mistake no lawman should make: I got caught up in her warped and bitter world. Maybe it was because Clayton had called me out on my first night in Haxan.

Clayton. Phaedra. Me. Like we were all tied together. Meant to happen, if you believe in things like that.

As I opened my mail and drank cold coffee—Jake had forgotten to stoke the iron stove—I decided life probably is like that. People are tied together in one way or another. Most men want to believe we are alone and dependent upon ourselves. But I had learned long ago life is like one big knot around your neck from the day you are born. Everyone in the world is tugging on their separate ends.

The trick is learning how to live without having the life choked from you.

"Have you seen Magra?" My preparation for the inquest had stolen my entire morning. And, naturally, she wasn't allowed to attend. Forget the fact she was a woman—Judge Creighton didn't allow Indians in his court unless they were being tried for a crime.

"Came in to sweep and make coffee," Jake answered. "Then she hoofed it back to the hotel. Wanted to tell you she wished you luck and would meet you for dinner."

"Sounds good." I was looking forward to it. Talking to Magra, and being in her company, always made me feel better. We had gone riding last night and stopped by Broken Bow to look at the water gleaming under the moonlight. She had told me not to worry about the inquest, that everything would be all right.

She had a way of grounding me. Making me see things straight no other person could.

The door to the office creaked open. A black man with a bald head and salted beard wedged on through. He had a broken nose and a cauliflower ear swollen twice its usual size. There were ugly cuts on his face and a long gash across his left temple that had been sloppily bandaged with a red kerchief.

He wore black pants with silver piping, a faded yellow shirt with blood on the front, and rough-cut boots. His shoulders were as wide as his waist. He looked a solid slab of leathery muscle.

"Yes, sir, help you?" I asked.

He walked over to my desk, thick legs thumping the floor. He solemnly removed his grey bowler and held it against his chest.

"The Little Missy," he rumbled in a sombre baritone, "she sen' me to fetch you, but you was at the inquest."

At first I didn't know who he was or what he was talking about. A light dawned.

"I bet you are Red Sam. Adele Bouvier's bouncer."

His resulting smile was fierce. I had the impression he flashed that terrible smile whenever he was about to toss someone out of the Topsy Tumble head first into a hitching post. If they got their neck broken in the process, well that was too damn bad.

"I sure am. The Little Missy, she wants you on a matter of importance. I come to fetch you because, well, Marshal, she's ailing some."

"Is Adele sick?"

"We had a speck o' trouble at the Tumble early this morning, an hour or two before daybreak. I guess you didn't hear about it 'cause we like to keep private house trouble to ourselves."

"I told Adele I wanted the law to handle these problems."

Red Sam turned his hat over in his large hands.

"Yes, sir, she remembered you said that. She kept her word. That's why I come to fetch you."

"All right. What happened, Sam?"

"The Little Missy, she got herself roughed up by the man you are looking for, Marshal."

"Conrad Rand is in town?" Jake asked, kicking forward off his chair.

Sam nodded with enthusiasm. "She caught this man robbing her cash box. When I heard the rumpus I ran down the hallway to break this bastard up good."

He fingered the bandage across his temple. "But the door to her office, it was locked. He buffaloed me when I crashed through the door and gave me this here crack with a horse pistol. After I went down he thought to hit me some more to make sure I stayed down." That explained the ugly marks on his face. "I tried to grab him, but he jumped through the window and disappeared in the night."

Red Sam's big face soured. "All that don't matter to me, Marshal. My hurts are my own and I can live wit' them. It's what he did to the Little Missy that sticks in my craw."

He swallowed in a half-embarrassed way. "That little gal, pardon my expression, but she was mighty good to me and my family. She gives the children books so they can read better than their papa. There are good people, and there are people who call themselves such. Miss Adele, she one of the good ones."

"I think I understand, Sam." I was already rounding the desk. I lifted my rifle from the gun rack and thrust a box of shells into my duster.

"Jake, get my horse saddled. I may need him after I talk with Adele. Sam, this man who pistol-whipped you, was he tall with white-blond hair?"

"That's him, Marshal. Miss Adele knows where you can find this here outlaw." He waited for me in the doorway.

"And if you don't mind my saying," he finished, "I 'spect you need to kill him so we can be shed of his vile presence once and for all."

CHAPTER 25

I am sorry to be so much trouble, Marshal."

Adele Bouvier's long body reclined on a green satin settee with ball-and-claw feet. Her dark hair was folded around her shoulders. The silver streak was stark. She wore a fashionable tan and white business suit that had become torn and rumpled during the night. Her bottom lip was split and swollen and one eye was blacked shut. She had purple bruises on her arms and finger marks around her neck where Rand tried to throttle her.

"Don't be ridiculous, Adele," I said. "We had a deal. You did right letting me know. Doc have a look at you yet?"

She nodded a fraction. It hurt if she moved her head too much. "He gave me a powder for the aches and pains and told me to use a cold pack for my arm. He said I'll mend." She paused, considering what to say next, how much to reveal.

"Doc talked me into calling upon you for assistance, Marshal. He urged me to do so as soon as the inquest ended. I couldn't reach you before then."

"I know, I'm sorry."

"I'd sure like to have another chance at Rand," Sam rumbled. He occupied one corner beside the shattered remains of the office door. "It don't sit right—I was close to taking him out and missed killin' him."

"Sam, no more of that talk." Adele reached for his thick hand. "Marshal, it was all I could do to hold Sam back. Given his druthers, Sam would like to tear that man apart as soon as eat breakfast."

Sam resembled a massive tree that had withstood a violent storm. You could tell he was disappointed he hadn't snapped

Rand's spine between his machine-like hands when he had the chance.

"Marshal, the Little Missy and me," he said, his voice rumbling like distant thunder, "we watch out for one another. Miss Adele, I want to say again I'm plumb mortified I didn't protect you better." His face was creased with shame. "I not blame you one bit if you fire me. No, ma'am. I understand that fine."

Adele lifted his giant hand and kissed a bruised knuckle. "Don't fret, Sam. We've been through worse than this. Remember?"

"I shore do, Missy ma'am. Them was bad days for certain during the war. Me and my family will be grateful to you forever for getting us out of there after we was set free."

"Not as grateful as I for your friendship, Sam. We'll get through this tribulation. Now, leave us, please, so I can talk to the Marshal alone."

"I'll be close by if'n you need," he promised. "I won't leave your side never again." Sam cut a meaningful glance my way. "You need help, Marshal, I be ready, day or night. I can ride some, and shoot if I have to. I kill whoever you need."

"Thank you, Sam," I said. "I appreciate the offer more than you know."

He plopped his grey bowler with its yellow band back on his head. He quit the office, closing what remained of the door—not more than a plank connected to the crooked frame. Adele uttered a sigh. "Sam and I have a long history. I trust him with my life. Tell me, what would have happened if Sam killed Rand last night?"

"A black man killing a white man, even an outlaw like Rand. You want me to draw that picture, Adele?"

"No. I guess you answered it straight enough."

I found a hard-backed chair angled off from her settee and moved it closer. "All right, Adele. Enough about Sam. What happened last night, and where can I find Rand?"

"He was with one of my girls last night." She paused. "I think you met her already."

"Bertha?"

"That's her. Rand came very late last night and paid for her time. I decided to send someone over to let you know. Somehow Rand got wind of it. He went wild."

"He runs with two other men. One is Silas Foote, a known *comanchero*. I don't know the other man's name."

"Rand was alone last night."

I considered this. "It wouldn't surprise me if they stayed outside as guards. Rand is a careful man."

"I don't know how careful he is. I know he's mean. He started breaking furniture and waving a pistol about. Bertha ran out the back door. She was smart. Rand pushed his way into my office and you know the rest. There was sixty dollars in the cash box but the money isn't important. Later, when we had a breather from all the commotion, I questioned Bertha. She said Rand was gloating how he had the Marshal of Haxan running on the end of a string. Bertha's not dumb. She let him talk and tried to steer the conversation around to where he was hiding out. She warned Rand you were a no-nonsense lawman who shot a woman you were so mean. Rand laughed. He said he had a hideout in an old line shack south of Cottonwood Butte. He wasn't scared of no marshal. Said he killed one in Palo Duro after leading him into a Comanche ambush."

I remembered Frank Polgar's story. So Rand was responsible for Breggmann's death—not that I was overly surprised. Quite a tally. Plus, it fit with the knowledge that Foote was a *comanchero* and used to ride line. He would know of any abandoned line shacks in the territory.

"What else did he say," I prompted Adele.

"Rand claimed he had the wagon he stole and was going to come back to Haxan to finish a job. His words were, 'Finish that breed bitch good, like he paid us to.'"

My guts felt like a ball of scorpions squirming in oil. "Those were his exact words?"

"According to Bertha."

"Where is Bertha?" I had need to question her. It was an axiom of lawing that second-hand testimony was as good as the paper it was written on. No matter how well meaning a witness was, they always got something wrong in the retelling.

"Adele," I snapped my fingers to get her attention. "I want to talk to Bertha."

"You're not going to like this, Marshal. Bertha left with another girl for Topeka on the morning train."

"Dammit, Adele, don't jerk my chain."

Adele put out her hands, pleading. "It couldn't be helped, Marshal. I had a previous business arrangement with a dance hall owner in Topeka. I had to get those girls on their way or I would be out two hundred dollars."

She bathed me with her best, liquid red smile. "That's why I'm telling you everything I know. I'm not holding anything back."

I stood up. "Damn right you're holding something back, Adele. But short of shaking you like a rag doll, I'll have to overlook it, I guess."

"Red Sam wouldn't like you catawhomping me, Marshal," she warned. Cat and mouse—her favourite pastime.

"That's another problem," I admitted. "I don't think I could take Sam in a fair fight. All right. A line shack, you say, south of Cottonwood Butte?"

"That's what he said."

"I'll find it." I loomed over her. She looked up with large, expressive eyes. Well, one large, expressive eye.

It wasn't the first time she had raised her eyes to a man. She knew how to do it and make you feel intoxicated with the willing transfer of sexual power.

Power. It was all about power.

"Addie," I said, "are you pulling strings on my behalf with the Haxan Peace Commission?"

Her eyes were guileless. You have to be a good actress in her profession. She was one of the best.

"Whatever do you mean, Marshal?"

"Don't play coy with me. Someone is keeping the commission tamped down." I decided to venture an open guess. "Threats of blackmail may be involved."

"My heavens. Blackmail. What an ugly word. Whoever gave you the idea I am involved in such illicit deeds?"

"Judge Creighton."

Her eyes lighted up. "*Samuel* Creighton?" She laughed. "How is dear Old Barleycorn? I haven't seen him in ages. Simply ages. Not since he shot the hand of a man who was pawing me in an Albuquerque dance hall."

"We talking about the same man?" I'd heard Creighton called many things. I'd called him some of them from time to time. Most would make men in a mining camp blush. I'd never heard him referred to as "Old Barleycorn."

"There are lots secrets in a town like this, Marshal. A woman working on the line eventually hears them all. Come now, do you think Connie Rand is the *only* man who likes to hear himself talk in a woman's bed?"

"Adele, I don't want any blackmail. Look at me. I'm serious. I catch you doing it, I'll close you down and post you and your circus of whores out of town."

She drew an offended hand to her throat. "I would never think of doing such a thing, Marshal. You wound me with your unwarranted accusation, sir."

"Sure. Just see you don't start. "

She favoured me with a simpering, cat-like smile, like she had swallowed the entire canary. Not even feathers were left.

I knew she was having sport at my expense, but I let her do it. There weren't many people in Haxan I could rely on. It was good to have at least one more person on my side.

"Marshal." Her voice caught me at the door. "You're going after him, aren't you? Rand."

"That's right." We would see who had whom on the end of a string. Or a hangman's rope.

"But not because of the things he's done," Adele put forth. "I mean his crimes have bearing. You're going after him because he tried to hurt that girl. Everyone knows how you feel about her. It's no secret."

"I never meant to keep it as one."

"I didn't mean to imply you did," she said.

"Rand broke the law, Adele. If he's not stopped he's going to keep on hurting people."

"And you're the man who's going to stop him?" she asked.

"That's right, Adele. I'm the man. And don't you forget that."

I touched the side of her face that wasn't bruised and walked out the door.

I stopped by the telegraph and post office.

"Got anything for me today?" I was hoping to hear from the lab in Chicago any hour.

The postmaster examined the slot reserved for the marshal's office and shook his head. "Nothing today, Marshal. Be sure to let you know the instant I have word." He looked past me and shouted, "Oliver, be careful with that package."

One of the clerks had tossed a box into a corner with other packages piled and awaiting pickup. It rattled and clinked when it bounced on the floor.

"What's in it?" Oliver asked. "Sounds like broken glass."

"Sounds like broken glass *now*," a customer chortled, counting his stamps.

"That's Oil of Cloves," the postmaster said off hand. "It came special delivery from St. Louis."

"Well, whatever it is," Oliver said, "I don't think they packed it good. One of them bottles was already broke. You could smell it when it came off the morning train."

A familiar aroma filled the tiny mail office. I couldn't remember when, or where, I had smelled that odour before. But it nagged me something fierce.

"Soon as I have word, Marshal," the postmaster promised, "I'll send a runner to your office."

"Deliver it to my deputy. I'll be out."

"Whatever you say, Marshal."

I stopped and read the address on the broken package. I left the mail office, strode across the plaza, and ducked inside the jailhouse. "Jake, I've got a lead on Rand. He's holed up in a line shack south of Cottonwood Butte."

"I'll come with you." He made to grab a rifle.

"No. You have to watch that prisoner. Stage is coming to get him at noon today. And there's a San Antone herd set to trail through Haxan either today or tomorrow. Town's gotta have law while I'm gone."

He frowned. "It ain't smart to go after three men by yourself, Mr. Marwood."

"I'll be fine. It's a feint. Rand has never been one to make mistakes. Not so far. It's not in his nature to let slip where he's hiding out. I think he told this Bertha that story and made a rumpus at the Topsy Tumble on purpose."

"What for?"

"To draw me out of town. I'm going to let him think he's done it. I'll make a big show riding out and swing back after a mile or two. Rand won't waste any time. I'm willing to bet he has a spy in town, probably that third man we've never seen. Once I'm seen leaving he'll pass word to Rand to come on in."

Jake's nodded with appreciation. "You're setting a deadfall for Rand."

"It's a long shot but I can't think of a better way to snare them all."

"I'll have the office guns loaded for bear while you're away, Mr. Marwood. But be careful. This Rand is more slippery than a mudcat."

"That's why I'm going to warn Magra before I leave." I took her father's scattergun from the rack and charged it with buck. "I aim to lock her in my room at the Haxan Hotel with her father's shotgun. Rand might know by now she sleeps in the storeroom. That's common knowledge. He'll never look for her upstairs in a room reserved for whites."

"You're sort of hiding her in plain sight where she can't be found. Neat trick."

"Only if it works, Jake."

"I reckon Alma Jean will kick about it, though." He laughed through his nose. "Better you than me."

I grabbed an extra box of ammunition. "She'll have to kick. In any case I saw her riding out of town yesterday. I'm not worried about her."

"Best of luck to you, sir."

"Like I said, once I pull out of town I'll circle around and come through the back door. Make sure you have it unlocked."

"Will do, Mr. Marwood."

I went through the motions of preparing for a long and arduous trail. I packed my war bag, saddled my horse, and stuffed *charqui*, hardtack, and camp supplies into the saddlebags.

I wanted to give the impression I might be gone for days. Perhaps an entire week.

After I went through my play-acting, I walked my horse to the Haxan Hotel. I dismounted and looped the reins over a pine hitch rail.

I kicked sand from my boots before stepping inside the big lobby. Alma Jean Clay was a stickler for people tracking mud and sand on her expensive carpets.

Hew Clay leaned over the reception desk, his weight resting on one thin elbow.

"Morning, Clay."

He glanced up and his eyes flew open in stark surprise. "Oh hello, Marshal. Say, what are you doing back home?"

"What do you mean, Clay?" My voice was strangled.

Hew Clay flinched at my words. "Magra got your message, Marshal. She went to meet you at her father's place."

"Hew, what are you saying?" My voice bounced off the walls, which felt as if they were closing in.

His quizzical eyes picked out my lone horse standing idly at the hitch rail. "Where is she, Marshal?" he asked with deep confusion. "Did you leave her all alone in the desert?"

I realized all my play-acting had been exactly that. Rand had not waited for me to ride out of town. He had made his move while I was busy at the inquest. With me giving testimony there was nothing to stop him from moving against Magra.

He had had been playing chess while I was playing with marbles.

PART 3

SAMSARA

CHAPTER 26

I mounted my blue roan, reined him around, and headed north out of Haxan. The sun was high overhead and beat down on the side of my face.

As I passed the livery Piebald waved jauntily from the blue shadow of a gnarled mesquite tree. He was sitting cross-legged at its base, eating a slice of melon. The sticky juices dripped off his chin onto his bare chest.

"You going after a man, Marshal?"

"That's right."

"Guess you're going to bring him in alive."

I didn't say anything. Piebald's smile slowly faded. I kept on riding, keeping my cold and bitter thoughts to myself.

I hurriedly crossed the railroad tracks and rode through the holding grounds where cattle were waiting to be loaded onto boxcars. I skirted a large herd and swung north.

Out of the desert haze I could see Cottonwood Butte rising in the distance. Grey and black, it shimmered against the blue sky like a nightmare.

Rand and his gang had a good three- or four-hour head start on me. The only lead I had was the line shack. I hoped I could pick up their real tracks along the way. That story about the line shack had to be a dodge as well.

Rand hadn't made many missteps up to now. If he told Bertha he had a hideout south of Cottonwood Butte he did it for a reason. The only one I could think of was he wanted to draw me along in that direction and dry gulch me somewhere.

I touched the wooden stock of my Sharps rifle. I was willing to oblige him the opportunity, if it meant I could get within shooting yardage.

My first stop was Shiner Larsen's place. I had no other choice. It would make sense if they brought Magra here. But there was nothing to see but our old tracks from days ago. I spent ten minutes kicking through the burned wreckage, searching for blood drops or anything else that might tell me where Magra was, or her fate. There was nothing.

I mounted up and rode on.

I kept a slow but steady pace. My instinct was to kick hell for leather. But my horse wouldn't last the day and I would fall farther behind Rand.

While I rode I tried to convince myself three horses and a buckboard shouldn't be hard to find in 4,000 square miles of desert country. Sure. Very simple. Do it in my sleep. But I was a lone man. That wagon would slow them down. Not much, but some. And it couldn't go where a single horse could step. When I was with White Hawk we perforce stayed on the trails a wagon could negotiate. Which is why we were able to find Morning Star with the odds stacked against us.

If Rand kept the wagon there were only so many places he could drive it. Southwest was out of the question. That pushed him against the San Andres Mountains, unless he went through the pass and whipped on down to Las Cruces or Mesilla. There was no reason to suspect he would do that, however. It wasn't likely he would go into another town—not with a kidnapped woman on his hands—which meant he either headed north or broke across White Sands. Maybe, just maybe, he turned off east between Fort Providence and Coldwater. Lots of empty country that way and he could sneak right through. Though this, too, was less likely in my mind because there was little in the way of water out that way.

It made sense Rand would stay as far away from civilization as he could. Leastways, as long he had Magra on his hands. Once he killed her she would be less of a handicap.

If all they wanted was to kill her they could have escorted her out of town, murdered her, tossed the body in an arroyo, and ridden for any part of the compass they wished.

Face it, Marwood. If that's what they wanted she was already dead and there is nothing you can do.

But if that's all they wanted, I argued, why didn't they shoot her soon as they got her out of town? Perhaps they had. Perhaps I rode past her and never saw. Maybe she heard my horse clop past while she lay in the bottom of a dry wash and couldn't call out because she was hurt. No. I would have noticed the tracks. That didn't happen.

Though it might have. People get lost in the desert all the time. It could have happened.

Or maybe they decided to bring her to the line shack and torture her like her father. Or they might keep her as a camp slut before selling her off to other *comancheros*. I'd never find her if that was their plan. Not ever. They didn't find that Parker girl for years.

If. If. If.

After many hours of this mental anguish I spotted the hazy block outline of a buggy with yellow wheels rolling toward me. Looked like a single horse in shaft. I only caught a glimpse before it dipped behind a dune.

I spurred my horse forward. He was blowing hard when I reached the buggy. I pulled abreast from behind, my pistol drawn and the hammer thumbed back.

"Hey, there," I called. "Hold that wagon or I'll shoot."

The driver turned in surprise, not expecting anyone to come up from behind at a right angle. It was a woman. I reined in, causing the head of my horse to whip, and stared in disbelief.

"Alma Jean Clay, what the hell are you doing out here?"

She heaved back on the lines. The buggy creaked to a stop. I had given her a fright when I emerged from behind ocotillo and cat's claw, my gun out and leaning over the neck of my horse.

"Marshal Marwood," she gasped. Her gloved hands clutched the reins close to her body. She wore black crinoline with a high collar and a dark bonnet that shaded her face.

"You gave me a dreadful fright," she chided. "Skeered ten years off me. I thought for sure you were a road agent."

I held the bridle of her horse. Alma Jean looked like she wanted to take off in a clatter. She had gotten over her initial fright and now she nervously fingered the buggy whip.

"Alma Jean, what are you doing way out here by yourself? Don't you know this is dangerous country? Here now, look at me. Does Hew know you're out here?"

She blinked at this. "Well, of course he does. What kind of husband do you think I have? One who doesn't know where his wife got to all night long?"

She stopped, realizing she had revealed too much.

"Alma Jean, you'd best tell me what you were doing. All night, you say? I can't believe that."

"I reckon a body has the right to go for a buggy ride in this country if she wants. Even at night." She had gotten over her initial fluster. Now she was back to her normal, combative self.

I frowned back at her. "Look here, Alma Jean. Despite what you think I am not your enemy. Like it or not your safety is my responsibility. Now, for the last time, what where you doing out here all night long?"

She looked like she had been up all night. That much was certain. Her eyes were red-rimmed and her face washed out, both emotionally and physically. Maybe that's why she didn't have as much fight as usual inside her.

"I will tell you, Marshal," she yielded. "I was camped on top of Cottonwood Butte."

"I can't believe that." Alma Jean did not strike me as the type of person who would night camp by herself.

"It's true," she insisted. "I brought a mess of mesquite wood and made myself a fire. I had water and warm blankets, too."

Something in her voice warned me we had entered very deep waters. This was an Alma Jean I had never confronted before. Vulnerable.

"What were you doing?" I asked, gentle.

She considered the plaited leather reins in her bony hands. "I was putting flowers on a grave." Her voice was small.

I recalled her buying Indian paintbrushes from that old blind woman in the plaza.

She looked up. "My boy Tommy would be twelve years old today, Marshal. That's near enough a man's age."

She waited for me to disagree with her.

"It sure is," I said. "Right enough a man's age."

She gave an abrupt nod of appreciation. Then she stared into the distance, occasionally glancing my way to gauge my reaction as she spoke.

"It was during the war," she said. "Tommy died of scarlet fever. I got it, too. It did something inside me so I can't have any more children. Hew and me, we had a nice little farm with green trees and cold crik water. We buried Tommy there. Hew dug the hole and I laid Tommy down wrapped in a blanket I had knitted."

The thin grass around us waved back and forth as the wind rippled across.

"I'm sorry, Alma Jean."

"When the railroad came through they bought us out. The surveyors laid a line right over Tommy's grave and cut down all the trees. So one night, before they started laying track, I dug my son up and wrapped his skeleton in a brand new blanket I had knitted. Then I rode to the top of Cottonwood Butte and I buried him under the stars."

I could not believe what I was hearing. Was this the same Alma Jean Clay I had known?

"Hew know about all this?" I asked in disbelief.

She nodded. "He couldn't stop me. No one could, though folks tried. They said it wasn't right. I knew Tommy wouldn't be happy with a train rattling over his grave. Those rich, ignorant folk riding their spanking new carriages and not knowing a good boy like Tommy lay under them. I wanted to bring him someplace quiet where he could rest proper and see the sun and sky, and feel the cool wind on his little face."

It was a long time before I spoke. "So you brought him to Cottonwood Butte. Why there?"

She reached for a canteen and drew a mouthful of water. "It's because I wanted my child buried nearer to heaven, Marshal. Because Haxan is too close to hell."

She took a handkerchief from her sleeve and touched her eyes.

"Why didn't Hew come with you last night, Alma Jean?"

She tucked the handkerchief back in her sleeve. "This is a mother's burden. I'm not saying anything against you, Marshal. Being a man maybe you wouldn't understand why this is something I must do every year."

She capped the canteen and placed it on the seat beside her. "Last night was Tommy's twelfth birthday," she said. "He deserved to have his momma with him on a special day like that."

"I think you're right, Alma Jean."

A flicker of a smile lightened her face a degree. "I'm glad you understand, Marshal. Most people don't want to."

"How did you reach the top of the butte?"

"Oh, that's not difficult," she answered. "There's an old switchback the Army used before the telegraph came through. They had an old adobe station up there where they raised these big signal flags. They don't use it anymore. The station is all deserted and vacated and it doesn't have a roof. It's not liveable except for a night camp."

"You didn't see anyone else around?"

She shook her head. "I make this trip at night, Marshal. Slow going, but it's easier to avoid people. I don't want to have to explain myself you see. But no, I didn't see anyone at all."

"I heard there's a line shack on the southern base of the butte."

"I seen that."

"Anyone there?" I asked.

"Not that I saw."

"No horses, nothing?"

"I rode right by it, Marshal. Not so much as a light from a single candle. Why do you keep asking me about that shack?"

"Magra Snowberry's been kidnapped. The men who killed her father have her."

Alma Jean's eyes became round. "Oh, dear Lord, no. The same men who hurt Piebald that day?"

"I heard a rumour they were holed up in this line shack we're talking about. I suppose I have to check it out, even though you claim it's empty. I just hope I can cut their tracks before then.

Otherwise, I'll never find them. Or Magra."

"I wish I could help you, Marshal," she put forth. She looked at the reins in her hands. "I know we've had cross words. But that don't mean I want anyone to be hurt."

I put my hand on hers. "It's all right, Alma Jean. I appreciate your offer and your confidence in me. And I won't tell anyone what you were doing on the butte."

She looked relieved at this. "When I get back to Haxan do you want the men to get a posse together?" she asked. "They can catch up to you quick."

"No. I just came from town. I want you to ride on, Alma Jean. Go straight home and don't stop. With these *comancheros* loose it's very dangerous for any woman to be out here alone. If you want, I'll escort you back to Haxan."

"No, Marshal, I'm fine, I promise. I will go straight home like you said." She hesitated. "Marshal."

"Yeah?"

"I sure hope you find Magra. I do."

"Thanks, Alma Jean. You get going now."

"Yes, sir, I surely will." She whipped up the horse and clattered off in a flurry of dust.

I turned for Cottonwood Butte.

I came upon the line shack as the sun was about to dip below the mountains. It was a low-roofed adobe hut with shuttered windows. The bricks had not been properly cured. They sagged on one side, making the hut lopsided. The single door hung ajar. I dismounted and used ground cover to steal up on the shack.

I went through the door ready to kill anything that jumped. The narrow, cramped room was empty of human habitation. There was a broken cook stove. Ragged linen and old animal bones littered the floor. I kicked through the accumulation of leaves and trash. I didn't find anything that looked like bloodstains or evidence of recent occupants. I tried to tell myself this was good news.

It meant Magra was alive. Maybe.

It was musty inside and hot as an oven. I stepped outside

and stood in the open air, my anger smouldering like the dying flames of the sun.

Rand had me in irons. I rode all this way on a wild goose chase and came up short. No sign of Rand. No Magra. Nothing.

They had her and they could do anything they wanted to her. There wasn't a damn thing I could do about it.

I angrily grabbed the reins of my horse and walked along the ground. The shadows were long, but the acute angle of the sun revealed each and every depression.

Think, Marwood. If Rand kept the wagon there were only so many places he could go. Even over hard ground like this. He was certainly intent on keeping the wagon. He could have gotten rid of it long before now and had not.

I found the old switchback Alma Jean had described to me. I picked out her buggy tracks right enough. Naught else.

It was certain. No one beside her was here last night.

I kept walking, using the slanting sun shadows to find imperfections in the stone-hard ground. I made a half-circle about a quarter mile in radius and found absolutely nothing. I was feeling panic starting to come on. I mounted and rode south in an attempt to back-slot them. I saddled down into a little canyon with high, rocky walls rising on either side. It was half a mile long and quite narrow in places. Any wagon would have to ride straight down the middle, if it passed this way at all.

I dismounted and canvassed the ground, yard by yard. Daylight was fading fast. One or two stars, or planets, I guess, since they didn't twinkle, rose in the east. I traversed the ground in the fading light. To add to my anxiety there were clouds building in the north, their bottoms reefed with blood.

I cut a single track just as the sun disappeared with a final spray of light.

I squatted on my haunches and studied what I had found. I got on the ground, length-wise, and peered eye-level across the flat, overlapping sheets of rock.

No doubt about it. It was them—or someone like them. I could make out the shadow of wagon wheels and hoof prints.

There was a bit of chipped stone where an iron horseshoe had scuffed the ground and a doodlebug hole on top of a second print.

So. They had travelled through this narrow valley after all. It was scaled with rock plates that overlapped like roof shingles. Damn smart way to break up their road sign. But now that I knew what to look for I could dog them.

It was easier to scout the cracks between the rock shingles, where dirt was piled from an ant bed, or stones dislodged from the recent rains. I followed the trail out of the valley and came upon patches of thin grama grass. Here and there blades and stems were broken or mashed. Not enough time had passed for the grass to spring back up. It was getting very difficult for me to see. When I spotted horse droppings I toed them apart with my boot, breaking the crust.

Judging from the moisture inside they were eight hours, maybe ten, ahead of me. They had gained a *lot* of ground. But I had their trail now. I would follow it to the end of the Earth if need be.

I had done it before, on other worlds, and in other times.

I made a cold camp that night amidst rustling cottonwood trees. There wasn't enough grass, other than a patch or two of Johnson weed, so I stripped bark off one of the trees and fed that to my horse.

I didn't like stopping but there was nothing else I could do. I couldn't follow this faint trail with only the stars for illumination. I knew of posses who used lamplight and torches to scout a night trail—I had ridden with some of them—but I was alone with no fire. Besides, if I built a fire, Rand would spot the glow from miles away. I wasn't about to give him that much of an edge over me.

Tracking a man through the back country is like that. You don't know where he is, and he doesn't know where you are, exactly. You know he's going to try and fox you, so you are always on the lookout for tricks. He knows you know it. He tries to keep one step ahead because he doesn't want to stand on the gallows. The mental aspect of this, trying to read the other man's thoughts, gets complicated between hound and hare. It's like playing a long distance game of tag with death for one, or both of you, as the only prize.

Of one thing I was certain. Rand knew I was coming after him. He knew I would not quit. Not with Magra's life in the balance.

Which must mean he had a card up his sleeve he hadn't yet played. I couldn't begin to imagine what it was. Only time would tell.

I had a bad fright when I saw the night sky start to flash off to the north. Those damn clouds. It went on for hours. It was heat lightning. My luck was holding. Rain, even the briefest of showers, would wash these tenuous tracks away. I would lose them for good.

The weather held and I caught an hour or two of sleep.

When morning came I used the slanting sun trick again, with the sun in the opposite sky, and picked up their trail. By breakfast time I was riding hard. I cut their tracks again, and then again twenty miles on the western side of Cottonwood Butte. I slipped off my saddle so I could study them.

This was Rand and crew. No doubt about it.

The tracks jinked north, then northeast. I followed them, keeping a sharp eye out for ambush. After five miles we were approaching Cottonwood Butte again. Rand was circling. At the western base the tracks split.

The wagon and one horse arrowed off toward the northeast. A single track broke west for the snow-white line of White Sands, miles and miles away.

I turned after the single track, knowing full well I was heading away from Magra. I had no choice. If I caught this man's horse I would be better mounted and could overtake the slower buckboard that much faster. If I turned away and left this man behind me, he could ride up while I was approaching Rand and shoot me in the back.

It was a hard decision to make but I had learned long ago never to leave an enemy behind. That was only asking for trouble.

It was obvious Rand wanted me to see he had split his forces.

HAXAN

He wanted me to come after him, giving this other man a chance to blind-side me from behind.

I wasn't going to fall into his trap. I rode on. It was hard, turning away from Magra like that, but I had absolutely no other choice. I had to kill this man first or he would kill me.

By midday I hit White Sands.

CHAPTER 27

I had no problem following his tracks through the white sand drifts.

He wasn't riding hard or fast at all. He wanted me to close up because he thought he could take me. If I didn't, if I lost my nerve and turned back for Magra, he would swing around and put a bullet between my shoulder blades.

I presumed he had drawn the short straw last night. Maybe they had a pow-wow, the three men huddled together, furtive eyes scanning the dark horizon for signs, when Rand decided that come morning one of them would saddle his horse and kite me east.

They knew I would go after the single man like a duck after a June bug. If I could eliminate him, it would cut their numbers by a third when I confronted Rand. Furthermore, it would ensure I didn't leave an enemy behind when I caught up to the wagon.

Either way, it worked out for Rand from a tactical standpoint. In his view if I took the single man first he had time, and more opportunities, to throw me off his trail.

This was the long distance game I mentioned earlier. Rand and I were trying to read each other's mind across miles of hard country. You get to know a man you're trailing. Even though there are miles separating you it's like you're closer to him than anyone else at that moment in time.

I followed the single line of hoof prints into White Sands. Their edges were crisp and had not degraded. He was four, maybe five hours ahead. Taking it real slow. Daring me to catch him.

The pristine, snow-white landscape was shattered here and there by a clump of yucca or tuft of wind-whipped grass. He headed deeper into the interior. Before long there was nothing but serried waves of frozen white sand marching into eternity all around me.

It was very quiet. The only sounds were my horse's hooves scuffing through sand and the creak of saddle leather. The sun glare off the white sand was awful. I found myself starting to go snow-blind. I had to blink rapidly and find small shadows, or concentrate on the back of my horse's neck, to break the monotony.

From what I could judge by the tracks, my prey remained hours ahead. Like a fool, I crested a dune instead of going around. It was a bad position. For a brief moment I was perfectly silhouetted against the flawless sky.

The rifle shot creased my left shoulder. I spun off the saddle, falling with a crunch in an awkward way, my gun hand trapped under me. My horse bolted.

Before I could spin over and clear my gun hand he was on top of me. I saw a grinning shadow before he crashed a rifle butt across the back of my head.

A splash of water on my face brought me back.

He stood with the sun behind him. Smart men always have the sun with them. He had a Barlow knife in one hand. His sorrel stood at ease a good piece away alongside my blue roan.

"What's your name?" I asked.

"What you need to know for?" His voice bubbled in his throat, like marbles rattling across dry wood. "You thinking to arrest me?" He laughed at the thought.

I was hogtied, lying on my right side. The white gypsum sand was eerily cool against my face and I was grateful for how it felt. My left shoulder was molten fire. I think the old wound in my side had opened up, too. I felt something wet trickle down my ribs. My leg was numb.

My captor squatted on his thin haunches, watching me like

a hungry lizard watches a doomed cricket. He had a bleak, wind-raw face. He pulled makings from his shirt and rolled a cigarette.

"I drew low card." He blew tobacco smoke and watched it drift over the white sand. "We figured you would try for the single man first." A crisp smile broke the brown skin and rough, three-day-old whiskers of his face. "Didn't think it would be this easy to take you, though. Hell, all I did was double back. Guess you thought I was still ahead. An easy trick."

He smoked and looked disappointed in me. I was disappointed in myself, too.

"I don't know." He took another drag on the cigarette. "Maybe you're not as good as they say."

I couldn't argue with that. I was the one hog-tied. He had a horn-handled knife and a gun on his hip. The rifle was back in the scabbard on his horse.

The cigarette bobbed in the corner of his mouth. "I woke you up, Marshal, because I wanted you to feel this here hurt I'm about to do you. I'll start once I finish my smoke."

"Take your time."

Ash dropped from the end of his cigarette. He tested the blade of his knife with the ball of his thumb. It wasn't quite up to snuff so he removed a whetstone from his shirt pocket and stropped it half a dozen times.

"Ain't fun skinning an unconscious man," he said, testing the blade again and grinning. "You can't hear him squeal and beg for you to stop the hurt."

I wondered if he was the one who drove the iron spikes into Shiner Larsen, or if they had all taken turns. No matter what happened this man would have wanted his turn doing that.

He picked the cigarette from his mouth, hawked and spat to one side. "Except, I never stop once I start to cutting."

I tested my knots. My hands were lashed near the tops of my boots. He had done a professional job. I was completely immobile.

"I'll start on your face." He pointed the knife at me and drew curlicues in the air. "Then I'll throw the skin over there on that dune so's you can see your own face while I slice the rest of you."

"Can I have water?"

"I don't waste water on a dead man." He took another drag on the cigarette. He rose to his feet and stretched.

"Gotta get limbered up. You know, it ain't easy, skinning a man. Human leather don't come off muscle easy like you'd think. Ain't that funny?"

His bones cracked as he worked his arms back and forth.

My fingers were numb from the leather thongs biting my wrists. I used them to search carefully along the top of my right boot, trying to interpret what I was feeling with their tips.

"Let's get this over." He flipped his cigarette away in an arc. "Gotta ride hard to catch the outfit once I'm done fixin' you. It's my turn to have me a slice of that squaw meat." He laughed. It was an ugly sound and I hated him for it. "I don't want to miss my chance before we sell her to the Comanches." His face twisted in a feral sneer. "Hell of a waste if you ask me. They'll just cut her up for dog meat. Goddamn savages."

The blade of his knife reflected silver as he started for me. I let him come. I wanted him close. I wouldn't have a second chance.

"Sometimes a man will piss himself when he's gettin' skun," he said. A bead of sweat rolled down his face into his dirty beard. I smelled his stink. His tongue touched his bottom lip in concentration. He bent low.

I rolled over quick, kicking up a flurry of sand and looking over my shoulder for the target. A professional would have done for me right there, but he dropped the knife and went for his gun when he saw what protruded from my fist. That was the mistake that killed him.

The little double-barrelled derringer from my boot barked twice. Both .41-calibre slugs hit him low in the stomach. His gun spun out of his open fingers. He folded to his knees and crawled off to die, one claw-like hand clutching his belly in unbelievable agony.

I rolled over toward the knife he dropped. I grunted with pain every time I came down on my bad shoulder.

No matter what I wanted that knife. He might be made of

sterner stuff and remember the pistol he left behind. He was dying, but he wasn't dead. Not yet. I sawed the blade through the knots fast as I could, flaying skin and not caring. When I had my hands free I cut the rope around my ankles and stumbled to my feet.

He had made a big, nasty mess in the sand, crawling around a high dune to hide himself in a patch of shadow and die in peace. I found my Colt Dragoon on his horse. I broke the cylinder open. It was loaded.

I walked around the opposite side of the dune.

He was hunched up trying to hold his guts in, his face a twisted mask of pain.

"I ain't heeled, mister," he wheezed between gritted teeth. "You shoot a dying man who is unarmed?"

I lowered my pistol and holstered it. I went back to my horse and dug through the saddlebag for a hand axe. When I came back to the dune he had crawled farther away, leaving a nasty blood trail.

Crimson on snow.

My shadow drew up on him. He was doubled up, knees drawn toward his chest. His bloodless lips skinned away from his teeth as he said, "Guess you don't stop, neither."

He breathed in hissing jerks of fear and pain.

"Never have yet," I told him.

He watched me come on.

When I finished I left him for carrion and put what I wanted in an old flour sack. I caught his horse along with mine and started out of White Sands. His bullet had cut me, but the blood was stanched and I didn't need to be sewn up.

It was a long, lonely ride out of that white, featureless desert. I was glad to leave the immense quiet behind. The pain in my shoulder crested in waves, like the dunes of white sand the two horses kicked through. Black clouds amassed over my head, like ladders with rungs made of feathers. I kept riding until they were behind me, towering.

All those clouds building up and no shadow to cut the sun.

HAXAN

Why didn't it rain if there were so many clouds in the sky, I wondered.

It was late afternoon when I emerged from the soundless desolation of White Sands. I came out of the northern edge of the waste. Only after I hit prairie scrub did I look behind me.

The desert sky was black with buzzards whirling over the feast I had laid out for them.

I reined my horse around and rode away.

CHAPTER 28

I rode his horse into the ground, slapped it loose, then mounted my blue roan and raced for the horizon. Salinas Peak crawled away to my left. The wagon tracks were pointed north by northwest. I slowed near sunset to let my horse blow and walk off his lather.

I found a spring as we were crossing through the mountains. Not more than a cup of rank water seeping from a bowl-like depression. I wouldn't have spotted it but for the thick vegetation around.

It wasn't much water. When you emptied it another cupful swelled from the razor-thin crack. I watered up. My head throbbed where that bastard had clubbed me. While I was rubbing down my horse I felt my stomach revolt and I brought up all the water I had drank. There was nothing else in my stomach but it kept trying to empty itself. Every time a spasm hit my head burst in blinding fragments of light and diamond. I remained on my hands and knees, head down like a sick dog. My head hurt so much it felt like blood was pooling behind my eyes, making my vision all red and watery.

I felt the back of my head, gingerly. The hair was caked and scabbed with dried blood. The skin underneath felt spongy. I had quite a lump and had to cock my hat to the side so the brim wouldn't press on it too hard.

I tried more water and this time I kept it down. My horse lowered his muzzle and drank from the stuff that seeped out to replace what I had taken. I let him keep drinking. When he had enough he browsed on the tender shoots growing around the bowl.

I didn't relish the idea of trying to climb back into that saddle, not in my condition. But the thought of Magra, and what she was going through, forced me to my feet.

The world rocked. I clung to the pommel like a drunken, shattered man. I was afraid if I fell I would never get up. I laid my head on my arms. I may have fallen asleep like that for a minute or two. When I lifted my head again a lot of the fuzziness in my vision was gone.

I don't know how long I stayed at that spring. It couldn't have been more than an hour but it felt like years. Finally, I gathered enough strength to pull myself into the saddle. My horse shook his head, jingling the bridle. He had cooled off, too, and was ready to go.

I drove my mount forward. I don't remember much of the ride. I felt something had snapped inside me back in White Sands, like when a broken guitar string twangs. I remembered what I had in the flour sack, tied to my saddle and thumping against my horse. I had become more animal than man.

I knew this and I didn't care.

I spotted their campfire as the rising moon was making its appearance like an orange lamp. The moon hung so close to the ground you felt you could touch the face of it.

I let my horse stand, pulled my Sharps Special from its scabbard, along with extra ammunition, food, and canteen. I marched across the scrub waste, boots whisking through brush, fighting every minute to keep myself upright and not fall in an ungainly sprawl.

My head throbbed, but at least I could think after a fashion.

I was far out of Sangre County. Somewhere west of the San Andres Mountains would be my guess. That looked like the Oscura Ridge over on my left, but I wasn't certain.

But if it was Oscura that meant I was thirty or forty miles southeast of Socorro. Give or take some miles.

Point being, I didn't know precisely where I was. It didn't look like the hard pan and scrag around would ever amount to anything.

It was as empty and as desolate as you could get in New Mexico Territory.

Maybe the whole world.

At least White Sands had white serried dunes against the big iron-blue sky. All I saw here was flat, limitless scrub with a slight depression or hollow now and then. A shallow ravine or wallow here or there. The land was as big as the night sky. It was that empty, and that wide.

However, empty as it was, you couldn't help but feel you were at the centre of something.

I hefted the rifle and kept walking. My horse followed me. I fed him a handful or two of grain from the saddlebags and chided him to stay ground tied.

After ten minutes I came on three rocks, each one the size of a big coffee can. They had white markings on them, similar to the pictographs around Shiner Larsen's place. I guessed they were of Indian make. Perhaps they were even older than that.

Maybe they were here when the Earth first formed and lava, or whatever, carved those markings into their faces.

I studied the pictographs by the light of the stars and moon, tracing my finger along them. I couldn't make out what they meant. I don't know why the stones were there, or if the markings meant anything at all.

But it was the one thing that was different around here. In my mind I called them Three Rocks and I memorized the lay of the land in case I wanted to find this trinity again.

I circled Rand's camp, coming upon them from the east. I used the yellow glow of their small fire as my lodestone. Rand must have been pretty damn sure of himself to build a fire. Even a small one, burning like that, could be seen for miles. Maybe he put a lot of store in the talents of the man he left behind to kill me.

I don't know what they used for fuel way out here. Perhaps they picked up chips or something while they were on the run and hoarded them for such an emergency. Didn't matter much to me. Nothing mattered anymore.

They weren't going anywhere.

I found a knoll two hundred yards from their camp and set up the rifle. It was difficult to make out faces from this distance and in that dim light. There were three figures sitting around the fire. I thought one of them might be Magra but I couldn't be sure.

No matter. Time was on my side. *They weren't going anywhere.* My .50-calibre Sharps would see to that.

All I had to do was wait for the sun to come up.

I settled down and waited out the night on the cold, uncomfortable ground. The desert was quiet and peaceful. Not even the howl of a coyote broke that deep stillness. There wasn't enough water out here to keep many animals alive, anyway, if the surrounding scrub was any indication. Any water there was likely reeked of alkali—there were several alkali depressions around.

The last good water had been that little depression I found fifteen miles back. I hoped I could find it again.

Even with the moon up I never saw so many stars. You could hold up your finger and count a hundred before you got to the first knuckle. The emptiness of the hushed waste made a sort of roaring sound in your head, until you changed position and heard the soft rustle of your clothes, or your boot leather pop as you adjusted your cramping legs.

It was a long, bitter night. But Magra was out there. I could feel her. Almost touch her.

I waited. From the position of the pointing stars on the Big Dipper I judged it about midnight. I felt dog-tired. I found small rocks and pointed them in an arrow toward the North Star. That way, if it got cloudy during the night, or I fell asleep, I would be compass-oriented come morning.

The weather held. Before sunrise I made a quick breakfast of hard biscuit and half a canteen of water. My head ached, but my thoughts were sharp and clear. I didn't mind drinking most of my water. If I lived, I could get my horse and ride past Three Rocks toward the spring I found. If not, then it wouldn't matter anyway.

I arranged my bedroll to rest the forestock of the rifle on for stability. I stretched out behind, legs splayed, boots flat for added support.

While I waited, the world woke up around me by degrees.

I checked the Sharps rifle once more as a band of red and orange coloured the sky behind me. Everything appeared in working order. I laid a handful of heavy cartridges with ninety grains of powder each in a line on my bedroll. They were within easy reach. I kept them on the bedroll because I didn't want sand or dirt on them. I didn't want there to be any chance of misfire.

I slipped a cartridge in the breech of the gun and raised the sights. I let my eyes and my body adjust to the morning air and the natural cycle of the desert as it awakened around me.

There was a breeze gusting out of the northwest, maybe five or seven miles an hour. The tops of the thin grass around me bent with the force of the wind. I told myself to remember to use them as windage when the time came.

The gun was ready. I was ready.

Morning came on fast. It always does when you're in the desert or any other flat and hard country by yourself. I watched them hitch the buckboard while Magra saddled the bay. I recognized her blue Union coat, but something was wrong. She was taller than before.

Even at two hundred yards I could sometimes hear their movements: clink of a coffee cup against an iron pan, snort of a horse in the cold morning, rough bark of harsh language or laughter.

They could afford to laugh. Things were looking up for them. I hadn't shown my face all night long. Their friend must have gotten me or I would have come in, guns blazing.

Sunlight lifted off the desert floor in bright waves. It worked out just right. By the time they had the team rigged I had a bright sun over my shoulder and I could make them out clear.

I settled down to work. The Sharps roared and the bay standing off to the side dropped. I loaded the single-shot action and the Sharps buffalo gun roared again. The outside horse on the team collapsed, his knees buckling. Another cartridge and the last horse went down, tangled in the traces.

I didn't like killing the horses this way because it might mean we had to walk out on foot. But I wanted to shock Magra's captors beyond the ability to think. To let them know they were under the sights of a killing gun, with a merciless hunter on the other end.

If I had gone riding into their camp, six-gun firing . . . well, they would expect that move. They were prepared for that. Few men, I don't care how tough they are, are ready to hear thunder rumbling out of a clear blue sky as three good horses drop in their tracks around them, a froth of blood spraying from their mouths and noses from the concussion of each shot.

You don't plan for that. No one does.

Of course, the little doll-like figures didn't stand around scratching their ass when this slaughter began. The man wearing Magra's coat grabbed her and leaped behind a raised hummock of turf. The other man, dressed in a blue shirt and brown trousers with long black hair hanging across his face, tried to use the buckboard as a screen.

It would have been a good idea had I been armed with a Winchester, or some other rifle like a Spencer, or even an old Henry.

I wasn't using any of those. I was using a Sharps Special.

I started pouring rounds through the wagon. It was no match for a .50-calibre buffalo gun powered by ninety grains of powder at 200 yards. Given enough time and ammunition I could chop it into kindling.

They had me spotted. They could see the puff of smoke a second or two before they heard the crack of the rifle. But I had the yardage on them. They couldn't reach me with their pistols.

I could reach them, though. Hell tapped on their shoulder every time I fired the Sharps.

It takes a lot of nerve to stick under that kind of remorseless fire. My victim behind the wagon didn't have that much sand. He broke cover and started running across the prairie, snap firing his six-gun wildly in my direction, wasting loads. I cut him down. He thrashed on the ground. I guess I just clipped him with that first shot. Watched the tops of the grass for windage. I put another slug into him. He stopped moving.

There was a stand of silence. I didn't have time to use a Fisher brush to clean the hot barrel so I breathed down it to moisten the powder cake. I laid out several more cartridges in case I needed them.

The reverberation of the big gun had stilled the land. I could put Rand under the same withering fire, but I didn't want to risk hitting Magra.

I grabbed my flour sack and walked toward their camp, right in the range of his six. I could see Rand's slitted eyes under the broken brim of his hat and Magra's cowed head pressed under his left hand.

"You take one more step, lawman, and I put a bullet in this witch's brain," he warned. He had a double-action Starr with the hammer drawn back. "What happened to Tanner?"

"Was that his name?" I flung the flour sack in Rand's direction. When the mouth of the sack opened up, Tanner's head rolled out and came to a stop on the incline, staring at the blue sky with sightless eyes.

"What kind of man are you?" Rand asked. There was waver in his voice. "You shot Silas when he was down. You murdered him."

"That's right. I did."

"What kind of man are you?" he asked again.

"I guess you're going to find that out in about one minute, Rand."

His dirty Adam's apple bobbed. "I don't want to cross guns with you, Marwood. Let me walk out with the girl. I'll leave her unharmed by a dry wash three miles west."

"No deal."

"Listen, you don't understand." He stopped to catch himself. He was rising close to panic and smart enough to know that wasn't going to help him way out here.

"We were paid one hundred dollars in gold to kidnap her," he said. "We could keep her or kill her, our choice. The d—" he stopped. "The man who bought our guns in Haxan said that was part of the bargain. But we never thought to kill her. We were going to sell her to Comanches in Palo Duro before you got on our trail."

Magra tried to look up. Rand pushed her face back down in the sand.

"Palo Duro," I said. "The same place you suckered Breggmann to die. You've got thirty seconds left, Rand."

"I'll give you all the gold double eagles I have, Marwood. Just let me walk out of here with a whole skin."

"No."

He pressed his revolver into Magra's hair. "I'll kill this girl, Marwood. I've never killed a woman before—you have. But I'll do it. Her death will be on your conscience. Not mine."

I put my rifle aside. "Time's up, Rand. Get to your feet."

"Marwood, listen to me, I—"

"I said stand."

He rose, dragging Magra with him and using her body as a shield. He kept the gun to her head. Her face was bruised and her doeskin dress was torn and ripped. She had been given an old pair of pants to replace her leggings. They hadn't been gentle with her. I didn't expect they would be. These kinds of men never are.

"Marwood, I was only doing what I was told." The wind blew his white-blond hair, revealing white scalp around his ears. His drooping left eyelid began to flicker with nervous tension.

"So am I, Rand."

"I don't want to pull on you," he said.

I didn't say anything.

He watched me for a long time. His face subtly changed. He was cornered. The only way he would live was if he shot his way out. He already had his gun free while my heavier Colt Dragoon remained holstered. The odds were on his side.

"Have it your way," he said.

He was good. His expression never changed and his eyes remained steady. He flung Magra aside and started to draw a bead on me. My first shot hit him in the head and took away most of his lower jaw. He stumbled back, arms windmilling as my second shot centre-cut his lungs.

I walked up on him. His tongue was moving in what was left of his lower mouth. He was most dead, but the flickering nerves that remained in his brain were trying to make him talk before they, too, died.

I raised my pistol. My third shot echoed across the flat desert.

I turned. Magra stood alone, trembling. Her dirty hands were pressed against her face. I walked to her and said soft, "It's over."

She took her begrimed fingers from her face. "They said someone in town paid them to kill Papa and kidnap me."

"I know."

"They never said a name."

"It doesn't matter." I already knew who hired them.

"They . . . I—" She swallowed hard. Watched me. Softened.

"I'm glad you came, John," she said at last.

The wind blew her loose hair across her face.

"Can you walk? I'm camped beyond that next rise."

"Don't you want their money? Connie, that man, he kept it in a leather satchel under the wagon seat."

I gave her a sidelong glance. "Why would I want their gold? Unless you want it."

She flashed a sick, angry look. "I don't want anything from them, ever again."

I took her hand. "Then let's go home."

CHAPTER 29

We rode in slow. I thought Magra needed time and I was right.

That same morning we reached the spring I had found earlier. I used a shovel found on the buckboard and dug down into the earth until I had a wide basin of clear water.

I cleaned my shoulder wound. The muscle was red and bruised where the bullet cut me. It was inflamed but didn't appear infected. The old wounds on my side had opened up and bled through, but they weren't too bad. I cleaned those, too.

I was achy and sore, but I was alive. So was Magra. Right now, that's all that mattered.

Magra washed her broad face and long hands at the water hole. She glanced my way briefly and, without a word or a blush, started to undress so she could wash her entire body. She started this process by scrubbing herself clean with sand and rinsing it off her glowing skin with handfuls of water.

I rummaged in the saddlebags and brought out a doeskin skirt, faded red blouse, and calf-skin boots.

"Got these from your poke in the storeroom before I left Haxan," I explained. "Thought you might want a change of clothes when I caught up with you."

"Thank you. Leave them there, will you?"

I gave her the privacy she deserved. Some time later, after she let the sun air-dry her, she called, "I am ready."

She had dressed in the plain white doeskin skirt and blouse. The boots came halfway up her calves, hugging her legs. Her face was scrubbed bright and her black hair, washed, was combed straight and hung down her back in long ropes. She pinned her hair behind her ears with a piñon stick.

Standing there, water dripping from her fingers and the sun

in her red-brown face, she looked like the wildest thing the desert had ever let loose on a man.

She didn't say anything as I helped her onto my horse. She rode behind me, her chin resting on my shoulder.

I tried to make small talk. I pointed out things she had taught me about the desert. She didn't respond. She was lost in her own thoughts. I let her be.

A high wind started up from the south, kicking dust in our faces. By the time night came on it died down and I was able to build a decent fire. There had been no game on the trail so we shared *charqui* and hardtack.

"I knew you were coming after me," Magra said. She tapped the hardtack against a rock to make sure there were no weevils in it. The firelight danced on her cheekbones and in her eyes. A breeze ruffled her blouse and hair. She turned her face to mine. Parts of her were in shadow like the open desert around us.

"Papa came to me last night and said you were nearby, hiding in the dark. He said you were waiting for morning to come."

I grunted. "Must have been good to have that kind of comfort."

"*Ai*, it was." She hugged her knees. "I think it's the last time he's going to visit me, John." Her tone was plaintive. "I got the impression he felt, well, because you were here he didn't need to watch over me anymore."

"I hope that's right, Magra."

A desert owl called across the night flat. Another answered, farther away.

"That first owl caught a mouse," she said.

She gave me her first real smile and tugged a black and white Mexican blanket over her shoulders. The night closed down around us. The stars were like handfuls of sugar flung against the black sky.

She didn't move for the longest time. Just watched the dancing fire while I smoked my pipe. "John, I want to ask you something," she said at length.

"You can ask anything you want, Magra. You never need my permission."

"Where are you from?"

I didn't wait to answer. "It's a place you'll never have to visit."

"That sea of time and dust you spoke of before?"

I nodded. I put my pipe away. Now it was my turn to stare at the fire. "Mostly."

"Is it old, this place?"

I nodded. "Very."

"How old?"

"Oh, I don't know." I made an expansive gesture. "As old as man's time in the world. Yesterday. An hour ago. There's no telling."

She wasn't put off by that. She knew I wasn't being evasive. I was only describing it with the words I had.

"But it's real," she pressed on, "this place you speak of?"

I remembered some of the people I used to know. Things they had said in languages long forgotten. Things they had told me about why we had come to the world.

"It's real, Magra."

"And you are from there."

"I am."

"Why?"

"Like I said before. We are called to stand against that which must be faced."

Her curiosity deepened. "You've been other places? These other places?"

"Some of them. Not all." I felt myself groping, trying to find a way to explain. "I guess in a way you could call it night-walking. We are made to night-walk between worlds that can't exist until something is put right. Then all these worlds are put together in a line, like glass beads on a string, and that's the history of man." I shrugged. "That's the best I can explain it. I'm sorry."

"*Ai*, but why you, John?"

I had one arm across my knee. The night air was fine and the fire felt good on my face and arms. My horse whickered behind us and pawed the ground.

"Because they don't choose anyone, Magra," I said with careful deliberation. "You have to have something inside you.

Something so big it could maybe devour worlds if you let it loose."
I shrugged again. "I don't let it. Leastways, not often."

"You have this thing inside you?" She wasn't afraid. She wanted to know.

"I do." Coiled and wintry. Asleep at the moment. But it had awakened in White Sands and again at Trinity.

She thought about this for a long time. "How do you carry something like that inside you and stay human, John?"

"That's easy." I looked at her, watched the flecks of dancing fire reflected in her liquid dark eyes. "Because it's more afraid of me than I am of it."

"I think I saw something of that power," she admitted. "When you shot Silas Foote after he was down. Again when you shot Rand. Rand only had seconds to live. You didn't do that to end his suffering."

"No, I didn't."

She rolled the blanket off her shoulders. Her eyes were dark. "John. Do I have any reason to ever be afraid of you?"

I smoothed her hair back. "Magra, the day you are afraid of me is the day I leave Haxan forever. That's all."

"I guess you will never have to leave."

I pulled her into my arms and she leaned into me at the same time.

Her hands went around my neck as I kissed her. She pulled me down, trying to cover her body with mine.

Night fell around us.

Her body lay warm under the rumpled Mexican blanket. I could feel the warmth of the dying fire on my exposed legs.

She rolled over and propped herself on her elbows. "He called you here, didn't he? Papa."

The glowing embers of the fire brightened and dimmed with the shifting wind.

"I never know that, Magra. Sometimes I think I can call myself and that's why I go where I'm needed."

Her fingertips explored my face. She touched the scars on my chest, shoulders, and elbows. "You really were living with the Mandans," she said.

"Yes."

"But you're here now. Maybe not only for me, but a lot of other reasons you don't understand."

I tucked the wool blanket around her shoulders. "Time to go to sleep. Let yourself heal."

She pressed her face into the open palm of my hand. "I'm doing that, John. You're helping me do that right now."

CHAPTER 30

When we arrived in Haxan I dropped Magra off at the hotel. Hew and Alma Jean came outside in the sunshine to meet her.

"It must have been quite an ordeal," Alma Jean said, bustling forward and clucking like a mother hen. "Thank God you are back safely among us, Magra Snowberry."

"Thank you, Mrs. Clay."

"Marshal," Hew said, "Mayor Polgar wanted to see you. Doc Toland got the lab results back the very day you left."

"All right." I paused in the open doorway to the hotel. The sun at my back cast a long shadow across the lobby. "Magra?"

"I'm okay, John."

"I'll be back for you as soon as I can."

She cast a shy smile my way. "I know."

"We'll keep an eye on her for you, Marshal," Hew promised.

"Indeed we will," Alma Jean echoed. She put a protective arm around Magra's shoulders and steered her away. "Hot food, bath, and a long rest will set you right, young lady."

I strode down Avenida de Haxan toward the freight office. Polgar was inside the station with Doc Toland. Word had spread like quicksilver as soon as I returned with Magra. Doc probably figured I would want him around.

He was right. He was going to be needed.

"How's the girl?" Polgar asked.

"It's going to be a long time before she's ever right again," I told him. "They hurt her bad." I turned to Doc Toland. "Mayhap you should examine her and make sure she's all right. But, don't leave just yet."

"All right, John," he said, catching my meaning.

"We saw you ride in alone, John," Polgar prompted. He had

a cigar going and was debating whether or not he had smoked it down far enough to toss it aside. "We saw you ride in without Rand."

"That's right, Frank, I guess you did."

"Those men still out there?" he asked.

"They're not going anywhere." I pointed through the window at a circular nailed to a post, flapping in the breeze. "We can take down those dodgers. I heard you got news for me, Doc."

"Indeed I do. Those men you found in the ditch at Shiner Larsen's place died in a very bad way. Poisoned until their kidneys shut down and failed. Their stomachs were full of—"

"Oil of cloves." That was what I had smelled on their bodies that night. They must have been held down and forced to swallow, but some had spilled on their clothes and soaked through.

"That's right, Marshal." I had impressed Toland with my deduction. "How did you know?"

"I smelled it a second time at the post office when a package carrying bottles of the stuff was smashed on the floor. That's when I knew for sure," I admitted.

"It's a nasty way to die," Toland remarked.

Polgar caught my attention. "John, there's only one man in town who uses that stuff in any definable quantity. Rex and I have been keeping an eye on him 'til you got back. We figured you would want to be the one to take him."

"I'll pick him up, Mayor."

"You need help? Jake is down at the office."

I opened the cylinder and checked the loads and percussion caps in my gun. Snapped it closed. "I'll take care of this alone. It's my job."

I walked through the empty street. The morning sun was hot and there was dust in my throat. A few Mexican women and their children lounged around the water well in the plaza, talking and fanning themselves from the heat.

I walked but a few buildings down in the direction of his office.

I hadn't been back in town long, but I wouldn't have been

surprised to meet him running out the door when I went through it.

I slammed the door behind me to announce my presence. The little wooden plate with the name "JOSIAH HARTLEBY: DENTIST" rattled in alarm against the glass pane.

I had caught him in the middle of packing. He had a threadbare carpet bag stuffed full of odds and ends, along with shirts that needed laundering and a pair of striped suspenders.

"Sir, I am closed for the day. You'll have to come back another time."

He saw me and his face sheeted white.

I felt cold and distant. "You have to answer for Shiner Larsen, tooth-puller."

He had sense enough not to try and talk his way out of it.

He drew himself up to his full measure, what there was of it. "And why not?" he snapped back. "Why shouldn't I have that crazy old Swede killed? Being a dentist is a hard enough trade. People don't like dentists much and his slander wasn't helping me eat. Besides, I was willing to marry that half-breed daughter of his, but he wouldn't have it. Said I was no good, that she didn't need the likes of me because one day he would call a man out of the dust of time to protect her. He was always talking crazy like that."

He moved across the room until a table stood between him and me.

"You have to understand, Marshal. Larsen wouldn't even broach the subject of my marrying Magra to her. He was crazy. So I made arrangements to have him pushed out of the way. Told the man I hired to teach her a lesson, too, since I couldn't have her to myself." He lifted his chin. He had cut himself shaving that morning and there was a stick of white plaster there.

"The way I see it," he said, "I did this town a righteous favour. Cleansed it of evil. If you know anything about the history of Haxan you know that much, Marshal."

"Law says you have to pay, Hartleby. You'll get a trial and then you'll be hanged."

"I was losing money and respect."

"You had more than enough money to hire three cold-blooded killers. Think about that. And I'm not sure you had much self-respect to begin with, seeing how you wanted Magra treated. No, Hartleby, I think you're a man who let his hate get the better of him. It happens."

His mouth worked a bit. He spit with indignation. "I don't like your high-minded tone, Marshal. Or your insinuations regarding my character."

"I don't care. As for your character, you're probably the sneak who tried to back-shoot me from the alley." I could tell by his reaction I had hit the mark.

"Come on, Hartleby. I'm taking you in. You're under arrest for murder."

His hand stole for the carpet bag.

I swept my grey duster aside, revealing the bone handle of my Colt Dragoon. "Don't try it, Hartleby."

"I won't hang from a rope, Marshal." He was facing the street. If he fired he might hit someone standing outside. Phaedra Finch all over again. I had to get him first.

"Don't pull on me, Hartleby," I warned. "You'll never live to see your own hanging if you do."

He wasn't hearing me. He was listening to the hate that bellowed in his heart. His hand flashed and our guns roared in the cramped room at the same instant. He slumped against the wall and left a smear of red.

Acrid gun smoke drifted between the high rafters. I kicked the smoking Walker from his hand and went outside.

Mayor Polgar and Doc Toland were there to meet me, blinking in the sun.

"Haxan's going to need a new dentist," I told them.

ABOUT THE AUTHOR

Kenneth Mark Hoover is a professional writer living in Dallas, TX. He has sold over sixty short stories and is a member of SFWA and HWA. His fiction has appeared in *Beneath Ceaseless Skies, Ellery Queen's Mystery Magazine, Strange Horizons,* and many others. You can read more at kennethmarkhoover.com, or follow his blog at kennethmarkhoover.me

EMB
RACE
THE
ODD

THE HEXSLINGER TRILOGY
GEMMA FILES

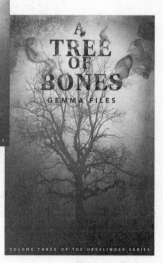

It's 1867, and the Civil War is over. But the blood has just begun to flow. For Asher Rook, Chess Pargeter, and Ed Morrow, the war has left its mark in tangled lines of association and cataclysmic love, woken hexslinger magic, and the terrible attentions of a dead god. "Reverend" Asher Rook is the unwilling gateway for the Mayan goddess Ixchel to birth her pantheon back into the world of the living, and to do it she'll force Rook to sacrifice his lover and fellow outlaw Chess Pargeter. But being dead won't bar Chess from taking vengeance, and Pargeter will claw his way back out of Hell, teaming with undercover Pinkerton-agent-turned-outlaw Ed Morrow to wreak it. What comes back into the world in the form of Chess Pargeter is a walking wound, Chess's very presence tearing a crack in the world and reshaping everything around him while Ixchel establishes Hex City, a city state defying the very laws of nature—an act that will draw battle lines between a passel of dead gods and monsters.

AVAILABLE NOW

WE WILL ALL GO DOWN TOGETHER
GEMMA FILES

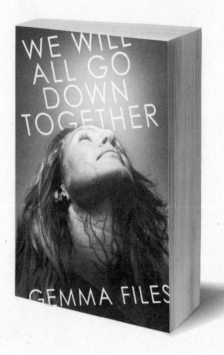

In the woods outside Overdeere, Ontario, there are trees that speak, a village that doesn't appear on any map and a hill that opens wide, entrapping unwary travellers. Music drifts up from deep underground, while dreams—and nightmares—take on solid shape, flitting through the darkness. It's a place most people usually know better than to go, at least locally—until tonight, at least, when five bloodlines mired in ancient strife will finally converge once more.

AUGUST 2014
978-1-77148-201-1

FEARFUL SYMMETRIES
EDITED BY ELLEN DATLOW

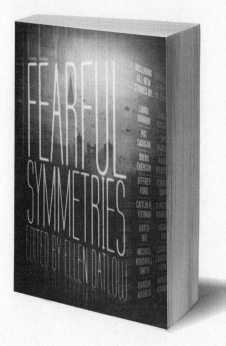

From Ellen Datlow, award-winning and genre-shaping editor of more than fifty anthologies, and twenty of horror's established masters and rising stars, comes an all-original look into the beautiful, terrible, tragic, and terrifying.

Wander through visions of the most terrible of angels, the Seven who would undo the world. Venture through Hell and back, and lands more terrestrial and darker still. Linger a while in childhoods, and seasons of change by turns tragic and monstrously transformative. Lose yourself amongst the haunted and those who can't let go, in relationships that might have been and never were. Witness in dreams and reflections, hungers and horrors, the shadows cast upon the wall, and linger in forests deep. Come see what burns so bright. . . .

APRIL 2014
978-1-77148-193-9

CHIZINEPUB.COM

IRREGULAR VERBS
MATTHEW JOHNSON

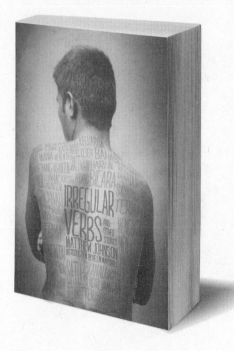

Meet a guilt-ridden nurse who atones for her sins by joining her zombified patients in exile; a lone soldier standing guard on a desolate Arctic island against an invasion that may be all in his mind; a folksinger who tries to unionize Hell; and a private eye who only takes your case after you die. Visit a resettlement centre for refugees from ancient Rome; a lost country recreated by its last citizen on the Internet; and a restaurant where the owner's ghost lingers for one final party. Discover the inflationary effects of a dragon's hoard, the secret connection between Mark Twain and Frankenstein, and the magic power of blackberry jam—all in this debut collection of strange, funny, and bittersweet tales by acclaimed writer Matthew Johnson.

JUNE 2014
978-1-77148-177-9

DAWN SONG
MICHAEL MARANO

A modern dark fantasy classic returns with this new, Special Edition of *Dawn Song*, the soul-haunting novel from a Bram Stoker Award-winning author with a deeply powerful—and prescient—vision. Set in Boston at the start of the First Gulf War, a larger, supernatural battle for Supremacy in Hell takes shape . . . but plays out on a personal scale as unassuming humans career into the path of a beautiful, terrible Succubus who has come to Earth to do her Father's bidding.

JULY 2014
978-1-77148-180-9

CHIZINEPUB.COM

HEAD FULL OF MOUNTAINS
BRENT HAYWARD

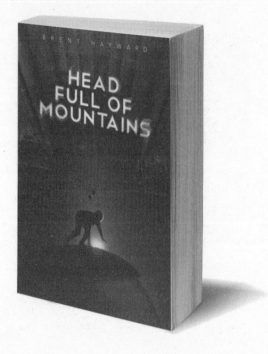

When Crospinal's ailing father finally dies, he is left utterly alone in the pen, surrounded by encroaching darkness. The machines that tended to him as a child have long ago vanished, and the apparitions that kept Crospinal company are now silenced. Struggling with congenital issues, outfitted in a threadbare uniform, he has little choice but to leave what was once his home, soon discovering that nothing in the outside world is how he had been told it would be. In his quest for meaning and understanding, and the contact of another, Crospinal learns truths about himself, about his father, and about the last bastion of humanity, trapped with him at the end of time.

JULY 2014
978-1-77148-181-6

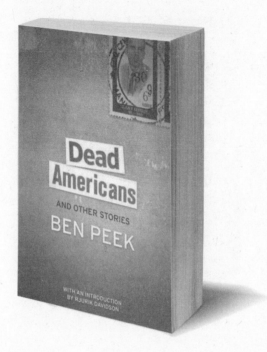

GET KATJA
SIMON LOGAN

Katja from Simon Logan's award-winning *Katja From the Punk Band* is back. Free and on the mainland, she emerges from hiding, only to find herself hunted by transvestite debt collectors, a mad surgeon and his voyeuristic fetish nurse and a corrupt detective, all of whom will stop at nothing to claim her for their own. And behind this scramble lies a twisted mind, desperate for revenge. Replete with dark humour, chaotic storytelling, and a fast-paced industrial thriller setting, Get Katja is the latest novel from the author of *Pretty Little Things to Fill Up The Void, Nothing Is Inflammable,* and *I-O*.

AVAILABLE NOW
978-1-77148-167-0

THE DOOR IN THE MOUNTAIN
CAITLIN SWEET

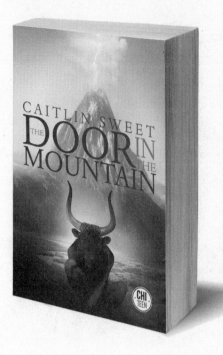

Lost in time, shrouded in dark myths of blood and magic, *The Door in the Mountain* leads to the world of ancient Crete: a place where a beautiful, bitter young princess named Ariadne schemes to imprison her godmarked half-brother deep in the heart of a mountain maze . . .

. . . where a boy named Icarus tries, and fails, to fly . . .

. . . and where a slave girl changes the paths of all their lives forever.

MAY 2014 IN CANADA/OCTOBER 2014 IN U.S.
978-1-77148-191-5

CHIZINEPUB.COM

FLOATING BOY AND THE GIRL WHO COULDN'T FLY

P. T. JONES

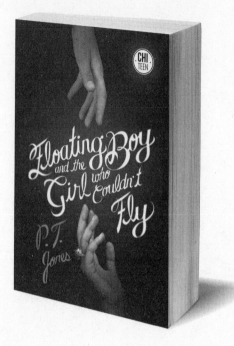

This is the story of a girl who sees a boy float away one fine day. This is the story of the girl who reaches up for that boy with her hand and with her heart. This is the story of a girl who takes on the army to save a town, who goes toe-to-toe with a mad scientist, who has to fight a plague to save her family. This is the story of a girl who would give anything to get to babysit her baby brother one more time. If she could just find him.

It's all up in the air for now, though, and falling fast. . . .

Fun, breathlessly exciting, and full of heart, *Floating Boy and the Girl Who Couldn't Fly* is an unforgettable ride.

MAY 2014 IN CANADA/OCTOBER 2014 IN U.S.

978-1-77148-173-1